The
Subterranean
Brotherhood

The Subterranean Brotherhood

Julian Hawthorne

ÆGYPAN PRESS

The Subterranean Brotherhood
A publication of
ÆGYPAN PRESS
www.aegypan.com

Footfalls

In the cell over mine at night
A step goes to and fro
From barred door to iron wall —
From wall to door I hear it go,
Four paces, heavy and slow,
In the heart of the sleeping jail:
And the goad that drives, I know!

    I never saw his face or heard him speak;
    He may be Dutchman, Dago, Yankee, Greek;
    But the language of that prisoned step
    Too well I know!

    Unknown brother of the remorseless bars,
    Pent in your cage from earth and sky and stars,
    The hunger for lost life that goads you so,
    I also know!

Hour by hour, in the cell overhead,
Four footfalls, to and fro
'Twixt iron wall and barred door —
Back and forth I hear them go —
Four footfalls come and go!
I wake and listen in the night:
Brother, I know!

Written in Atlanta Penitentiary,
May, 1913

Preface

These chapters were begun the day after I got back to New York from the Atlanta penitentiary, and went on from day to day to the end. I did not know, at the start, what the thing would be like at the finish, and I made small effort to make it look shapely and smooth; but the inward impulse in me to write it, somehow, was irresistible, in spite of the other impulse to go off somewhere and rest and forget it all. But I felt that if it were not done then it might never be done at all; and done it must be at any cost. I had promised my mates in prison that I would do it, and I was under no less an obligation, though an unspoken one, to give the public an opportunity to learn at first hand what prison life is, and means. I had myself had no conception of the facts and their significance until I became myself a prisoner, though I had read as much in "prison literature" as most people, perhaps, and had for many years thought on the subject of penal imprisonment. Twenty odd years before, too, I had been struck by William Stead's saying, "Until a man has been in jail, he doesn't know what human life means." But one does not pay that price for knowledge voluntarily, and I had not expected to have the payment forced upon me. I imagined I could understand the feelings of a prisoner without being one. I was to live to acknowledge myself mistaken. And I conceive that other people are in the same deceived condition. So, with all the energy and goodwill of which I am capable, I set myself to do what I could to make them know the truth, and to ask themselves what should or could be done to end a situation so degrading to everyone concerned in it, from one end of the line to the other. The situation, indeed, seems all but incredible. Your first thought on being told of it is, It must be an exaggeration or a fabrication. On the contrary, words cannot convey the whole horror and shamefulness of it.

I am conscious of having left out a great deal of it. I found as I went on with this writing that the things to be said were restricted to a few categories. First, the physical prison itself and the routine of life in it must be stated. That is the objective part. Then must be indicated the subjective conditions, those of the prisoner, and of his keepers — what the effect of prison was upon them. Next was to come a presentation of the consequences, deductions and inferences suggested by these conditions. Finally, we would be confronted with the question, What is to be done about it? Such are the main heads of the theme.

But I was tempted to run into detail. Here I will make a pertinent disclosure. During my imprisonment I was made the confidant of the life stories of many of my brethren in the cells. I am receiving through the mails, from day to day, up to the present time, other such tales from released convicts. The aim of them is not to get their tellers before the public and win personal sympathy, but to hold up my hands by supplying data — chapter and verse — in support of the assertions I have made. They do it abundantly; the stories bleed and groan before your eyes and ears, and smell to heaven; the bluntest, simplest, most formless stuff imaginable, but terrible in every fiber. Before I left prison I had accumulated a considerable number of these narratives, and had made many notes of things heard and seen — data and memoranda which I designed to use in the already projected book which is now in your hands. Such material, however, would have been confiscated by the Warden had its existence been known, and none of it would have been permitted to get outside the walls openly. The only thing to do, then, was to get it out secretly — by the "underground railroad."

There is an underground railroad in every penal institution. There is one at Atlanta. I attempted to use it, but my freight got in the wrong car. A prisoner whom I knew well and trusted came to me, and said he had found a man who would undertake to pass the packet through the barriers; he had already served such a need, and was anxious to do it in my case. This man was also a prisoner of several years' standing, and with several years yet to serve; he had recently applied for parole, but had been refused. I met and talked with him, found him intelligent and circumspect, and professedly eager to do his share toward helping me get my facts before the world. He intimated that he was on favorable terms with one of the guards or overseers who was inclined to help the prisoners, and would take the packet out in his pocket and mail it to its address. I addressed it to a friend of mine living near New York and on a certain prearranged day I handed it to my confederate. He hid it inside his shirt, and that was the last I saw of it.

The packet never turned up at its address, and it was only long after that I was told what had occurred. My confederate wanted his parole badly, and made a bargain with the Warden, by the terms of which his parole should be granted in return for his delivering to the Warden my bundle of memoranda. The terms were fulfilled on both sides, and my data are at this moment in the Warden's safe, I suppose, along with the letter that I wrote during my confinement to the Editor of the New York *Journal* (mentioned in the text of this book).

The Warden thought, perhaps, that the lack of my accumulated data would prevent or embarrass me in writing my book. I thought so myself at first, but had not long been at work before I found that the essential book needed no data other than those existing in my memory and supplied by the general theme; my material was not scant, but excessive. My knowledge of prison and my opinions and arguments based upon that knowledge were not subject to the Warden's confiscation, and they were quite enough to make a book of themselves, without need of dates, places, names and illustrations. Indeed, even of such supplementary and confirmatory matter I also found an adequate amount in my own unaided recollection — more than I cared to give space to; for it was my belief that such things were not required to secure confidence in the truth of what I had to say in the minds of persons whose confidence was worth my winning. They would believe me because they couldn't help it — because truth has a quality which compels belief. Moreover, of illustrations of my statements the public had of late had more than enough from other sources; what was now wanted was not so much instances of the facts, as a general presentation of the subject into which special and apposite cases could be fitted by the reader according to his previously acquired information. Finally, I reflected that the introduction of names, places and dates might injure the men thus pointed out; secret service men, post office inspectors and other spies, and the prison authorities themselves, would be prompted and helped to give them trouble. Accordingly, I was sparing even of such data as I had; and I noticed, as the chapters appeared serially in the newspaper syndicate which published them, that they were criticized in certain quarters as of the "glittering generality" class of writings; I made assertions, but adduced no specific proof of them. The source of such criticisms was obvious enough, but they did no harm, and were not accompanied by denials of my facts. The only other form of attack brought against the book is comprised in the claim that I am a writer of fiction and as such incapable of telling the truth, about anything; that I was the dupe of designing persons who made me the mouthpiece for their factitious grievances or spites; and that I was myself animated by a spirit of revenge for the injury of my imprisonment, which must render anything I might allege against prisons and their conduct worthless.

I have touched upon the two latter counts of the indictment in the text of the book; of the assertion that fiction writers cannot stick to facts or convey truth, I will say that it is unreasonable upon its face. Fiction writers, in order to attain any measure of success in their calling, must above all things base their structures upon facts, and to seek and promulgate undeniable truth in their descriptions and analyses. The "fiction" part of their stories is the merest outside part; all within must be true, or it is nothing. A novelist or story writer, therefore, is more likely to give a true version of any event or condition he may be required to present, than a person trained in any other form of writing, with the exception, perhaps, of journalism. And I have been a journalist, as well as a story writer, for more than thirty years past, and what success I attained was due to the accuracy and veracity of the reports I sent to my papers. In short, I am a trained observer of facts if ever there were one; and no facts in my experience have been so thoroughly hammered into my mind, heart and soul, digested and appreciated, as were the facts of my prison life. Whatever else that I have written might be caviled at on the plea of inaccuracy, certainly this book cannot be. Whether the statements which it contains be feebly or strongly put may properly be questioned, but none of them can be successfully denied.

But this aspect of the matter gives me small uneasiness. The important consideration is, will the book, assuming that it is accepted as the truth, do the work, or any large part of the work, which it was designed to do? Will readers be influenced by it to practical action; will it be an effective element in the forces that are now rising up to make wickedness and corruption less than they are? The proposal toward which the book points and in which it ultimates is so radical and astounding — nothing less than that *Penal Imprisonment for Crime be Abolished* — that the author can hardly escape the apprehension that the mass of the public will dismiss it as preposterous and impossible. And yet nothing is more certain in my opinion than that penal imprisonment for crime must cease, and if it be not abolished by statute, it will be by force. It must be abolished because, alarming or socially destructive though alternatives to it may appear, it is worse than any alternative, being not only dangerous, but wicked, and it breeds and multiplies the evils it pretends to heal or diminish. It is far more wicked and dangerous than it was a thousand or a hundred years ago, because society is more enlightened than it was then, and the multitude now exercise power which was then confined to the few. Whatever person or society knowingly and willfully permits the existence of a wickedness which it might extirpate, makes itself a party thereto, and also inflames the wickedness itself. And the ignorance or the impotence which we could plead heretofore in history, we cannot plead today. We know, we have power, and we must act; if we shrink from acting, action will be taken against us by powers which cannot be estimated or controlled. This book is meant to confirm our knowledge and to stimulate and direct, in a measure, our action; and to avert, if possible, the consequences of not acting. Its individual power may be slight; but it should be the resolve of every honest and courageous man and woman to add to it the weight of their own power. Wonderful things have been accomplished before now by means which seemed, in their beginning, as inadequate and weak as this.

In the sixth chapter of the Book of Joshua you may read the great type and example of such achievements, the symbol of every victory of good over evil, the thing that could not be done by man's best power, skill and foresight, accomplished, with God to aid, by a breath. The defensive strength of Jericho was greater, compared with the means of attack then known, than that of Sebastopol in the fifties of the last century, or of Plevna in the seventies, or of Port Arthur a few years since. Those walls were too high to be scaled, too massive to be beaten down, and they were defended by a great king and his mighty men of valor. From any moral point of view, the enterprise of destroying the city was hopeless. Nor did the Lord add anything to such weapons of offense as Joshua already possessed. Seven trumpets of rams' horns were the sole agents of the destruction provided; and not the trumpets themselves, but the breath of the mouths of the seven priests who should blow through them, should overthrow those topless ramparts, and give the king and his army and his people into the hand of the men of Israel. Were such a proposition presented to our consideration today, we can imagine what would be the comments of the Army and Navy departments, of Congress, of the editors of newspapers, of witty paragraphers, and of the man on the street. Possibly the churches themselves might hesitate before giving their support to such a plan of war: "We must take the biblical stories in a figurative sense!" But stout Joshua had seen the angel of the Lord, with his sword drawn, the night before; and he knew nothing of figures of speech. He got the seven trumpets of rams' horns, and put them in the hands of the seven priests, and led the hosts of the Israelites round and round the walls of Jericho day after day for six days, the trumpets blowing amain, and the hosts silent. And on the seventh day, the hosts compassed the walls of the city seven times; "And at the seventh time, when the priests blew with the trumpets, Joshua said unto the people, Shout; for the Lord hath given you the city. . . . So the people shouted when the priests blew with the trumpets; and it came to pass, when the people heard the sound of the trumpets, and the people shouted with a great shout, that the walls fell down flat, so that every man went up into the city, every man straight before him, and they took the city. And they utterly destroyed all that was within the city."

Yes, the biblical stories are to be taken in a figurative sense; they stand as symbols for spiritual actions in the nature of man; though that is not to say that the events narrated did not actually take place as recorded. But Joshua had faith; and faith in the hearts of the champions of right begets fear in the hearts of supporters of wrong, and the defenses they have so laboriously built up tumble distractedly about their ears when the trumpets of the Lord blow and the people who believe in Him utter a mighty shout. Our jails are our Jericho; the evils which they encompass and protect are greater than the sins of that strong city; but a breath may shatter them into irretrievable ruin. Not compromises; not gradual and circumspect approaches; not prudent considerations of political economy, nor sound sociological principles; but simple faith in God and a blast on the ram's horn.

My business in this book was to show that penal imprisonment is an evil, and its perpetuation a crime; that it does not reform the criminal but destroys him body and soul; that it does not protect the community but exposes it to incalculable perils; and that the assumption that a criminal class exists among us separate and distinct from any and the best of the rest of us is Pharisaical, false and wicked. The "Subterranean Brotherhood" are our brothers — they are ourselves, unjustly and vainly condemned to serve as scapegoats for the rest. What the criminal instinct or propensity in a man needs is not seclusion, misery, pain and despotic control, but free air and sunlight, free and cheerful human companionship, free opportunity to play his part in human service, and the stimulus, on all sides of him, of the example of such service. Men enfeebled by crime are not cured by punishment, or by homilies and precepts, but by taking off our coats and showing them personally how honest and useful things are done. And let every lapse and failure on their part to follow the example, be counted not against them, but against ourselves who failed to convince them of the truth, and hold them up to the doing of good. Had we been sincere and hearty enough, we would have prevailed.

I do not underrate the difficulties; they are immeasurable; the hope seems as forlorn as that of the Israelites against the walls of Jericho. But they are forlorn and immeasurable only because, and so long as, we let our selfish personal interests govern and mold our public and social action. Altruism will not heal the inward sore, but at best only put on its surface a plausible plaster which leaves the inward still corrupt; for altruism is a policy and not an impulse, proceeding not from the heart but from the intelligence — the policy of enlightened selfishness. It has already been tried thoroughly, and proved thoroughly inefficient; it is the motive power behind charitable organization; it breeds a cold, impersonal, economic spirit in charity workers, and coldness, ingratitude and resentment in those who are worked upon. It will not do to speak of Tom, Dick and Harry as cases Nos. 1, 2 and 3. You must call them by name and think of them as flesh of your flesh and blood of your blood, to whom you owe more than they owe you, or than you can repay. Put a heart into them by giving them your own heart; do not look down on them and advise them, but at and into them and take counsel with them; or even up to them, and learn from them. They know and feel much that you have never felt or known.

The book is full of shortcomings, imperfections, omissions, and repetitions. But there is meaning and purpose in it, and I hope it may do its work.

JULIAN HAWTHORNE

I

INTRODUCTORY

Conspiracies of silence — it is a common phrase; but it has never been better illustrated than in regard to what goes on in prisons, here and in other parts of the world. The conspiracy has been attacked sometimes, and more of late than usual, and once in a while we have caught a glimpse of what is occurring behind those smug, well-fitting doors. But they have been mere glimpses, incoherent, obscure, often imaginative, or guesswork based on scanty, incorrect, at any rate second-hand information; never yet conclusive and complete. In England, Charles Dickens and Charles Reade have personally visited prisons, talked with prisoners, written stories that have stirred the world, and forced improvements. Great prisoners like Kropotkin have related their experiences in Russia, and our own George Kennan prompted us to congratulate ourselves, in our complacent ignorance, that our methods of generating virtue out of crime were not like those of the Russians. It was annoying, after this, to be assured by writers in some of our magazines — called muckrakers by some, pioneers by others — that after a sagacious, eager, well-equipped investigation into our own prison conditions, peering into depths, interrogating convicts, searching records, they had found little difference in principle between our way of handling offenses against law, and that of our Cossack neighbors. The latter are more sensational and red-blooded about it, that is all. These revelations compelled some removals and a few reforms; but they too failed to bring home livingly to public knowledge and imagination the whole ugly, sluggish, vicious truth.

Then, only yesterday, an amiable, naïve and impressionable young gentleman underwent a week of amateur convictship in one of our jails, and came forth tremulous with indignation and astonishment; though, obviously and inevitably, he did not have to endure the one thing which, more than hardship or torture, is the main evil of penal imprisonment

— the feeling of helplessness and outrage in the presence of a despotic and unrighteous power, from which there is no appeal or escape. The convict has no rights, no friends, and no future; the amateur may walk out whenever he pleases, and will be received by an admiring family and friends, and extolled by public opinion as a reformer who suffered martyrdom in the cause. Yet what he has experienced and learned falls as far short of what convicts endure, as the emotions of a theatergoer at a problem play (with a tango supper awaiting him in a neighboring restaurant) fall short of the long-drawn misery and humiliation of those who undergo in actuality what the play pretended.

Meanwhile, scores of animated humanitarians, penologists, criminologists, theorists and idealists have consulted, resolved, recommended, and agitated, striking hard but in the dark, and most of their blows going wide. Commissioners and inspectors have appeared menacingly at prison gates, loudly heralded, equipped with plenipotentiary powers; and the gates have been thrown wide by smiling wardens and sympathetic guards — tender hearted, big brained, gentle mannered people, their mouths overflowing with honeyed words and bland assurances, their clubs and steel bracelets snugly stowed away in unobtrusive pockets — who have personally and assiduously conducted their honored visitors through marble corridors, clean swept cells, spacious dining saloons, sanctimonious chapels, studious libraries and sunny yards; and have stood helpfully by while happy felons told their tales of cheerful hours of industry alternating with long periods of refreshing exercise and peaceful repose; nay, these officials will sometimes quite turn their backs upon the confidences between prisoner and investigator, lest there should seem to be even a shadow of restraint in the outpourings. "Is all well?" — "All is well!" — "No complaints?" — "No complaints!" What, then, could inspectors and commissioners do except bid a friendly and apologetic adieu to their ingenuous entertainers, and go forth bearing in each hand a pail of freshest whitewash? And if, during the colloquies, any malignant prisoner had happened, in a burst of reckless despair, to venture on an indiscreet disclosure, the visitors were allowed to get well out of earshot before the thud of clubs on heads was heard, and the groans of victims chained to bars in dark cells of airless stench, underneath the self same polished floors which had but an hour before resounded to paeans of eulogy and contentment.

This is not a fancy picture — no, not even of what is known to judges and attorneys (but not to prisoners) as "The model penitentiary of America," down in sunny Georgia. Fancy is not needed to round out the tale to be told of conditions existing and of things done and suffered in this age and country, behind walls which shut in fellow creatures of ours whom facile jurors and autocratic courts have sent to living death and to worse than death in accordance with laws passed by legislatures for the benefit of — What, or Whom? — Of the community? — Of social order and security? — Of outraged morality? — Of the reform of convicts themselves? — These questions may be considered as we go along. Meanwhile we may take notice that a number of persons, more or less deserving, gain their livelihood by the detection, indictment, arrest, conviction and imprisonment of other persons more or less undeserving; and whether or not these proceedings or any of them are rash or prudent, straight or crooked, just or tyrannous, lenient or cruel, honest or corrupt — is of secondary importance. What is of first importance is to supply fuel for the furnace of this unwieldy machine which operates our criminal system. Our costly courts must have occupation, our expensive jails must be kept full. We have succumbed to the disease which has been called legalism — the persuasion that the craving for individual initiative born of the unsettling of old faiths and the opening of new horizons, as well as the consequences of poverty, misery, ignorance, and hereditary incompetence — that this vast turning of the human tide, manifesting itself in many forms, some benign, many evil — that this broad and profound phenomenon can be met and controlled only by force, suppression, punishment, the infliction of physical pain and moral humiliation.

This disease perverts that beautiful and ideal impulse toward mutual order and self-restraint, which is Law, into lust for arbitrary and impudent power to control the acts and even the thoughts of men down to petty personal details; so that human life, at this very moment when it most needs and aspires to enlightened liberty, is crushed back into mechanical conformity with statutory regulations to which no common assent has been or can be obtained, and the logical consequences of which are as yet but obscurely recognized, even by the limited portion of the community which has been active in establishing them. To give it its most favorable interpretation, it is a sort of crazy counsel of perfection, incompatible with the healthy tenor and contents of human nature, and sure in the end to involve in its errant tentacles not only those who are the avowed objects of its pursuit, but likewise the lawmakers and enforcers themselves. Like all abuses, in its own entrails are the seeds of its destruction. Laws now on our books, if radically applied, would land almost every mother's son of us behind prison bars. And no doubt, when the murderer, forger, swindler, or white slaver, in his cell, begins to recognize in his new cell mate the judge who sentenced him, the attorney who prosecuted him, the juryman who convicted him, or the plaintiff who accused him, we shall find it expedient to subject our legal nostrums to a system of purgation, and our fever of legalism will abate. But if we will take thought betimes we may meet the trouble halfway, and thus avert, perhaps, the danger that the fever will be checked only by the overturning of all law, sane or insane. The following chapters are designed to help in defeating a catastrophe so unlovely.

Be it observed, first, that the only persons competent to reveal prison life as it is are persons who have been sentenced to prisons and lived in them as prisoners. Such showings might have been made long ago and often but that those who knew the facts were afraid to speak, or could not win belief, or had not education and capacity for expression requisite to get their facts printed. Others, exhausted or unmanned by their sufferings, wished only to hide themselves and forget and be forgotten; others have indictments still hanging over them, to be pressed should they betray a disposition to loquacity. Seldom, at any rate, has a man trained as a writer lived out a prison sentence and emerged with the ability and determination to throw the prison doors ajar and expose what has hitherto been invisible, unknown, and unsuspected.

Such a story has importance, because there is no group of persons anywhere but has some relation near or remote to what goes on in prisons. And the constant output of new laws, creating new crimes (so that one might say a man goes to bed innocent and wakes guilty) — this delirious industry must goad us all into feeling a personal interest in the administration of our penal machinery. You saw your friend tried and sentenced yesterday; you may yourself stand in the dock tomorrow, knowing yourself morally innocent, astounded at finding yourself technically guilty. Yet you yourself by your civic neglect or ignorance contributed to the enactment of the statute which now catches you tripping. You had better search into these matters, and find out what the authorities whom you helped to office are doing with their authority.

I have served my term in prison. The strain of that experience has not sharpened my appetite to bear testimony; my desire, as evening falls, is for rest and tranquility. But I owe it to my American birth, parentage and posterity, which connect me with what is honorable in my country, and to my individual manhood, to do what I hold to be a duty. Especially am I sensible of the claim upon me of those voiceless fellow men of mine still behind the bars, who cannot help themselves, who have honored me with their tragic confidences, who have believed that I would do my utmost to let the truth be known and show the world what penal imprisonment really means. I will keep faith with them.

I do not know that my attempt will succeed. Not every reader has imagination or sympathy enough to step into another's shoes — especially into the sorry shoes of a convict — and to realize facts which, even if we credit them, are disquieting and unpleasant. They make us uncomfortable and keep us awake at night. It is pleasanter to ignore or forget them, to say that they must be exaggerated, or that their purveyor has some ax of his own to grind; besides, do not abuses cure themselves in time? — and there is always time enough!

Three or four men, while I was spending my months in jail, had time to die of broken health and broken hearts, due to physical assaults or neglect, combined with a system of mental torture yet more effective and barbarous. Hundreds more are in similar plight, in Atlanta jail alone, who might be saved by timely attention and common humanity. Of this, more anon. I wish now to say that I undertake this work with a purpose as serious as I am capable of; and that among the inducements that move me, personal grudge and grievance are not included. Individual enmities are foolish and sterile for the individuals, and a bore for everybody else. Individuals are never so much to be hated as are the conditions which prompt them to act hatefully. Improve the environment which produced the murderer, robber, corrupt judge, rascally attorney, cruel warden, brutal guard, and you are likely to get a creature quite humane and tolerable. On the other hand, however, in the process of opposing evil conditions, one cannot avoid contact with the human products of them — sometimes in a stern and conclusive manner. Without going the length of the Spanish Inquisition, which tortured the body on earth in order to save the soul for heaven, it is not to be denied that punishment for evil deeds is latent in the bowels of the evil doer and will make him suffer in one way or another. We cannot strike a bad condition without hitting somebody who is carrying it out; and I am in the position of the Quaker who went to war: "Friend," he admonished his foe-man, "thee is standing just where I am going to shoot!"

I am not disposed to present here, in the way of credentials, any account of the circumstances that landed me in prison; still less to plead anything in the way of extenuation. The District Attorney, in his address, described me as a member of one of the most dangerous band of crooks and swindlers that ever infested New York. The government of this country authorized his statement; the news was bruited afar, wherever men read and write and invest money on the planet, and it appealed to every city editor and scandal-monger. Julian Hawthorne, son of the author of "The Scarlet Letter," a pickpocket. Well, what next!

If ever I cherished the notion that the charge was too preposterous to be believed, I was abundantly undeceived. To jail I went, and there served out my time to the uttermost limit allowed by the law. But in this connection I must touch on a matter which caused me some annoyance at the time.

In June of 1913 an editorial appeared in a New York newspaper endorsing some petitions which had been circulated asking the President of the United States to pardon me, mainly on the ground that in my ignorance of business I had been more of an innocent dupe than a deliberate malefactor. I had known nothing of these petitions; had I known of them, I would have omitted no effort to prevent them.

But I did get hold of the editorial; and found myself placed in the position of admitting myself guilty of the crime charged against me, but cowering under the pitiful excuse of having been bamboozled by others. What was even less tolerable, it presented me as entreating pardon of a government from which I would in fact have accepted nothing short of an unconditional apology. The Government had done me an injury under forms of law; I am only one man, and the Government stands for a hundred millions; but justice has no concern with numbers. My mining company and I were ruined; the iron and silver which we tried to put on the market will enrich others after we are gone; but I knew that what I and my partners had said of them was true. What had I to do with "pardons?" Pardon for what?

I lost no time in writing a letter to the editor of the paper, defining my attitude in the matter; but it never reached him. It is in the private safe of Warden Moyer, of Atlanta — or so I was informed by the Deputy Warden, when I was released in October — and for aught I know or care it may remain there forevermore.

Whether my respect for Law is higher or lower than is that of those persons who are responsible for my being sent to prison and kept there, may appear hereafter. But if crime be the result of anti-social impulses, then I hold that our present statutes fail to include under their categories, numerous and inquisitive though they be, a class of criminals who do, or intend, quite as much harm as was ever perpetrated by any man now under lock and key. Many of these persons occupy high places; most of them are respectable. We meet them and greet them in society. I know them, and also the murderers, highwaymen and yeggs of the penitentiary; and when I want sincere, charitable, generous human companionship, my choice is for the latter.

II

The Devil's Antechamber

*T*he judge pronounced our several prison sentences; that they were not also sentences of death was due to circumstances which developed later. The jury had previously dispersed, clothed in the sanctity of duties discreetly performed, knowing why they did them, and enjoying whatever consolation or advantage appertained thereto. Marshal Henkel cast upon us the look of the turkey buzzard as he swoops upon his prey, and we found ourselves being hustled down the familiar corridors, and into a room which we had not visited before; a few assistant marshals were there, and ere long a knot of newspaper men entered, observant and sympathetic, ready to receive and record the last words of the condemned.

It was about six o'clock of a dark and rainy March evening. "Any statement you would like to make?" One stands upon the brink of the living world, facing the darkness and silence, and hears that question.

Here is an end of things, a nothing, a sort of death. The support and countenance of one's fellow creatures are withdrawn; you are no longer a part of organized social existence. The rights, privileges and courtesies of manhood are stripped from you. You are adjudged unfit to touch the hand of an honest man in greeting; you are made impotent, disgraced, consigned to the refuse heap. The helpless shame put upon you is borne tenfold by those who bear your name, those you love and who love you. All that touches you henceforth shall be sordid, base and foul.

The prison officials who stand near you meet your eye with a leer of familiarity; they have handled thousands of men in your situation; they will have a grin or a growl for any remonstrance or protest you may make; power over you has been given to them; in you there is no power. You cannot blame them; their authority was deputed to them by men above them, who in turn received it from others; they are parts of the great machine, working irresistibly and automatically.

The judge is blameless; he had said, "The verdict of the jury makes it my painful duty to sentence you!" The jury is not to blame; they had decided upon the evidence, in accordance with their oath. The witnesses who bore testimony against you — did they not testify upon a solemn adjuration to utter nothing but the truth, at the peril of their immortal souls? The indictments to whose truth they bore witness — were they not made and brought by officers appointed by law to seek only impartial justice, and sworn to seek it without fear or favor?

Go back yet another step if you will, and consider the inspectors and detectives who gathered the complaints against you — is the beginning with them? No: they did but act for the protection of the community against a crime of which you were suspected, which was resolved to be a crime by the representatives of the nation in Congress assembled — that is, by the nation itself. You yourself, therefore, as part of the nation, share with the rest the responsibility for your present predicament. Then, whether the verdict against you were right or wrong — whether you be innocent or guilty — the blame at last comes home to you.

Such is the *reductio ad absurdum* — the lawyers' argument, technically flawless, though proceeding upon a transparent fallacy. That fallacy I shall consider hereafter; the question of the moment is the reporters' — "Have you any statement to make?"

Of what avail to answer? Has not enough been said during the trial of the past four months, and in vain? The young fellow stands there, courteously inquisitive, not unsympathetic perhaps, his pencil suspended. Have I any last words for the world which I am leaving? Shall I declaim of injustice, outrage, perjury? Shall I threaten revenge, or entreat mercy? Shall I "break down," or shall I "maintain an appearance of bravado" — he is ready to record either.

No, I will do none of these futile things. In such extremities, a man's manhood and dignity come to his support. I am helpless, to be sure, but only physically so. All this portentous paraphernalia of court and prison can touch nothing more than my body — my spirit is unscathed. It is the ancient consolation, coming down through poetry and history even to me. The Government — the Nation — can destroy my life, separate me from my people, throw mud on my name; but they cannot take away one atom of my consciousness of the truth. And it is better to have that consciousness than to retain all the rest without it. Blessed ethical truisms, which come to our succor when all else falls away!

Accordingly, the reporters were supplied with a few grave, not sensational words, suggested by the spur of the moment; they receded into the background, and Marshal Henkel, zealous to do his whole duty, and prevent the escape of an elderly gentleman through locked doors, echoing corridors, and the resistance of half a dozen lusty guards, advanced to the front of the stage and gave the order, "Handcuffs!" Knowing my marshal as I did, I was prepared for him, and extended my arm, till I felt the steel close round it with a solid snap. I was a manacled convict, and the community was saved.

But no time was to be lost; it was already after hours for the city prison; and the stout party of the other part of the handcuff and I passed out through the opening door promptly. As we turned the corner of the corridor, I suddenly saw the face of one of my sons-in-law, pale in the electric light; he forced a smile to his lips, and threw up one hand in greeting and farewell. Ah, those who are left behind! who can compensate them, and how can the injury done them be forgiven? I smiled a moment to myself as I thought of the ready answer of the august purveyor of the law — "You should have thought of that when you committed your crime!" That answer is also a part of the automatic machinery, and comes out, when the button is pressed, as inevitably as the package of chewing-gum from its receptacle — even more so!

I felt the rain on my face as we emerged from the old post office building, and saw the slanting drops as we passed through the rays of the street lamp on the corner. It was a memorable journey for me, short in its material aspect, long otherwise; and I noticed the particulars. Newspaper Row loomed on the right, strange in its familiarity, my work-place of many years. Here was the Third Avenue terminal, whence, a few hours before, I had confidently expected to take the train homeward, a free and vindicated man. There were glimpses, in the wet glare, of black headlines of newspapers, and the shrill professional cries of the gamins, "Hawthorne convicted!" It was like living in a detective story — but this was real!

But then came the thought that had often visited me in the past months, as I sat in the dingy courtroom, and listened perfunctorily to the legal wrangle, the abuse and defense, the long-drawn testimony of witnesses, the comment of the precise and genial judge, and contemplated idly the jaded, uncomfortable jury, the covert whispering of Assistant District Attorneys and post office inspectors, the dangling maps and the piles of documents — when I had asked myself, "Is all this real, or are they transient symbols importing a concealed significance?" Then, to my imagination, the empty walls would seem to melt away, and I saw a great, benign face and figure above the bench of the judge, holding a trial of those who labored so busily — a trial not entered in the books, and alien from that which occupied us; and recording judgments, unheard here, but eternal.

Was that the reality? Then let come what might on this plane of foolish contention, where we strive to cover the Immutable with the petty mask of our mutabilities. We sweat and toil for ends which we know not, and our paltry and blind decisions, our triumphs and failures, determine nothing but the degree of our own ignorance and impotence. The Lord's aims and issues are not ours, and ours do but measure our spiritual stature, and direct our immortal destiny, in His sight.

Yes, but this palpable world has its place and function nevertheless, to be accepted and used while time lasts. If those who tried me were on trial, I had no personal concern in the matter. My business, now, was to keep pace with my companion, who obligingly allowed his arm to swing with mine, so that passers-by, even if they could afford to divert their attention from their own footing on the muddy pavements, and from the management of their umbrellas, would not have noticed the bond uniting him and me. For this courtesy — the only possible one in the circumstances — I took occasion to express my recognition, to which he responded with easy friendliness. "We don't never make no trouble for them as don't go to hunt none," was his remark.

We were now in Center Street, and the Tombs was close at hand; and I drew into my lungs full drafts of the open air, murky though it was, reflecting that my opportunities of doing so in future would be limited.

Here were the steps supporting the tall steel gate, through which, in former days, I had seen many a poor devil pass; it was now others' turn to commiserate, or to jeer, the poor devil that was myself. There was no delay — we seemed to be awaited; and in the next minute I had felt what it is to be locked into a prison. I was behind bars, and could not get out at my own will — nor at anyone else's, for that matter; only at the impersonal fiat of the machine.

My marshal chatted and laughed a moment with the keeper, then gave me his buxom paw in farewell. I was led through stone passages, past rows of barred cells from which peered visages of fellow prisoners, incurious and preoccupied, or truculent and reckless — men under indictment and without bail, convicts making appeal, and culprits jailed for minor offenses. Such men were to be my comrades for the future. Some were out in the corridors, pacing up and down or chatting with friends; for the laws of the Tombs are unsearchable.

It is a unique place, a Devil's Antechamber, where almost anything except what is decent and orderly may happen. It is not so much a prison or penitentiary as a human pound, where every variety of waif and stray turns up and sojourns for a while; murderers, pickpockets, political scapegoats, confidence men, old professionals, first-time offenders, even suspects afterwards to be proved innocent. There is nothing that I know of to prevent thorough-going convicts from getting in here permanently;

the Tombs is of catholic hospitality. But they do not properly belong
here; it is but their halfway house — the antechamber.

And discrimination must be observed in classifying the inmates; no
one here likes to be regarded as beyond hope of bettering or escaping
from his restricted condition. He wears his own clothes, for one thing
— and no small thing; he is not known by a number; it is not, I believe,
en regle to club him into insensibility at will and with impunity, or to
starve him to death, or so much as to hang him up by the wrists in a
dark cell. The guards or keepers do not go about visibly armed with
revolvers or rifles; talking and smoking are not prohibited; the grotesque
assemblage is let out into the corridors occasionally, where they shamble
up and down and exchange observations and confidences; and they have
an hour outdoors in the stone paved, high-walled yard.

Moreover, extraordinary liberties can be obtained, if you know how
to go about it, and possess the means of bandaging inconvenient eyes.
Not only are we permitted to stampede our quotas of bedbugs, but leave
may be had to decorate our cells with souvenirs of art and domesticity,
to soften our sitting-down appliances with cushions, to drape the curtain
of modesty before the grating of restriction, to carpet our stone flooring,
to supply our leisure hours with literary nourishment, to secrete stealthy
cakes and apples for bodily solace, to enjoy surreptitious and not
overhazardous corridor outings when others are locked up, to write and
receive any sort of letters at any times, without having them first read
and stamped by licensed letter-ghouls.

More, there was at least one man among my companions there who
contrived, by devices which I never sought to fathom, to pass the
immitigable outer gates themselves every day, attend to his business in
the outer world for as many hours as might serve, returning quietly in
time for last roll-call. He took a keeper with him, of course, but only in
order to assuage possible anxiety on the part of those responsible for
his security; and one cannot help suspecting that as soon as the two
found themselves under the free sky, the keeper betook himself to some
friendly saloon, moving-picture palace, or other inviting retreat, and
only saw the other again when they met by appointment in their trysting
place.

It was safe enough no doubt; the prisoner would hardly think it worth
his while to attempt actual disimprisonment; he was content to sleep
at night in his cozy and comfortable cell. But the Moral Powers who
live in white waistcoats and saintly collars might have been restless in
their innocent sleep, had they known what things are practicable under
the austere name of incarceration in the City Prison.

Revolving these matters, I could only come to the conclusion that they pointed in one direction, namely, toward the anachronism and absurdity of our whole theory of punishment by imprisonment. As I shall have plenty of cause to give full discussion to this subject later on, I will only touch it here; but the fact is that we imprison malefactors or law-breakers (not always synonymous by any means, since there are a score of artificial crimes for one real one) not because we believe that to be the right thing for them, but simply by reason of our inability to imagine anything more suitable and sane. Moreover, there are the steel and stone jail buildings themselves, which cost much in money and more in graft; what shall be done with them? The wardens and guards, too — all the fantastic appanages of these institutions — are they to be cast incontinently upon a frigid world?

The law, in short, lags leagues and ages behind the moral sense of the community, so encumbered with its baggage train that it can never fetch up lost ground. We know perfectly well that the only punishments that can improve men are punishments of conscience from within, and of love from without — which is practically the same thing; and that punishment by imprisonment is punishment by hate in fact, whatever it may be in theory, and therefore diabolical and destructive. It can only inflame and multiply the evils it pretends to heal; and this is no theory, but a certified and established truth. Everybody who has been through it, knows it, everybody who dares to think may know it.

The whole thing is ridiculous, a huge and clumsy absurdity, stepping on its own feet and smelling to heaven. And here in our America it is today worse than in Italy or Russia, in some respects, because we know better that it is wrong, and therefore try to hide its enormities from open daylight. We lie and dissimulate about it, investigators whitewash it, conservative citizens deprecate exaggeration about it, wardens and guards — some of them, not all — are more wicked in their secret practices with convicts than they would be if they did not know that they would be stopped if the community knew of them. And it was inevitable that only a low type of men would accept positions as guards and wardens, because no honest man worth his salt could afford to work for the pay that these officials get; and the latter themselves would not work for it, did they not depend upon stealing twice as much, or more, by the graft.

But the system, inwardly rotten, crumbles; and in the interval remaining before it falls, the devil is getting in some of his most strenuous work. I know, and rejoice, that enlightened and magnanimous methods are obtaining in some places; hearty and brave men, here and there, are making themselves wardens of the good in men instead of exploiters of the evil. But in most prisons — among them, in that one down in Atlanta, whence I come — the devil is laboring overtime, conscious that his time is short.

The worst criminals there — as God sees criminals — are not the men in branded attire who sit in their cells and slouch about their sterile tasks, but men who walk the ranges in uniform, and who sit in the rooms of managers; for the crimes of the former are crimes of poverty or of passion, but those of the latter are voluntary, unforced, spontaneous crimes against human nature itself. They are upheld in high places; they are fortified by difficulty of "technical proof"; they are guarded by the menace of the spy system, and of criminal libel; but there is some reason to think that their term is near.

But let us return to that queer Antechamber of the Devil at the corner of Center and Franklin Streets.

There is a picture by that strange and unmatchable English artist of the Eighteenth Century, William Hogarth, of the mad house in London know as Bedlam. If he were here, he might draw a companion picture of the Tombs. The one is as much as the other a crazy, incoherent, irrational, futile place, yet embodying very accurately a certain aspect of the civic attitude toward the insanity of vice and crime of the day. There is nothing intelligent, purposeful, trenchant or radical about it; it is planted in ignorance and grows by neglect.

The keepers of it are good natured people enough, with a sense of humor, and free from trammels of principle, official or ethical. Their greatest severity is exercised toward those who stand outside the gates and crave permission to visit their friends within; these find the way arduous and beset with pitfalls of "orders," hours, and other mystic rites, except where they blow in miraculously, enforced by some breath from on high.

The inmates themselves, meantime, get on quite prosperously, so long at least as their money or money's worth holds out. There is no license or aptitude on their guardians' part to club them for relaxation's sake, or to kick them into underground dungeons for "observation" (you will understand that term by and by), or in any manner to hold a carnival of wanton brutality with them. The general idea is merely to keep them somewhere inside the building for the appointed or convenient time; beyond that, a liberal view is adopted of the conditions of their sojourn. They can buy eats to suit themselves, and have them served to them in their cells; they can hold communication with one another and with the outer world; I suppose they might wear evening dress after six o'clock if they wanted to. They are not victims of despotic and irresponsible power, and this is not only good for them, but also for the keepers, who are not led into the degradation and monstrous inhumanities which the possession of such power breeds in regular prisons.

Most of these prisoners expect to get out before long, either to go on to more permanent quarters, or to be liberated altogether; many of them emerge with comparatively small loss of social standing; for, indeed, highly respectable persons occasionally stray in here. The Tombs is not regarded as a final or fatal misfortune in a man's career. Yet it has its drawbacks.

Dirt is one of the more obvious of these; I might call it filth, but it depends on how one has been brought up. The impurity, at any rate, is not confined to the surfaces of the cells, floors and walls, but it creeps into the current language, and permeates the atmosphere. I am convinced that there never has been or could be a houseful of people who hear or use fouler and more unremitting obscenities than are those which flow sewer-wise and unhindered from the lips of many of this population.

It dribbles and exgurgitates, black and noisome, at the slightest provocation — nay, at none whatever, but with the delight of the past master and artist in verbal nastiness, anxious to display his erudition. It is a corruption of thought and expression so foul and concentrated, and withal so limited in its vocabulary and scope, that it fastens itself in the ear by a damnable iteration which no diverting of the attention can overcome; and it announces a depth of moral and mental debasement which seems as far from human as from merely animal possibilities; it is of the uttermost soundings of Tophet, and would probably be modified by fresh-heated gridirons even there.

This speech, or verbosity rather — for it has none of the logic or continuity of mortal utterances — does not continue uninterruptedly during the day, but observes special hours, when the guards are paying even less than their usual attention to the vagaries of their charges. Of these periods, the hours of early dawn are the most fertile.

When I dwelt in the environs of the city, it was my fortunate habit, in summer, to awake at dawn, just before sunrise, when the wide pasture outside my window was still obscure with the shadows of night, but the sky had begun to kindle with the splendors of day. In a group of darksome trees beside a little stream two hundred paces distant a song thrush was wont to trill forth the holy soul of awakening nature in such a paean of deathless Pan as inspired John Keats to utter the melodies of his magic ode. It consecrated the footsteps of the approaching sun, and the hearer was borne back on its swelling current to those pure early aeons of the human race, when love was the lord of life and innocence went forth crowned with rapture.

For this hymn of the primal gods was now substituted the hideous strophes and antistrophes of the grimy spirits of darkest New York. As one performer after another took up the strain, to and fro and from upper to lower tiers of cells, one awaited some seismic cataclysm to put an end to it and them; and the pauses of it were punctuated by bursts of dreary laughter, applausive of the incredible gushings of blighting depravity. They were the heralds of the prison day — the tune to which its steps were set. After it was over — when the yawning keeper had rattled the bars and threatened a twelve-hour close confinement to the perpetrators — one was amazed to identify with the latter persons outwardly in human shape, instead of malformed and sooty fiends from the bottomless abyss. I doubt whether anything to range with this occurs in any other criminal cauldron in the world; and therefore, with stopped nostrils, have I tried to give some faint adumbration of its character.

The head keeper of the menagerie I saw but once or twice; he was of Falstaffian proportions, with a clear and steady masculine eye and a demeanor of genial and complacent authority. He knew what and when to see and not to see, and had his own measure of the legalities and the proprieties. Little gusts of investigations and reforms passed by him as the eddying dust of the street sweeps by granite skyscrapers. *"J'y suis — J'y reste!"* was his motto. The subordinates had a general Irish complexion to my feeling; they were there to gather tips under the humorous guise of marshals of order. They were affable and easy, going as far as they could with only so much show of resistance as might lend more value to their yielding.

The prisoners were as heterogeneous as the contents of a rag-picker's auction. Yet they associated with little friction, herding uniformly kind with kind, only rarely lending themselves to transient ructions. They played little jokes on each other; a fat and serious captive was sitting of an evening at his cell door, absorbed in the perusal of a wide-spread newspaper; a gnomelike passerby in the corridor lit an unsuspected match, and suddenly the newspaper was a sheet of flame.

There were uglier spectacles; we had among us a fresh murderer, who after killing his wife had retained grudge enough against her to hack off her head. He kept darkly to his cell, sitting hour after hour with his head leaning on his hand, and eyes unswervingly downcast. His crime was not popular in that company, and none sought his companionship. At the other end of the scale were dazed, foreign creatures, guilty of they knew not what, gropingly and vainly striving to understand and to make themselves understood. There was the scum of the gutters; and there were men of intellect and high breeding, arming their hearts to resist shame and despair, and bending to soften the plight of children of misery below them.

The soul of the newcomer blenches and shivers occasionally as he contemplates the grisly, crazy scene, and thinks of all that menaces the women at home. And when, in the visiting hours, the women come and stare palely at the faces of those they love between the bars, wishing to cheer them, but appalled and made giddy by the abject and sordid horror of the solid fact, those who stare back at them and try to smile feel the grating of the wheels of life on the harsh bottom of things. But a man's manhood must not give way; there must be no triumph over him of these assaults and underminings of the enemy. Soul gazes at soul; but the talk is superficial and trivial. He is drowning in the gulf, and she stands yearning on the brink, but there shall be no vain outcries or outstretched arms. It is a condition wrought by men, not countenanced by God, and the spirit must command the flesh to endure.

Punch the button and listen once more to the refrain — "You should have thought of that before!" But can our posterity ever be induced to believe that such inhumanities could have been committed in the divine name of Law!

I am not qualified to write the epic of the Devil's Antechamber; I abode there but ten days, as we reckon time. On a cool and clear Easter Sunday morning the summons came to go forth to further adventures. Accompanied by three deputies, but free of the Henkel handcuffs, we passed the gates and trod the sunny pavements. Not a cloud in the blue sky, nor a taint upon the pure wings of the free air. None that saw us pass suspected our invisible fetters. Yet to me at least the thought that had ministered to me in the actual courtroom and prison, that the fetters were a dream and freedom the reality, was not accessible then. The absence of physical bonds seemed to render the imprisonment more, not less undeniable.

But we stepped out briskly, and breathed while we might.

III

THE ROAD TO OBLIVION

*F*ive of us stood on the platform of the Pennsylvania station; one stayed behind as the train moved out. He was the answer to the question, *"Quis custodiet ipsos custodes?"* — "Who shall watch the watchman?" Our two marshals were to see that we did not escape; he was to see that they saw. But his function ended when the departing whistle blew. He was a lean, pale, taciturn personage in black; Marshal Henkel had perhaps substituted him for the handcuffs. There was nothing between us and freedom now but our brace of tipstaves, the train crew, the public in and out of the train, the train itself moving at a fifty mile an hour pace, the law, and our own common sense. Moreover, we had decided to see the adventure through. Something more than nine hundred miles, and twenty-six hours, lay between us and Atlanta.

The elder of our two guardians was a short but wide gentleman of forty-five, of respectable attire and aspect, as of one who had seen the world and had formed no flattering opinion of its quality, yet had not permitted its imperfections to overcome his native amiable tolerance. He was prepared to take things and men easy while they came that way, but could harden and insist upon due occasion. Human nature — those varieties of it, at least, which are not incompatible with criminal tendencies — was his "middle name" (as he might have phrased it), so that in his proper social environment he was not apt to make social mistakes. This environment, however, could not but be constituted, in the main, of convicts either actual or potential; and there was probably no citizen, however high his standing or spotless his ostensible record, who in this official's estimate might not have prison gates either before him or behind him, or both. To be able to maintain, under the shadow of convictions so harsh, a disposition so sunny, was surely an admirable trait of character.

His assistant in the present job was still in the morning stage of his

career; a big, red-headed, rosy-cheeked, and obtrusively brawny youth of
five and twenty. He might be regarded as the hand of steel in the glove
of velvet of the combination. He may have carried bracelets of steel in
his rear pockets; but his associate earnestly assured me that such was far
from being the case. "I don't mind telling you the truth, Mr. Hawthorne," he confided to me with a companionable twist of the near
corner of his mouth, "I'd as soon think of cuffs, for gentlemen like you
two, as nothin' in the world! Why, it's like this — as far as I'm concerned,
I'd just put a postage-stamp on you and ship you off by yourselves —
I'd know you'd turn up all right of yourselves at the other end! That's
me; but of course, we has to foller the regulations; so there you are!"
And the ruddy youngster stretched his Herculean limbs and grinned,
as who should say, "Cuffs! Hell! What d'yer know about that? Ain't I
good for ten of yer?"

As the comely Pennsylvania landscape slid by, my friend of a lifetime
and I looked out on it with eyes that felt good-bye. For us, the broad
earth, bright sunshine and fresh air were a phantasmagoria — we had
no further part in them. From college days onward, through just fifty
years of life, we had traveled almost side by side, giving the world the
best that was in us, not without honor; and now our country had
stamped us as felons and was sending us to jail. It had suddenly
discovered in us a social and moral menace to its own integrity and
order, and had put upon us the stigma of rats who would gnaw the
timbers of the ship of state and corrupt its cargo. The end of it all was
to be a penitentiary cell, and disgrace forever, to us and to ours.

But was the disgrace ours and theirs? When you kick a mongrel cur
it lies down on its back and holds up its paws, whining. But the
thoroughbred acts quite otherwise; you may kill it, but you cannot
conquer it. We would not lie supine under the assault of the blundering
bully. Disgrace cannot be inflicted from without, — it can only come to
a man from within. And the disgrace which is attempted unjustly must
sooner or later be turned back on those who attempted it; the men
whom our country had deputed to handle the machinery of law had
blundered, and had convicted and condemned those who had done no
wrong. I had never felt or expressed anything stronger than contempt
for any particular persons actively concerned in our indictment and
trial — the pack that had snapped and snarled so busily at our heels. Till
the last I had believed that their purpose could not be accomplished, —
that the nation would awake to what was being done in the nation's
court, under sanction of the nation's laws. The public must at last realize
the moral impossibility that men who had all that is dearest to men to
lose, should throw it away for such motives as were ascribed to us —

ascribed, but, as we felt, not established. And when the public realized that, thought I, they would perceive that the shame which the incompetent handling of the legal machinery aimed to fix on us must finally root itself not in us but in the public; since the world and posterity, which, more for our names' sake than for our own, would note what was being done, would not distinguish between the employee and the master — the country and the country's attorneys, and would hold the former and not the latter accountant.

I was mistaken; the public took the thing resignedly to say the least. And though I consented to no individual animosities — for individuals in such transactions are but creatures of their trade, subdued to what they work in, like the dyer's hand — I could not so easily absolve the impersonal master. The fault inhered of course not in any grudge of the community against us, but in the prevalent civic neglect (in which, in my time, I had participated with the rest) of duties to the state, theoretically impersonal, but which cannot proceed otherwise than on personal accounts.

Man is frail; but, next to sincere religious conviction, no principle exists so strong to control him as *noblesse oblige* — the impulse to keep faith and to deal honestly imposed not by his individual conscience alone, but by the pure traditions of his inheritance. The man who has the honor of his forefathers to preserve — an honor which may be a part of the nation's honor — is a hundred-fold better fortified against base action than is the son of thieves, or even of nobodies. The latter may find heroism enough to resist temptation, but the former is not tempted; he dismisses the thing at the start as preposterous. It is no credit to him to put such temptation aside, but it is black infamy and treachery to make terms with it. If he do make terms with it, no punishment can be too severe — though I take leave to say that the external penalties which state or nation can inflict are trivial compared with those deadly ones which torture him from within; but before crediting him with having yielded, the state or nation should not merely assume his innocence — a stipulation which our law indeed makes, but which is notoriously disregarded by prosecuting attorneys — but should weigh and sift with the most anxious and jealous scrutiny anything and everything which might appear inconsistent therewith. A son of a thief who steals does but follow his inborn instinct; but a thief whose ancestors were gentlemen is a monster, and monsters are rare.

In England and the other older countries, the principle of *noblesse oblige* still has weight with the public as well as with the individual; here, the welter of democracy, which has not evolved into distinct human form, uniformly ignores it; leveling down, not up, it is quick to see a scoundrel in any man. Meanwhile, instead of taking thought to abate the public mania for success in the form of concrete wealth which multiplies inducements to crime, it creates shallow statutes to punish acceptance of such inducements, with the result that while in its practical life it rushes in one direction, it erects in its courts a fantastic counsel of perfection which points in a direction precisely opposite. Our law tends not merely to the penalizing of real crimes, but to the manufacture of artificial ones; and the simple standard of natural or intuitive morals is bewilderingly complicated with a régimen of patent nostrums, conceived in error and administered in folly.

Sitting in the car window with my friend, I revolved these things, while the sunny landscape wheeled past outside, and our guardians chewed gum in the adjoining section. After all was said and done, amid whatever was strange and improbable, he and I were going to the penitentiary in the guise of common swindlers. A pioneer on the western plains, in the old days, riding homeward after several hours' absence, found his cabin a charred ruin, his property destroyed, his wife lying outraged with her throat cut, his children huddled among the débris with their brains dashed out. Sitting on his bronco, he contemplated the immeasurable horror of the catastrophe, and finally muttered, "This is ridiculous!"

"This is ridiculous!" I remarked to my companion; and he consented with a smile; when language goes bankrupt, the simple phrase is least inadequate. "We may as well have lunch," he said; and we rose and journeyed to the rear of the train, sedulously attended by our deputies. The spontaneous routine of the physical life is often a valuable support to the spiritual, reminding the latter that we exist from one moment to another, and do wisely to be economical of forecasts or retrospects. We journeyed back, through innocent scenes of traveling life, to the smoking compartment, which happened to be vacant; and under the consoling influence of tobacco our elder companion sought to lighten the shadows of destiny.

"You gentlemen," he said, uttering smoke enjoyingly through mouth and nostrils, "don't need to worry none. It's like this: the judge figured to let you off easy. He's bound, of course, to play up to the statute by handin' you your bit, but, to start with, he cuts it down all he can, and then what does he do but date you back four months to the openin' of the trial! All right! After four months you're eligible for parole on a year and a day's sentence, ain't yer? Your trial began on November 25th, and today is the 24th of March. That means, don't it, that you make your application the very next thing after they gets you on the penitentiary register tomorrer! Why, look-a-here," he continued, warming to his theme, and becoming, like Gladstone as depicted by Beaconsfield, intoxicated with the exuberance of his own verbosity, "it wouldn't surprise me, not a bit, sir, if you and your mate was to slip back with us on the train tomorrer evenin', and the whole bunch of us be back in little old New York along about Wednesday! That's right! An' what I says is, that ain't no punishment — that's no more'n takin' a pleasure trip down South, at the suitable time o' year! An' I guess I been on the job long enough to know what I'm talkin' about!"

We guessed he knew that he was talking benevolent fictions; and yet there was plausibility in his argument. The law did not allow parole on sentences of a year or under, but on anything over one year, a convict was eligible, and our sentence of twenty-four hours over the twelve-month therefore brought us within this provision. In imposing that extra day, the judge could hardly have been motived by anything except the intention to open this door to us; and although the regular meeting of the parole board at the prison was not due just then, we were informed that an extra meeting might be summoned at any time. The board consisted of the warden of the prison, the doctor, and the official who presided at all parole board meetings at the various federal penitentiaries throughout the country, — Robert LaDow. The law declares that a majority of the board decides the applications that come before it; and as two members of the board make a quorum, it seemed obvious that the warden and the doctor of Atlanta Penitentiary would serve our turn — if they wanted to. Mr. LaDow, of course, might be appealed to by telegraph if expedient.

Turning the thing over, therefore, with the cozening rogue in front of us drawing our attention to the buttered side as often as it appeared, we could hardly avoid the conclusion that there was a possibility of his being right. We might be required to remain in Atlanta barely long enough to don a suit of prison clothing and to have our bertillons made, and forthwith make a triumphal return home, with our scarlet sins washed white as snow. Of such an imprisonment it might be said, as wrote the poet of the baby that died at birth,

"If it so soon was to be done for,
  One wonders what it was begun for,"

but it would not be the first thing that we had noticed in Federal administration of justice which might have been similarly criticized.

My allusion to this subject here is only by way of leitmotif for a thorough discussion hereafter. The juggling with the parole law, by the Department of Justice and the parole boards, is one of the most inde-

fensible and cruel practical jokes that "the authorities" play upon
prisoners. It caused two deaths by slow torture while I was at Atlanta,
as shall be shown in the proper place; and there is no reason to suppose
that the percentage at other prisons was not as large or larger. The
sufferings short of death that are due to it cannot be calculated. A
practical joke? — yes; but there is a practical purpose back of it. The
miserable men who are practiced upon by this means, helpless but
hoping, are led to believe that they may buy freedom at the price of
treachery to their fellows. Can it be credited that a convict in his cell,
with perhaps years of living death before him, — you do not yet know
what that means, but if I live to tell this story, you will be able to guess
at its significance before we part — will refuse the opportunity offered
to end it at once in return for merely speaking one or two names? — a
convict — a creature outlawed, crushed, damned, dehumanized, de-
spised, — can we look from him for a heroism, a martyrdom, which
might shed fresh honor on the highest name in the community? I
confess that I would not have looked for it a year ago, and I doubt
whether you look for it now. But, I have to report, with joy in the
goodness and selflessness in men whom you and I have presumed to
look down upon, that in very few instances that I have heard of, and in
almost none that I know, has a convict thus terribly tempted even
hesitated to answer — NO! But many an old and cherished prejudice
will begin painfully to gnaw its way out of your complacent mind before
we are done.

The City of Brotherly Love flickered by and was left behind, like the
sentiment which it once stood for. We were headed for Washington,
where the will and conscience of the nation take form and pass into
effect. Government of the people by lawyers, for lawyers; did they know
what they were doing? The Constitution, bulwark of our liberties; the
letter of the law, technicalities, precedents, procedure, the right of the
individual merged in the public right, and lost there! The House — five
hundred turbulent broncos, each neighing for his own bin; the Senate
— four score portentous clubmen, adjusting the conservative shirt-front
of dignity and moderation over the license of privilege and "the interests"; the Executive — dillydallying between nonentity and the Big Stick;
the Supreme Court — a handful of citizens and participators in our
common human nature, magically transmuted into omniscient and
omnipotent gods by certificates of appointment! And the rest of our
hundred millions, in this era of new discoveries and profound upheav-
als, on this battlefield of Armageddon between Hell and Heaven, in this
crumbling of the old deities and the looming of the Unknown, — are
we to lie down content and docile and suffer this hybrid monster of

Frankenstein, under guise of governing, to squat on our necks, bind our Titan limbs, bandage our awakening eyes, gag our free voices, sterilize our civic manhood, and debase us from sons of divine liberty into the underpinning of an oligarchy?

My friend and I — while our licensed proprietors napped with one eye open — smiled to each other perhaps, recognizing how the prick of personal injury and injustice will arouse far-reaching rebellion against human wrongs and imperfections in general. But our famous American sense of humor may be worked overtime, and, from a perception of the incongruity and relative importance of things, be insensibly degraded into pusillanimous indifference to everything, good or bad. The soberest observer may concede that there is a spiritual energy and movement behind visible phenomena, whose purport and aim it is the province of the wise to understand. The peril of Armageddon lies in the fact that evil never fights fair, but ever masks itself in the armor of good. Not only so, but good may be changed into evil by hasty and misdirected application, and do more harm — because unsuspected — than premeditated evil itself. Public endowment of chosen persons with power is good and necessary in our form of civilization, and the chosen ones may accept it in good faith. But in a community where everybody has business of his own to mind, and is put to it so to conduct it as to keep off the poor rates, deputed powers, designed to be limited, always tend to become absolute. It is heady wine, too, and intoxicates those who partake of it. And it is only a seeming paradox that absolute and irresponsible power is more apt to develop in a democracy than under any other form of human association. Holders of it, moreover, instead of fighting for supremacy among themselves, and thus annulling their own mischievousness, as would at a first glance seem likely, soon learn the expediency of agreeing together; each keeps to his own area of despotism, cooperating, not interfering with the rest. But the system inevitably takes the form of rings within rings, each interior one possessing progressively superior dominion. At last we come to a central and small group of men who are truly absolute, and are supported and defended in their stronghold by the self-interested loyalty of the rest. But they do not proclaim their supremacy; on the contrary, they hide it under clever interpretations of law, and, at need, by securing the enactment of other laws fitted to the exigency of the occasion. If there is remonstrance or revolt among their subjects, they subdue it partly by pointing out that it is the law, and not themselves, that is responsible; and partly by employing other legal forms to put down the resistance. You cannot catch them; they vanish under your grasp as principles, not men. Their voice is never heard saying, "I will!" but always, "The law requires." And these autocrats — this oligarchy — are only men like ourselves, with like passions, limitations and sinful inheritance. They were not born to the purple — they just happened to get to it. But being possessed of it — and apart of course from any crude and obvious malfeasance in office — they cannot be "legally" dislodged; and if they step aside, it is only to let alter egos take their place. The King of England — the Emperor of Germany — can be deposed by the people, and his head cut off; but the free and independent — but law-abiding — citizens of the United States cannot throw off this subtle tyranny, because it is identified with legal provisions which we have insensibly allowed to creep into the inmost and most personal fibers of our lives. As for modifying or abolishing the law itself — that would be anarchy!

It would be foolish to contend that our rulers are actuated by any personal malevolence or even, at first, by unlawful personal ambition; they are, as I have said, for the most part lawyers, and law is their fetish — their magical cure-all and philosopher's stone. They almost persuade themselves, perhaps, that we the people make the laws; whereas not more than one man in ten thousand — even of lawyers — knows what the law in any given case is, nor would the majority of us approve any particular law, if we were afforded the chance. Any one of us will support the law against his enemy, but not, in behalf of his enemy, against himself. But our legalized sultans and satraps, Councils of Ten and Grand Inquisitors, keep an easy conscience; the Law is King and can do no wrong. A few centuries ago it was law in England to kill a man for taking any personal liberties; there was not much harm in that, for most of the persons that counted were above the law, being nobles or gentlemen. But our way is far more injurious; if a man takes a personal liberty, the cry is, Put him in jail! Death is a penalty which only disposes of a man forever; but jail is poisonous; the man survives, but he becomes criminal, and an enemy of society. And this cry for jail does not appear to emanate from legal tribunals merely, but we the people ourselves have caught it up, and invoke cells and chains for the lightest infraction of public or personal convenience; nay, we clamor for more laws to supplement our already overburdened statute-books. Thus do we thoughtlessly strengthen the hands of our masters. The nostrum which they manufactured to govern us withal, and which at first had to be administered to us willy-nilly, has now become like that notorious patent medicine for which the children cry. We kiss the rod — as long as it is laid across our fellows' backs and not our own. And the rule of Law, by lawyers, for lawyers, shows no signs of vanishing from our earth. Only convicts and ex-convicts dissent; for they know what they dissent from. As an unidentified friend wrote to me of late, "No thief ere felt the halter draw, With good opinion of the law"; but the thief had reason on his side. And it may yet come to pass that his reasons may be listened to.

Darkness set in as we entered the sacred soil of Virginia; night lay before us — our next night would be spent inside penitentiary walls. Was it a dream, or would some cosmic cataclysm occur in season to prevent it? No: the ancient routine of one fact after another, of cause and effect, would keep on with no regard for our sensibilities; however important we might appear to ourselves, we were but specks infinitesimal in the vast scheme of things. Miracles and special providences are for story books; if you are the victim of abuses, be sure that the remedy will come not through averting them, but by carrying them out to the finish. On the morning of his execution, it seemed incredible that Charles I should be beheaded; but he mounted the scaffold, laid his head upon the block, and the masked man lifted his sword and cut it off. All that is left for you is not to falter — to keep down that tremor and sickening of the heart; when Danton of the French Revolution reached the guillotine, he was heard to mutter, "Danton, no weakness!" And many an unrecorded Danton, on the night before his appointed death, has lain down and slept soundly. It recurred to my memory that my father, shortly before his death, had said to an old friend of his, "I trust in Julian." On the day following his death, that friend had journeyed to Concord to tell me those words — returning to Boston immediately. My father's son had lived to be proclaimed a felon; but I slept sound that night.

All next day we were passing through the raw red soil of the South, with its cotton plantations, forlorn at this season, its omnipresent idle Negroes, and its white folks, lean and solemn, standing guard over what fate had left to them. At stopping places we would step out for a few minutes on the platform of the observation-car, to breathe the air and feel the sunshine, — the affectionate deputies close at our elbows. Some of our fellow passengers were bound for Florida or Cuba, to escape the crudity of the northern March; "May be we'll meet up again there!" some of them said, innocently unsuspicious of what sort of characters they were addressing. Paradise and the Pit travel side by side on this earth, and find each other very tolerable company.

Into Atlanta station the train at last rolled; the journey to oblivion was all but finished. The restless little city, turmoiling in its boom, swarmed around us; we had to wait half an hour, our gripsacks in our hands, for the surface-car to the prison, three miles or more beyond the town. We awaited it with some impatience — such is the unreasonableness of our mortal nature. At last we were rumbling off on our trip of twenty minutes, sitting unnoticed in the midway seats, our considerate but careful guardians on the watch at the front and rear platforms. The car took its time; it stopped, started again, stopped, started, after the manner of ordinary cars; oh, for a magic carpet or pneumatic tube, to make an end of this! or for a thousand years! It was as if the headsman were making preliminary flourishes with his sword, ere delivering his blow. These were difficult minutes.

They ended; "Here we are!" We alighted, and advanced to the entrance of an expanse of ornamental grounds, with a cement pathway leading up to an extensive fortified structure — a wall thirty feet high sweeping to right and left from the tall steel gateway, with the summits of stone towers emerging beyond. I stepped out briskly, in advance of the others; I noticed some bright-hued flowers in a bed on the right. In a few moments I was ascending a wide flight of steps; as I did so, the gateway yawned, and two men in uniform stepped out. There was a transient halt, a few words were exchanged; we went forward, and the gate closed behind us.

IV

Initiation

"*P*ut the fear of God in his heart!"

This phrase, impious and ironic, is used by officials in prisons, and repeated by prisoners. It has no religious import. The naming of God in that connection reminds me of a remark I heard from a moonshiner — as the distillers of illicit whiskey in the mountain regions of the South are called — who had lately arrived at the penitentiary. He said, "I allus thought this here Jesus Christ was a cuss-word; but these folks say he was some religious guy!" His enlightenment was doubtless due to the first aid to the unregenerate administered by our chaplain.

To "put the fear of God in a man's heart" means to break his spirit, to cow him, to make him, from a man, a servile sneak; and this is effected not by encouraging him to remember his Creator, but by instilling into him dread of the club, the dungeon, and the bullet. He must learn to fear not God, but the warden, the captain and the guard. He is to be hustled about, cuffed, shoved, kicked, put in the hole, punished for not comprehending surly and half inarticulate orders, or for not understanding gestures without words; all of which encouragements to obedience are, indeed, specifically forbidden by the rules which were formulated in Washington and disseminated for the information of the investigation committees and of the public, but which are disregarded nevertheless by the prison authorities from the highest to the lowest. For they risk nothing by disregarding them; there is no one except prisoners to complain of illegal treatment, and there is no one for them to complain to except the very persons who are guilty of the illegalities; and the warden at Atlanta, at any rate, has repeatedly stated that he would not accept the oaths of any number of prisoners against the unsupported denial of a single guard. To do otherwise would be to "destroy discipline." Moreover, these unverified complaints – such is their inevitable category in the circumstances – are themselves fresh causes of offense, and productive of the severest punishments – not only clubbing and close confinement, often in the dark hole, but loss of good time, which of course is more dreaded than anything else.

But may not the prisoners complain to the committees or inspectors, appointed precisely to enquire into and relieve abuses of this sort?

I shall have a good deal to say about these agents of humanity presently. I will only say here that no prisoner who cares whether he lives or dies, or who possesses common sense or the smallest smattering of experience of prison affairs, ever is so reckless as to impart any facts to the persons in question. If he accuses any guard or other official of cruelty, the entire force of prison keepers can and will be at need marshaled to deny point-blank that any such thing occurred, or, if any did, it was because the accused official was at the time quelling a dangerous revolt, and deemed his own life in peril. If this evidence be insufficient, it is a pathetic truth that some prisoners can always be found so debased by terror and abject as to perjure themselves against their comrades. It is among Negro prisoners that such traitors are commonly sought and found. White men uniformly have a sense of honor – thieves' honor, if you please – which keeps them loyal. There are exceptions to this rule, and there are also exceptions to the rule that Negroes betray. I have the pleasure and the honor of the acquaintance of some Negro prisoners at Atlanta who would sooner die than ingratiate themselves with the officials by a falsehood.

Accordingly, complaints of brutal treatment at Atlanta are not frequent, either to the officials or to investigators; otherwise, I need not tax your imagination to picture what happens to the complainants after the investigators have departed.

Order and discipline — as appertaining to prisoners, not to officials — must be preserved; of course they must, if we are to have any prisons at all. And since there is no way for the prisoners to compel the guards to keep within the license accorded to them, we must compel the prisoners to accept whatever injustice or outrage the unrestrained despots of the ranges have the whim to inflict upon them. There are desperate revolts at times — desperate in the literal sense, since they have no hope of relief in them, but only the tragic rage against tyranny which will sometimes blaze up in victims — and on the other hand there are officials who will resign their positions rather than connive at abuses. But every means is taken to avert this last; for guards know things, and the System could be shaken by men who not only know, but, unlike prisoners, have a chance to make what they know believed.

All this time we have been waiting just inside the prison gates. The difference between just inside and just outside is important; for nine convicted men out of ten, it would be punishment for their misdeeds more than sufficient to be taken no further on the way to retribution than that. Whatever humiliation and disgrace they are capable of feeling or have cause to feel is at that first moment at its height; it strikes upon them unaccustomed and defenseless — never so acutely sensitive as then. Afterward, familiarity with misery and shame renders them progressively more and more callous, without adding one jot to the public odium of their position. They can never forget that first clang of the closing gates in their ears; the whole significance of penal imprisonment is in that. Many a man, the moment after that experience, might turn round and go forth a free man, yet with a soul charged with all the mortal burden that man-devised penalties can inflict upon him. Moreover, not having been unmanned and his nature violated by physical insults and outrages, he might find strength and spirit to begin and pursue a better life thereafter. The "lesson" (word which our shallow and officious moralists roll so sweetly under their tongues) would have been taught him to the last tittle, and withal enough of the man remain to profit by it. Whereas, under the existing conditions, no more than four or five years in jail destroy any possibility of future usefulness in most men; they have been hammered into something helpless, dazed, or monstrous; and even if they have courage to attempt to take hold of life again, they are defeated by the unremitting pursuit of our spy system, which depends for the main part of its livelihood upon getting ex-convicts back to jail — whether on sound or on perjured evidence is all one to the spies. So, as I said some time ago, most prison sentences are life sentences, to all practical intents. To the manhood of the man, prison means death.

Do some of the above statements appear extreme? Read on, and decide. Meanwhile I will observe that so long as prisons endure, such abuses as have been hinted at must persist. Whatever reforms have in special instances ameliorated them, have in so far only gone to show that the whole system is vicious and irrational.

My friend and I looked at our new masters with curiosity; they looked at us with what might be termed arch amusement. With such a look do small boys regard the beetles, kittens, or other animals, power to torment whom has been given them. It was after prison hours – the men had been already locked in their cells, and the warden and deputy had gone home. It was left to the subordinates to put the fear of God in our hearts; we could only surmise how far they would go in that instruction. We did not then know that their power was limited only by their good pleasure. But it is an accepted and reasonable principle with them that the sooner one begins to take the nonsense out a prisoner, the better. The strangeness of his surroundings intimidates him at the start, and he more readily realizes that he has no friends and that he is in prison – not (as one of the guards afterward took occasion to remark) in a "sanitarium for decayed crooks." A good scare thrown into him now will bring forth more fruit than greater pains taken – and inflicted – hereafter.

Our anticipations, however, were the less formidable, because we had been exhaustively assured during the past ten days that Atlanta Penitentiary was not so much a penitentiary as a sort of gentlemen's summer resort and club, where conditions were ideal and treatment almost foolishly humane and tender. This information came not only from all court officials with whom we had held communion on the subject, but from our own counsel at the trial; the judge himself seemed to believe it, and if you ask the prison authorities at Atlanta, they will earnestly assure you that prisoners there are treated like gentlemen, are given every material comfort consistent with their being prisoners at all, are sumptuously fed and housed, and are helped in all ways to build up their manhood, maintain their self-respect, and prepare themselves for a career, after liberation, as valuable and industrious citizens. We were naturally disposed to credit assertions so emphatically and variously made, – some basis for them there must be. And it was obvious, at a glance, that the corridor in which we stood was spacious and airy, with a clean limestone pavement; that the disorder and shiftlessness of the Tombs was absent here. The guards who attended us wore neat dark uniforms of military cut; and if their caps were tilted back on their heads, or cocked on the northeast corner, that was a pardonable expression of their authority and importance. I saw no firearms and no blood, nor were the groans of tortured convicts audible. I remembered the flowers in the garden outside, and was prone to think that things might have been very much worse; they were certainly better, at a first glance, than at Sing Sing, which I had visited on a newspaper assignment about fifteen years before. I had resolved beforehand to make the best of everything, and it seemed already possible that I might not have to make believe very much to do so.

No resolve, however, could overcome the influence of that locked and barred gate, nor the realization that I was a convict, and that nobody inside the penitentiary had any doubt that I was justly convicted. Friends were remote and helpless; the support of former good repute was annulled; I stood there impotent, one man against the Federal Government, with nothing to aid me but the weight of my personal equation (whatever that might be worth) and my private attitude on the question of my guilt, which the trial had not modified, but which could be of no practical benefit to me here. The sensation of confronting everywhere a settled and hostile skepticism as to one's integrity was novel, and hard to meet with a firm countenance. And I felt how easily this sensation might crush the courage of one who was conscious of being justly condemned. How many men must be sitting yonder in those cells who lacked the moral consolations that I had! The thought sharpened my perception of the horror of all imprisonment, but at the same time stiffened my fortitude; for if these men could live through their ordeal, how much more could I!

Meanwhile we were being hurried through the handsome corridor, and down a flight of iron steps to a less presentable region. There was no aggressive brutality, only a peremptory curtness, entirely proper in the circumstances. Our only defense against physical severity was a bearing of cheerful but not overdone courtesy, and we gave that what play we might. I could not foretell how I might behave under a clubbing, and would not bring the thing to a test, if I could decently avoid it. In a long, low, shabby, ill-lighted room we were lined up against a counter, on the other side of which were two or three of our fellow prisoners — the first we had seen — whose function it was to fit us with prison suits. They consisted of a sack coat and trousers of grey-blue cloth — rather heavy goods, for the warm season had not yet begun — and this was obviously far from being their first appearance on a convict; suits are handed down from one generation of prisoners to another until they are entirely worn out; my own was of an ancient vintage and a good deal defaced, but I had no ambition to be a glass of fashion in jail. Of course I could only conjecture what diseases previous wearers of it might have suffered from; but I hoped for the best. Every new arrival at the penitentiary is presumed to be dirty until he is proved clean, and the only way for him to prove his bodily purity is to submit to a bath. The regulation is commendable, and was welcome to us after our day and night in the train; but a comrade of mine from the mountain wildernesses of South Carolina, where bathing is still regarded as a degrading innovation, described to me long afterward what a sturdy battle he had put up against the disgrace, and being a lusty youth, it had taken the best efforts of several guards to hold him under the spout long enough to wet him — and themselves into the bargain. Though this was the first time since infancy that I had bathed under compulsion, I complied very readily, and even said to my friend, "This isn't so bad!" It is not permitted, under the law, to give out any news about prisoners to the world without, after they have once passed the portals; nevertheless, this memorable remark of mine was printed next day in the New York newspapers, together with the scarlet hue of my necktie, and some other details, — my registered prison number among them, my own first knowledge of which was derived from the published paragraph. It was my first intimation of a fact which afterward exercised no small influence on my destiny in the prison — that I was a "distinguished," or at least a notorious prisoner. This influence had its good as well as its bad aspect, in the long run, but the latter was in the beginning the more conspicuous. The unidentified press-agent who disseminated to an eager world the news about the bath and the necktie, continued to be active during our stay in Atlanta, but his other communications were not even approximately so accurate as the first one, and nearly all of them were children of his imagination exclusively, and were more likely to be gratifying to the officials than to my fellow prisoner and myself.

From the bath to the bedchamber. Up the darksome stairs again into the stately corridor; through an inner gateway, and into a wide hall which communicated to right and left, through small steel doors, with the west and east ranges (dormitories). The west door was unlocked, and we were pushed into a huge room, about two hundred feet by a hundred and twenty, with tall barred windows along each side. Inside this space had been constructed a sort of inner house of steel, seven or eight stories in height, with zigzag stairways at either end, leading to narrow platforms that opened on the individual cell doors. These doors were barred, and were locked by throwing a switch at the near end of the ranges; but any particular door could also be opened by a key. The cell doors of the inner structure were at a distance of some twenty feet from the walls and windows of the outer shell, and got what light and air they had from these — none too much of course. Also, the guard on duty in the range, if the weather be chilly, will close the windows, against the protests of the prisoners, and against the regulations too; but most of the guards are thin-blooded Southerners, and diseased into the bargain, and do not like cold air. The consequence is that the four hundred pairs of lungs in each range soon vitiate the atmosphere; the prisoners turn and toss in their cots, have bad dreams, and rise in the morning with a headache.

We mounted three or four flights of iron steps, and were introduced into a cell near the corner. It was, like all the others, a steel box about eight feet long by five wide, and seven or eight high. On one side, two cots two feet wide were hinged against the wall, one above another; they reduced the living space to a breadth of three feet. The wall opposite was made of plain plates of steel, and so was the inner end of the cell, but in this, at a man's height from the floor, was a round hole an inch in diameter. That was a part of the spy system; for between the two rows of cells is a narrow passage, in which the guard can walk, and, himself unseen and unheard, spy upon the prisoners and listen to their conversation. All prisoners are at all times of the day and night under observation. This seems a slight thing; but the cumulative effect of it upon men's minds is disintegrating. At no moment of their lives can they command the slightest privacy. And what right to privacy, you ask, has a prisoner? Would he not use it to cut his way through the chilled steel walls with his teeth and nails, or to plot revolt with his cellmate? — Possibly; but even a beast seeks privacy at certain junctures; and to deny all privacy tends to bestialize human beings. It is a part of the "put-the-fear-of-God-in-his-heart" principle — to break, humiliate, degrade the man, and render him unfit for human association. There are a washbasin and a toilet seat at the foot of the cot, facing the barred door. What difference can it make to a convict if the guard, or any other passer-by, watches him while he uses them?

There had been issued to us sheets, a pillowcase, and a grey blanket of the army sort; our first duty was to make our beds. Mattress and pillow were stuffed stiff with what felt like wood chips, and was probably straw and corn-husks; the pillow was cylindrical; the mattress was hil-locked and hollowed by the uneasy struggles with insomnia of countless former users. There was a campstool whose luxuries we might share. We had, each, a prison toothbrush, and a comb. In the ceiling of the cell, beyond reach of an outstretched arm, was an electric bulb which would be darkened at nine o'clock. But all this was welcome; I had often roughed it in conditions quite as severe; my spirits could not be dashed by mere hardships or inconveniences. We put our domestic ménage in order cheerfully, glad that we had been celled together, instead of doubling up with strangers. Nor would it have discouraged us to know that the west range was the one occupied by Negroes and dangerous characters. The place was silent; none of the demoniac chantings and hyena laughter of the Tombs. We had our little jests and chucklings as we made our arrangements; Courage, Comrade! the period of suspense and anticipation is passed; we are at grips with the reality now!

Moreover — "Every prisoner, on installation in his cell, is supplied with rolls and hot coffee, and with pipe and tobacco!" Thus would the statement run in the report to the Department. What if the bread be uneatable, the coffee undrinkable, and the tobacco unsmokable? The mere idea of such things is something; besides, prisoners do contrive, being hard put to it, to consume them. We ourselves at least tried all three; if it proved easier to be abstinent than self-indulgent, that was our own affair. Meanwhile, our mental appetites were appeased by a little grey pamphlet, containing the rules governing the conduct of convicts in the penitentiary. There were a great many of them, and not a few required thought to penetrate their significance. Why, for instance, should special emphasis be laid upon the injunction to rest one's shoes against the bars of the door upon retiring? We were never informed; but I presume it must have been to prevent a man being tempted to reach out an arm a hundred feet long through his bars, throw the switch, steal along the platform, open the steel door, unbar the two outer gates, climb over the thirty-four foot wall, and escape — all the while avoiding the notice of the range guard, of the guards in the corridors, and of the watchman on the tower outside, all of whom were armed with magazine rifles and were yearning for an opportunity to use them. Of course, he would want to have on his shoes for such an enterprise, so that if the shoes were visible inside his door, it was prima facie evidence that he himself was also within. Another rule was italicized — *"Do not try to escape — you might get hurt!"* I refrained from testing the validity of either prohibition.

In the midst of our perusal, we were interrupted by the arrival of a visitor. He was a slight-built, slope-shouldered young fellow, in prison garb, with a meager visage heavily furrowed with sickness and suffering — he had tuberculosis, chronic bronchitis, and the indigestion with which all prisoners who eat the regular prison fare are afflicted. Not that Ned (as I will call him, since it was not his name) mentioned his condition; it was determined long afterward by the diagnosis of my friend; Ned's object in visiting us was not to air his own troubles, but to assuage, so far as he might, the gloom and uneasiness of the new arrivals. In his haggard face shone a pair of very intelligent and kindly grey eyes, and above them rose a compact, well-filled forehead. I was fortunate enough to keep in touch with this young man during my stay, and I found no more lovable nature in the penitentiary. He made no secret of the fact that he had been guilty of a Federal offense, and he never expressed contrition for it; "I made a mistake in taking another man in with me," he remarked; "you are never safe unless you go it alone." He had not been systematically educated, but he had read widely and judiciously, talked correctly, though with occasional colloquial idioms thrown in, and he was a concentrated and original thinker. His opinions were bold, independent, and sound, his insight was very penetrating, and his knowledge of matters of criminal procedure and of prison conditions was accurate and ample. Facts which I afterward learned for myself were never out of accord with information he had given me; and the sanity and clarity of his judgments were refreshing and remarkable. His courage was undemonstrative but indomitable; he never complained of his own condition and experiences, but was instant in his sympathy with the misfortunes of others. No more welcome and valuable counselor than he could have come to us in those first hours of our durance.

That he was able to visit us was due to his being a "runner," as those prisoners are termed who are assigned to carrying messages and doing odd jobs in the ranges. He leaned against the bars and spoke manfully and pungently, with touches of gay humor now and then; advised us to our conduct — what to do and what to avoid; and when he noticed the little grey pamphlet, said scornfully, "Don't muss up your ideas with that! There's a hundred rules there, and everyone of 'em is broken every day. Those rules are for show; what happens to you depends on who the guard is, and how he happens to be feeling. You can go as far as you like sometimes, and other times you'll get hauled up if you turn your head sideways. The screw" (guard) "on this range is decent; he won't crowd you too much. Keep quiet, and do what they tell you, and the odds are you'll get by all right. Of course, if some fellow gets a grudge against you, he's liable to hammer you like hell; there are some prisoners here that get on the wrong side of a screw, and — well, it goes hard with 'em! But if you're a little careful, I guess you'll get through all right.

"I've read all about your case in the papers, and I know you oughtn't to be here; and Bill" (the Warden) "likely knows it too, and as folks on the outside are on the watch for what happens to you, he'll think twice how he treats you. Bill is a cunning one; he keeps his ear to the ground; when he sees that the reform people are going to put something across, he backs it up, and gives out that he suggested it himself; but up to a year or two ago, he did the worst sort of things to the men; even in his early reports and addresses he advocated treatment that he'd never dare stand for now — except on the quiet! He gets himself written up in the local papers here as the model warden — warm-hearted and broad-minded, and all that flap-doodle! But if he had his way, you'd think you were back in the dark ages in this penitentiary. Wickersham threw a bit of a scare into him a couple of years back; and there have been others; but most of the inspectors that are sent here stand in with him; he gives them good feeds in his house, and takes them out in his auto, and fills 'em up with soft talk — about 'his boys,' and his fatherly interest in 'em, and all that — but he keeps the dark cells and the rest of the dirty work out of their sight, and of course none of the men dares say anything to 'em — it would be all day with them if they did — as soon as the inspector turned his back. That's what gets the men's goat — that he puts up such a humane front, and all the while hammers them on the sly. They'd prefer being told at the start they were going to get hell, and then getting it; but it goes against their grain to get it, and meantime have folks outside believe they're in a gentlemen's country club!"

Ned imparted his information by fits and starts; ever and anon he would break off abruptly and walk off down the range, to give the guard the idea that he was about his ordinary business; then he would return, squat down on his hams beside the door, and murmur along in his rapid, distinct tones. All that he said was abundantly confirmed later.

Finally — "Good night — sleep well — they'll put you on some job in a few days; it's the first days that go hardest with most men, but you'll get used to it; you might get out on parole, too — but don't count on it; of all the frauds in this prison, parole is the worst! And if they ever pass that 'Indeterminate Sentence' law — good-bye! Imagine Bill with that thing to use as a club over us! He'd make every other man here a lifer!"

He laughed in the prison way — silently, in his throat — and went away, after warning us that it was near nine o'clock. Our watches had been taken away from us; no doubt, a prisoner might commit suicide by sticking his watch in his windpipe, or he could bribe a guard with it to bring him cigarette papers, or "dope." Besides, what has a man in jail to do with time? Our warm-hearted and fatherly masters desire their charges to exist so far as practical in a dead, unmeasured monotony, where a minute may seem to prolong itself to the dimensions of an hour; to feel themselves utterly severed from the world they have annoyed or injured. That is the penitentiary ideal; but it has of late become impossible fully to realize it. A prison will always be a prison; but at any rate, light shall be let in on it.

Meanwhile, our cell light went out; and we waited for the dawn.

V

ROUTINE

I lay in the upper bunk. It was a six-foot drop to the cement floor below. The mattress, though irregularly dented and bulged, was upon the whole convex, and not over two feet wide. A vertical fence or bastion, six or eight inches high, along the outer brink of this precipice would have averted the danger of rolling off in the night; but nothing of the sort had been provided. One must remember not to roll, even in the nightmare. Convicts educate the subliminal self to a surprising degree, and do not fall victims to this trap as often as one would expect; but occasionally one of them forgets, and down he comes, sometimes getting bruised only, but generally with a broken bone or so. I do not have nightmares, and I lay prone, gripping the sides of the mattress with my knees, as if it were a bucking bronco. So I journeyed, Mazeppa-wise, through the abysses of that first night, and was not unhorsed.

Light glimmered obscurely through the bars of the cell from the night-burner below. Odd sounds broke out at intervals. Half suppressed coughs, sudden, brief cries, irregular wheezings and gurglings, due to defective plumbing, occasionally a few muttered words; then a man in an upper tier began to moan and groan dismally – a Negro with a colic, perhaps. Long, dead silences would be interrupted by inexplicable noises. In the dead vast and middle of the night the prisoner in the cell over mine began to pace up and down his floor, eighteen inches above my head. Four paces one way, four back, over and over interminably. Who was he? What was he thinking about? Something seemed to goad him intolerably; that forging to and fro, like a tormented pendulum with a soul in it, gave a stifling impression, as of one tortured for air and space. How many years must he endure – how many centuries? Was his wife dying, his children abandoned? Up and down he padded; had he committed some ugly crime, for which he longed to atone – but prison is not atonement! Had his conviction been unjust, and was he raging impotently against injustice? Let him not rage too loudly, for there was a guard yonder, indifferent to tortured souls, but licensed to stop noises. A prison is a prison, not a sanitarium for diseased crooks. But if the world could hear those footfalls, and interpret their significance, how long would prisons last? A jail at night is a strange place — eight hundred men packed in together, each terrifyingly alone!

Some of the earlier workers had been roused at six or five o'clock or earlier; but for the majority the six-thirty bell was the reveille. It screeched violently and was silent. The watching devils or the guardian angels of the night vanished, and up got the eight hundred members of the Gentlemen's Country Club, to live as best they might through one day more; coughing, hawking, spitting, murmuring — but all with a sense of repression in it, the life-sapping drug of fear in its origin, but long since become a mechanical habit with most of them. Eight hundred criminals, herded beneath one roof to be cured of their crimes by indifferent or threatening and hostile task-masters and irresponsible discipline-mongers, and by association with one another — a régimen of hell to extirpate deviltry! The twentieth century solution of the problem of evil, unaltered in principle after thousands of years!

Civilization has progressed wonderfully, but always with this death-house on its back. And the death-house gets bigger and more populous every year. Reformers, exhorters, Christian Endeavorers, humanitarians, Salvation Armies, social reformers, penologists, scientific experimentalists with surgical apparatus, together with parole laws, indeterminate sentences, commutations, pardons, not to speak of a good warden here and there and a kind guard — all toiling and tinkering to make prisons better, to sweep them, to air them, to instill religion and education, to supply work and exercise and to pay wages — and all the while the tide of criminals gets larger and the accommodations for them less adequate. What can be the matter? Are we to end by discovering that everybody is a criminal, and ripe for jail? or shall we be driven to the realization that the fundamental idea of imprisonment for crime is itself the most monstrous of crimes — and try something else? What else is there to be tried? Are we to leave criminals to their liberty among the community?

There will be time enough to discuss these riddles. It is time now to get into your prison suit, with its "U.S.P." on the back of the coat, and your number; its "U.S.P." on the back of the shirt, with your number; its "U.S.P." on the front of your trousers-legs, and your number; your canvas shoes and your visored cap. But beware of putting on the cap within prison walls, lest the guard report you to the captain, the captain to the deputy, the deputy, if necessary, to the warden, and ye be cast into the inner darkness. There shall there be thin slices of bread, and water, and gnashing of teeth.

With a guard acting as cowboy, shepherd dog, or convict compeller, we shuffled in a continuous line down the iron stairways and across the hall into the dining room, a cement-floored barred-window desert sown with tables in rows, seating eight men each; guards with clubs standing at coigns of vantage or pacing up and down the aisles, and in one window, commanding the whole room, a guard with a loaded rifle, licensed to shoot down any misbehaver. At no time and in no part of this model jail are you out of range of a loaded rifle, in the hands of men quick and skillful in their use. They are the sauce for meals and the encouragement to labor. But casualties seldom happen; when they do, they are hushed up, and the body of the man is buried next day in the prison graveyard.

I will postpone to a future chapter the subject of the dining room and what is done there. As we filed out, I noticed "MERRY CHRIST-MAS," and "HAPPY NEW YEAR" emblazoned in green above the door. It was to remind us, perhaps, of what we lost by being criminals. As we debouched into the inner hall, separated from the corridor leading to the warden's office, and to freedom, by a steel-barred gate, we saw a guard seated in a chair with a rifle across his knees. Rats in a steel trap might have mutinied with as much hope of success as we at that juncture; but the guard had to be used for something, and convicts must not be allowed to forget that they are in prison. At all events we forbore to mutiny, and were rounded into our cells and locked up for half an hour, during which we might smoke Golden Grain tobacco, fifty percent, dirt, and the rest the refuse of the weed, supplied to the prison by contract; or we might read, or comb our hair, or do calisthenics, or invoke the Divine blessing upon the labors of the coming day.

The interval is really provided as a measure of security; many of the prisoners do their work outside the main buildings; but it is deemed unsafe to unlock the outer gates while the whole body of prisoners is on the move. They might make a concerted rush, and get out in the yard, to be shot down in detail by the guards in the towers.

Mr. Sidney Ormund, to be sure, a special writer on the *Atlanta Constitution,* makes the following statement in an issue of the paper shortly after I had left the jail and recorded my opinion that "Warden Moyer was unfit." — "It is safe to assume," Mr. Ormund affirms, "that if all the prisoners at the Atlanta federal penitentiary were life-termers and each had a voice in the selection of a warden to serve for a like term, William Moyer, the present incumbent — a man who has done more to make prison life bearable than any man in this country — would be selected without a murmur of opposition."

That is a fine, explicit statement of Mr. Ormund's, such as any warden in dire trouble and perplexity might be glad and proud to have a faithful friend make concerning him. It has no strings to it, and is followed up by similar sentiments throughout the article. But why, in that case, are the gates into the yard locked, and the man with the rifle provided? If Warden Moyer renders life at Atlanta prison more bearable than at any other in the country, what conceivable grounds are there that his affectionate inmates should wish to run away from him? That warm-hearted and big-brained gentleman would hardly put the Government to the expense of supplying safeguards against a contingency which his own tender and lovable nature renders unthinkable, even if the thirty-four foot wall outside does not. There seems to be a non-sequitur here, which Mr. Ormund, perhaps, may feel inspired to clear up. When he has done that, it will be time to call his attention to a score or more other incongruities which a residence of only six or seven months in this humane institution has been sufficient to disclose.

At the expiration of the half hour, we laid aside our pipes, or our prayer-books, and were ready for the activities of the day. The others were detailed to their regular work; but my friend and I had our final rites of initiation still to undergo. A young official, whose countenance readily if not habitually assumed a sullen and menacing expression, beckoned to us with his club, and we followed him downstairs to an elevator, in which he ascended to the upper floor, while we pursued him upward by way of the staircase. The cap of Mr. Ivy — such was his poetic given name — was worn on the extreme rear projection of his head, and he used his club in place of speech; not that he actually pummeled us with it, but by wavings and pointings he made it indicate his will, and kept us mindful how easily we might afford him a pretext for putting it to its more normal use. Mr. Ivy, as I afterward learned, was a Southerner by birth, as are the majority of the guards in the penitentiary, and may have been, like most of them, a graduate from the Army. In reporting the case of Private George, of the U.S. Army, now a prisoner in stripes in the Leavenworth Penitentiary, it was stated by Mr. Gilson Gardner that "The common soldier in the U.S. Army has no rights. When he enlists, he gives up the guarantees of the Constitution, the protection of jury trial, and even his right to petition for a redress of grievances. He may be unjustly charged, secretly tried and cruelly punished, and he has no remedy."

As regards unjust, cruel and despotic treatment, the status of the U.S. soldier and of a penitentiary convict are on all fours, though of course the former has the advantage of belonging to a service traditionally honorable, of open air service and exercise in all parts of the country or abroad, of reasonable freedom when off duty, and of whatever glory and advancement campaigning against an enemy may bring him. But we may readily perceive that a soldier who has felt the rough edge of discipline and finds his health broken, perhaps, by indiscretions incident to Army life, might say to himself, on receiving his discharge, "I am bred to no trade, I am good for nothing, but I should like to get back at somebody for the humiliations and hardships I have endured. Why not take a job as a prison guard; the pay is only $70 a month, but instead of being the under dog, I shall be on top, licensed to bully and belabor to my heart's content, to insult, humiliate and berate, and to get away with it unscathed!"

For my part, I can imagine no reason more plausible to explain the large number of ex-soldiers among prison guards, and their conduct in that position. With some shining exceptions, they are petty tyrants of the worst type, sulky, sneering, malignant, brutal, and liars and treacherous into the bargain. Their mode of life in a jail, immersed in that sinister and unnatural atmosphere, hating and hated, with no sane or absorbing occupation, encouraged by the jail customs to play the part of spies and false witnesses, ignorant and demoralized, — tends to create evil tendencies and to confirm such as exist. No worse originally than the average of men, they are made baser and more savage by their circumstances. And no man able to hold his own in the free life and competition of the outside world, would stoop to accept a position as guard in a jail.

I know nothing of the private biography of Mr. Ivy, and it is quite possible that he may have possessed endearing traits which he had no opportunity to manifest in our intercourse. It would be foolish and futile for the ends I have in view in this writing to cite or comment on individuals, save as they may illustrate the point under discussion. But I am the less reluctant to animadvert upon this or that employee of the penitentiary, because I feel satisfied that, so far from compromising him with the higher prison authorities, abuse from me would only recommend him to their favor. — Mr. Ivy, such as he was, conducted us to a bench outside a closed door, already partly occupied by three or four half naked convicts, white and black. We gathered from his gestures of head and club that we were to remove our upper garments and our shoes and stockings, and place them on the floor in front of us. It was a cold morning, and the floor was of limestone. We obeyed instructions, and for the next twenty minutes sat there, objects of pardonable curiosity or amusement to our fellow benchers and to passers-by in the hall, and with nothing to keep us warm but the genial influences of the occasion. Finally, each in his turn, we were passed through the door into a sort of office, with clerks and Dr. Weaver, the prison physician, at $1500 a year, — a tall, wooden faced young medical school graduate, who cultivated a skeptical expression and a jeering intonation of speech. He and an assistant put us through a physical examination, and took a series of measurements, all of which were entered by the clerks in ledgers. Our photographs were then taken, and afterward (it was the next day, but may as well be told here) we were further identified by taking the impressions of our finger prints, and by a second photograph without our mustaches — these having been removed in the meantime. We were now convicts full-fledged and published, and our pictures were disseminated to every prison and penitentiary in the country, to be enshrined in the rogues' gallery and studied by all police officials.

This may sound silly, in the case of two men much nearer three score and ten than three score, and untrained to gain a livelihood by crime. Bertillon measurements were not needed to identify us, nor photographs without mustaches. But, in the first place, prison rules apply to the mass, not to individuals; and secondly, it has been resolved by the wisdom of our rulers that a man who reverts to crime after one or more convictions shall be more severely punished than a first offender. Nobody stops to question the logic of this ostensibly prudent provision. But the convict knows that his chances of making an honest livelihood after a conviction are many times less than before. Spies are on his trail at every turn, and if ever he succeed in securing legitimate employment, an officer of the secret service presently informs his employer that he has a jail-bird on his pay-roll. Naturally he is promptly paid off and dismissed, and he may go through the same experience as often as he is foolish enough to try it. But even if he be inactive, he is not safe — far from it. He is known to the police and liable to arrest at any moment as a vagrant, without visible means of support. Nor is this all. Suppose him to be recorded in prison archives as a safe-blower, and that a safe is blown somewhere and the culprits escape. The credit of the police department demands that an arrest be made, if not of the person or persons actually guilty of this particular crime, then of someone who may be plausibly represented as guilty of it. Accordingly, our friend is apprehended and charged with the crime; there is his record, and it is easy to secure "evidence" that he was on the spot at the time, though he may have been, in fact, a hundred or two miles away from it. Detectives are experts at providing this sort of evidence; and it frequently happens that they get the corroboration of the victim himself by assuring him that, if he will confess, the judge will let him off with a light sentence, whereas if he prove "stubborn," it will go hard with him — a matter of ten years or so. Ten years in jail for something you did not do! Six months or a year if you confess! Perjury is wrong no doubt; but, were you who read this placed in that predicament, which horn of the dilemma would you select? If you have never served an actual jail term, you might virtuously hesitate; but it is the world against a mustard seed that you wouldn't hesitate if you had. The crisp of the joke is, however, — and of course it serves you right, — that the judge, after all, gives you the ten years, and that means life, for you will never be long out of jail afterward. As I write this, I have in mind several instances of it among my personal acquaintances at Atlanta.

If then our convict, upon his release, cannot keep himself in any honest employment, and cannot avoid arrest even when he is doing nothing at all, good or bad, it seems plain that he must either hunt out a quiet place where he may starve to death before the officer can arrest him for starving, or commit suicide in some more sudden and active manner, or he must accept the opportunity which is always at hand in "revert to a career of crime," as the saying is. Ex-convicts are often still human enough to be averse from starvation, and even from easier forms of self-destruction; and they yield to the temptation to steal. Like the idiots they are, they may hope to make a big strike and get away with it, and in some remote or foreign place, under another name, live out an unobserved and blameless existence.

Thereupon there is rejoicing in the ranks of the secret service; armed with their bertillons, they swoop upon their quarry and bear him away. "May it please the Court, this man is an incorrigible; not deterred by previous punishment, immediately upon release he plunges again into crime; he should receive the limit!" The Court thinks so too; the limit is imposed, and the malefactor is led out to the living death which will end with death in reality. And now will some righteous and competent person arise and proclaim that this man's yielding to his first temptation to crime did NOT involve greater moral turpitude than did his yielding to the second temptation or to the third — greater or at least as great — and that therefore the severer sentence is justified? His first misdeed was prompted by hunger, ignorance, drunkenness, or cupidity; the others were the fruit of desperation itself — and how many of you have known what desperation means?

You perceive that this story proceeds by digressions; such value as it may have it will owe mainly to such digressions, so I will not apologize for them. My friend and I, our ordeal completed, were returned to our cells to think it over. The walls and ceiling of the cells are painted a light grey color; it is against the rules, except by special indulgence, to affix pictures or other objects to them. The "coddling of criminals," so widely advertised, does not include permission to give a homelike look to their perennial quarters; it is more conducive to moral reform that they should contemplate painted steel. There was one camp-stool in our cell; later, cells were supplied with two wooden chairs, the seats sloping at such an angle with the backs as rendered sitting a penance; cushions were not provided. I remember seeing similar contrivances in old English cathedrals, relics of a day when monks had to be kept from falling asleep during the religious rites. We might also sit upon the lower bunk, bent forward in such an attitude as would avert bumping our heads against the upper one. Each convict, early in his sojourn, has a religious interview with the Chaplain, who presents him with a copy of the New Testament — not also of the Old; you may remember that the latter records certain regrettable incidents of a sinister and immoral sort, calculated, I presume, to shock the tender budding impulses toward regeneration of prison readers. One may get other books of a secular kind from the library, upon written application; and prisoners of the first grade may subscribe for newspapers that contain no objectionable matter. But only a small proportion of the inmates is addicted to reading, and the opportunities for doing so are limited. And as months and years go by, the desolation and sterility of the place weigh heavier upon the spirit, the mind reduces its radius and grows inert, and stimulants stronger than current fiction are needed to rouse it. Prison, prison, prison; steel walls and gratings; the predestinate screechings and clangings of whistles and gongs; the endless filings to and fro, in and out; the stealthy insolence of guards, or their treacherous good-fellowship; the abstracted or menacing gaze of the higher officials; the dreariness, aimlessness, and sometimes the severity of the daily labor; the sullen threat of the loaded rifles; the hollow, echoing spaces that shut out hope; the thought of the stifling stench of the dungeons beneath the pavements, hidden from all save the victims, whose very existence is officially denied; the closing of all personal communication with the outer world, except such as commends itself to the whims of the official censors; this morgue of human beings still alive — the impenetrable stupidity, futility and outrage of it all — slowly or not so slowly unbalance the mind and corrupt the nature. Meanwhile, newspapers clamor against the coddling of criminals, and the too indulgent officials smile sadly and protest that they have not the heart to be stern. "Coddling criminals" — the alliteration makes it roll pleasantly off the tongue!

But do I forget the many indulgences given to prisoners — and so profusely celebrated in every mention publicly made of Atlanta Penitentiary? Let me name them once more. Saturday being a non-working day, it used to be the custom to lock the prisoners in their cells from Saturday morning till Monday morning — a custom still followed at many penitentiaries; for how could they be controlled if not split up into working gangs, and thus prevented from conspiring to mutiny? It is one of the obsessions of prison authorities that the prisoners are severally and collectively a sort of wild beast, always straining at the leash, and ready at the least opportunity to break forth in wild and deadly disorder. It is obviously expedient, too, to impress the public with this conviction, and therefore, in part, we have the clubs, rifles, and general parade of watchfulness. As a matter of fact, meanwhile, nothing is more easy to handle than a prisonful of convicts, if the most elementary tact be used; and they are eagerly grateful for the smallest unforced and spontaneous act of kindness.

Until about eighteen months ago, however, severe restrictions were in vogue, and the warden declared that it was his belief and policy that men in prison should be taught by precept and illustration to regard themselves as dead to the world; that they should be held practically incommunicado, no visitors, letters at most but once a month, no conversation between prisoners — silence, solitude, suffocation in this terrible quicksand of jail for months, years, or a lifetime, at the mercy of men to whom mercy is a jest. Such a régimen is still in force at many jails, and when combined with contract labor, nothing in the age-long history of penal imprisonment shows a blacker record. It is advocated as the best way to induce men to reform, and become, after release, useful and industrious members of the community.

A couple of years or so ago, Atlanta was visited by an Attorney-General, who was not prepared for what he saw, nor had the things he should not have seen been removed from sight before he saw them. He demanded some improvements on the spot, and soon after a new deputy warden was appointed — a young man, of kindly disposition, though weak, not inured as yet to the conventional brutalities, and with a backing in Washington which gave him unusual powers. Among good things which he instituted and insisted on were — two and a half hours outdoors on Saturday afternoons, for baseball and general relaxation; conversation at meals; music at dinner by a band made up from convicts; regular bi-weekly letters, with extra letters allowed between times by special request to orderly convicts; concerts or vaudeville performances every month or so in the chapel, by professionals.

Insanity became less frequent after this, and the general health of the men improved. They had something to look forward to, and to look back to, and the freedom of the baseball concession led to no disorders; something like hope and cheerfulness began to appear, like green blades of grass in spring. The warden cleverly seized the opportunity to take credit to himself for all the improvements, and to circulate industriously in the local papers the praise of the model penitentiary. But neither did he fail to take advantage of the new situation to tighten his grasp upon the reins of control. The majority of jails, in addition to the ordinary spy system operated by officials, organize a supplementary one composed of convicts themselves — stool pigeons — certain carefully selected prisoners, who are rewarded for treachery to their fellows by various indulgences and secret liberties. The principle is detestable, and has evil effects. The stool pigeons themselves are of course the basest members of the community, and the other prisoners, soon learning to suspect them, come at last to a miserable distrust of one another — for the comrade apparently most sincere may be at heart only a more artful traitor. In this, they play into the officials' hands, whose theory of government is fear, and who find aid to themselves in the mutual misgivings and hatreds of their charges.

Evidently, the relaxations of the baseball afternoons afforded a capital opportunity to the stool pigeons, and the results were soon apparent. The spies, in order to curry favor with their employers, reported not actual infringements of discipline only, but guessed at what might be, and even invented what was not, often by way of retaliation against personal enemies. I shall return to this subject hereafter; enough, for the present, that it counterbalanced in a degree the physical benefits of the new concessions by engendering mental disquiets and animosities among the entire population, and especially inflaming them against the officials. I am not myself sure, for example, whether or not one or another of my most intimate acquaintances among the prisoners may not all the while have been on the watch to betray me behind my back. For aught I know, it may have been to some such sordid treachery that I owe the refusal of my parole, when it became due. And any respect for constituted prison authorities, upheld by such means, was impossible.

When the coddling of prisoners involves feeding them on poison, they would prefer Spartan severity and fair warning.

VI

SOME PRISON FRIENDS OF MINE

*V*ague noises are at all times audible in jail — stirrings, foot-falls, a subdued voice now and then, the sharp orders of an official — "bawlings out" as they are termed; the clanging of steel gates, the murmur of machinery, the cacophony of musical instruments during practice hours in the chapel; as well as the periodical screeches and ringings of whistles and gongs. The general impression on ear and eye alike is of stealthy repression, a checked unrest — a multifarious creature, uneasy but kept down. The place is perhaps hardly less silent than a cloister; but the peace of the cloister is utterly absent. An atmosphere of animosity and contention pervades all — a constant apprehension of sinister things liable to happen, a breathless struggle, the sullenness of hate, the whispering of treachery. The eyes of officials peer, watch and threaten; those of the convicts are downcast but privily rebellious, or deprecatingly servile.

It is the everlasting pregnancy of war between slave and master, quite different from submission to rightful authority. Whatever the law may say, the rightfulness of prison authority is never admitted by prisoners. Honest authority is tranquil and secure; prison authority goes armed, conscious of its unrighteousness, and there is unremitting nervous stress on both sides. Both sides seem secretly to await a signal to sudden conflict.

At dinner, soon after my arrival, amid the omnipresent murmurous palaver of conversation, there fell an unusual noise. The unusual is always formidable in jail. The noise was nothing in itself, and would have passed unheeded in a hotel dining room. But over us, crowded together there, spread an instant hush. All knew that men had been stabbed, frenzied affrays had broken out in that room. What was it now? The guard in the window stiffened and poised his rifle. The guards on the floor caught their breath, but assumed a confident air. The men sat staring in the direction of the noise, tense and waiting.

Nothing happened; somebody had dropped a plate and broken it, perhaps. But had some natural leader of the enslaved leaped up and shouted at that juncture, murder would have followed the next moment. Among every hundred convicts there are eight or ten whom misery and wrong have made reckless, whose morbid rebelliousness needs, to break forth, only the shadow of opportunity to kill before being killed, and they accept it. But it was not to be that day, and we relaxed, and grinned, nervously or grimly, and resumed our meal.

Eight hundred men, clad in a shapeless monotony of dingy blue, labeled on the back with their disgrace, stepping lightly or shuffling hastily to and fro, heads bent and eyes downcast, performing various offices, menial, clerical or industrial, with a certain obsequiousness and ostensible zeal that was yet inwardly repulsion and protest — these were men born under the great flag, Americans, my countrymen, and now my companions! What a change, what a degradation from the free American citizen of the streets and boundless expanses! Not men, now, but slaves, condemned to penal servitude; not citizens, but a class apart and alien; felons, criminals, no longer entitled to life, liberty and the pursuit of happiness, but existing in shame and on sufferance, ruined, nameless, parted from friends and families, with present physical pain and mental misery, and with a future of hounding and helplessness, of fear and hiding, of uselessness and aimlessness, of insanity and base death!

Upon what plea are these conditions established? Because the slaves had broken the law — been guilty of crimes. But what crimes? Some had done murder, others committed rape, some had held up a train, another had blown a safe, another was a pickpocket, another a white-slaver, this one had stolen food to avert starvation, that was a confidence man or bank embezzler, here was one snared in some technicality of new finance laws, yonder an ignorant moonshiner from the hills, who had grown corn in his back yard and thought he had a right to make whiskey out of it — he had no other means of livelihood. Breakers of God's laws; of man's; victims of tricks and legal technicalities, of torturing want and of headlong passion, and of sheer court errors or of perjured testimony — here they were, all on the same footing, no discriminations made! To what end? So that they might be punished and repent and go forth better men and useful workers, and so that society might be protected and its integrity vindicated. That is the ostensible reason; no other is alleged.

It sounds like a jest; but the men are here, the thing is done. In some moods I would say to myself, "It's too preposterous — it can't be — it's an hallucination — a bad dream!" But there it was, visible and palpable. Was it protection for society to shut up a man from ability to support those dependent on him, who were thus themselves driven to want and perhaps crime, multiplying the original criminality by three or four or half a dozen? Could any injury which the culprit could do to the community equal the injury thus done by the community to him and his, and indirectly to itself, by such treatment? Or could the technical and perhaps unconscious violator of an obscure and whimsical law be reformed by putting him on an equality with a cold-blooded murderer, or with a man who had grown rich by selling the shame of women? Was the punishment equable which handled with equal severity a brutish Negro from the cotton fields, and a man brought up in refinement and gentleness?

But I would go further, and challenge the right of the community to inflict penal imprisonment as we know it at all. Some criminals belong in hospitals, others in insane asylums, for others the thoughtless neglect and selfishness of society is responsible, and they should be succored, not punished; and the remainder should be constrained, under surveillance but not in confinement, to compensate for the harm they did by labor or self-denial aimed directly at that result. But of this hereafter.

Meanwhile, I paid attention to my companions themselves.

In their intercourse with one another there was a singular amenity or pleasantness, and with some who had been prisoners for a long time, a sort of childlikeness. But it was like the childlikeness of a person partly dazed, or recovering from a severe illness or shock. They greeted one another with a covert smile, an unobtrusive movement of head or hand; only when under direct observation of an official would they pass without a sign. The usual words were, "How're you feeling?" or, "How're they comin'?" not in the perfunctory tone of greetings in the outer world, but with an accent of real interest and solicitude. The answer would be, "Good!" "Fine!" with as much heartiness as could be thrown into it — though it might be obvious enough that the truth was far from being that.

There was one dear old fellow who had a variation on these forms; he was an alleged moonshiner, though, as he said, "Yes, I did make some whiskey, but I never sold none!" "How're you feeling, Joe?" I would say; and he would reply, with his pathetic smile, and his high, soft voice, "Pretty well — pretty well, for 'n old man!" with a drawling emphasis on the "old." He was about seventy, with the soft brown hair of youth, but bent and stiff and wrinkled with hard years and rheumatics; and if I questioned him more closely, he would confess that he suffered from "lots o' misery here!" — passing his gnarled old hands over his digestive tract. Indeed, four-fifths of the men had that trouble in more or less acute form, owing to the atrocious food supplied as our regular diet.

Joe's face, though lined with the hardships and privations of a long life, was beautifully formed, aristocratic in its delicate contours; and he possessed, and constantly used, one of the most delectable, contagious and genuine laughs that ever made music in my ears. The men would ransack their humorous resources in conversation with Joe, merely for the sake of making him laugh. He would fix his old eyes squarely on yours, and laugh and laugh with infinite mirth and good nature. Such a sound in such a place was rare and wonderful, and helped one like fresh water in a desert.

The general friendliness among the men — so contrasted with their demeanor toward the officials — was due to the identity of their common interests; they were in the same boat, facing the same perils and disasters, united in the same aims and hopes, and leagued against the same oppressors. They lived in the constant dread of some calamity; and if I met the same man three or four times in the same day, he would never fail to make the same enquiry — "How're you feeling?" recognizing that I might have received some ugly blow in the interval. There was a spontaneous courtesy and a charitableness in it that touched the heart.

The same sentiment was manifested at meals; if anybody got hold of anything that seemed to him a little better than usual, he could not rest till he had offered some of it, or all of it, to his neighbors at table. "Here, take this — take it — I got more'n I want!" Or, watching his opportunity, Ned the runner, who had comforted us on our first night in prison, would come to the door of my cell, with his Irish humor and cordiality shining in his eyes. "Say, Mr. Hawthorne, there's a dividend been declared!" and out of some surreptitious receptacle he would produce three or four crumpled cigarette papers — of all contraband articles in the prison the most prized. "No — take 'em — I got no end of 'em!"

A peculiar consideration was manifested by the men toward "the old man"; my hair was white enough, to be sure, but it had been so for nearly twenty years, and I was in much better physical condition than most of them. I accepted their kind offices with gratitude and emotion, and, when I saw that to do otherwise would hurt their feelings, their concrete gifts, too.

But there were many instances of self-sacrifice greater than these; men would go to the hole sooner than betray a comrade; and you are fortunate in being unable to comprehend what that means. If a comrade in his range was sick and unable to come to meals, I have constantly seen a man secrete half of his miserable breakfast or dinner in his pocket, to be carried up to the invalid and smuggled into his cell. It was a matter of course, nobody remarked it. Any mistake or indiscretion committed by a prisoner would be instantly and almost mechanically covered by the man nearest him, though at the risk of punishment – and the punishment for betraying human sympathy in this way is – of course it is! – especially severe; it is conspiracy to cheat the Government.

The traditional tale of a prisoner's devotion to animals is also true; a man next me at table – a yegg – for two weeks poured half his allowance of milk (he was on milk diet for acute indigestion) into a surreptitious bottle, and bore it off for the sustenance of a couple of little forlorn kittens that he was acting as special providence for. The meditative smile with which he perpetrated this theft upon the prison authorities was a wonderful sight. Another convict, a hardened old timer, for several weeks lavished cargoes of tenderness upon a rat which he had laboriously conciliated and tamed. "What makes you so fond of that animal?" enquired one day a sentimental and statistical old lady visitor to the prison. After struggling with his emotions for a minute, he burst out, "Yah! he bit the guard!" This dialogue was overheard, and enchanted the whole penitentiary for months.

But one reflects that, whatever humane or lovable traits prisoners may exhibit, they are after all criminals! The existence in a lost soul of good qualities or impulses side by side with evil ones has long been recognized. Victor Hugo illustrated the discovery in his Jean Valjean, it was a staple with Dickens, Bret Harte's heroes are all of that type, it was the inspiration of much of Charles Reade's eloquence, Kipling has more than a touch of it, our contemporary fiction-mongers sentimentalize over it, and the train-robber in the movies usually has a full line of sterling virtues up his sleeve. The lost soul, in short, brims over, upon occasion, with the wine of regeneration. Therefore (so runs the moral) let us of the elect furbish up our charity, and be as tolerant toward this non-human class of people as may be consistent with our own safety and respectability. Scraps of our own lustrous impeccability have somehow found their way into them, and we cannot afford wholly to disavow them, in spite of their wretched lodgings.

This phariseeism is so inveterate with us, that I may fairly say that one has to be sentenced to jail as a criminal in order to correct it. From that vantage ground or Mount of Vision it presently dawns upon us that these men are no more lost souls than we are – are, in fact, woven out of the same yarn and cut from the same cloth. And from this same vantage ground it also gradually dawns upon us that, in one respect at least, the aggregate in a jail is better than the same number of men taken haphazard from the city streets. For the former have now laid aside self-righteousness and dissimulation, which are of the essence of our unrestrained civil life: "I killed a man, yes; I robbed a bank, I picked a pocket, I lived off a woman, I swindled my stockholders, I counterfeited a banknote." No disguise here — no evasion.

But when you go into the details of the transaction, weigh the causes which led up to it, consider the conditions surrounding it, realize the temptations or provocations that precipitated it, you step into your confessional: "Lord, my nature and heart are not different from this sinner's, and but for accidents and good fortune which were none of my providing, I should stand accountant today as he does!" You bring the whited sepulcher home to you, and find that you have been living in it yourself. And if you have a little intelligence you will acknowledge in your convict the scapegoat who — not more and perhaps less blame-worthy than you — is bearing your iniquities as well as his own.

So, instead of condescending, with supercilious eyebrows and spotless broadcloth, to concede that these unfortunate members of a non-human class sometimes betray traces of saving grace after all, it might better become you to wish that some of their saving graces appertained to yourself. At your best showing, you are a Pharisee and a hypocrite, and he is not; he stands confessed; your sin is still secret in your soul. By what right do you look down upon him?

These things which I now say to you, I said first to myself, sitting in my cell, or watching the endless grey-blue files shuffle past me on their way to and from meals. It was of small help or significance that I claimed innocence of the particular offense that happened to be charged against me; I was as indistinguishable from these men in heart as I was in outward garb and rating. And I had manhood enough to feel glad that, since they had to be here, I was here with them. The burden of the scapegoat has its compensations.

On my first Sunday in the chapel, there came an exhorter or revivalist, accustomed to dealing with prisoners from the platform, and dubbed "The Old Warhorse of Salvation," or some such title. He had his white waistcoat, his raucous, shouting voice, his phrases, his anecdotes, his "my men," "my friends," "fellows"; his "I'm saved, I hope, and you can be!" Oh, the phariseeism of that "I hope!" At the end of his uproar, he called upon those of his hearers (we had all sat quite silent and impassive during the performance) who were willing to be saved, to stand up in their places. All the stool pigeons arose (poor devils), and a few other bewildered persons who fancied it expedient to be on the side of the angels, "Thank you — thank you — thank you!" hoarsely cried the exhorter, naïvely accepting their response as a personal compliment to himself.

But that great audience sat dark, silent and impassive, and it could only have been the tough hide of the Old Warhorse that made him immune to their cold contempt. I said to myself, "What a terrible audience it is! Who is fit to stand before it?" These men had seen, known and suffered the terrible, nameless things; the Unknown God, perhaps, had spoken to many of them in their solitude; and now this being of white waistcoat and phrases must get up and urge them to wash their sins in the blood of the Lamb! In their silence they were preaching to him a sermon such as no mortal pulpiteer ever uttered; but his ears were deaf to it. "One – three – six – nine souls saved tonight! Thank you – thank you – thank you!" And he turns to receive the polite congratulations of the distinguished guests who sat behind him on the stage.

In prison, and only in prison, the veil is lifted or rent in twain, and men are revealed as they are. As they stand before their Creator, they stand now before their fellows. They are helpless – so warden and guards think – but they have gained a power beyond any physical might of man. They are voiceless, but they challenge mankind. They endure every indignity and outrage; but an account will be required of those responsible for it.

I wish to emphasize this dropping of the mask – this stop put to posturing and pretending – this going forth in rude nakedness before one's fellows. The man in the church pew chants out with the rest of the congregation, "We are sinners, desperately wicked, and there is no health in us;" but he says it with his tongue in his cheek, and fitting his mask on only the more tightly. Or the man "convinced of sin" on the anxious seat at the revivalist meeting frenziedly accuses himself of all the sins in the decalogue, but finds protection in the very generality and promiscuity of his confession, which includes and at the same time conceals the particular fact that he robbed the till and got away with it. We seldom hear of a penitent of this kind being indicted by a Grand Jury, tried, convicted and jailed on the basis of his salvation outcries. He talks figuratively.

There is nothing dramatic or hysterical in the attitude of the felon in his cell. He robbed the till, he admits to you; but he does not drag in the rest of the decalogue to divert your attention. And his penitence, when he feels any, is not, in nine cases out of ten, prompted by the expectation of getting a clean bill of health on his entire life-account (the empty till included) from a good natured Savior not too keen about details. He tells you, as a rule, "I was foolish and took too many chances!" or, "If I'd handled the thing by myself, instead of admitting a partner, it would have been all right;" or, "Oh, of course, I was a damned fool; what's the use of bucking up against the fly cops!" In the case of a murder, it might be, "I'm sorry I killed him, but I guess any fellow would have done the same in my case."

Duration of confinement does not modify this attitude; the man of ten years says the same as the man of ten months, except — and the exception is worth noting — that the former's moral sense, whatever he originally had of it, has been blunted or discouraged, and he has conceived a settled animosity against human authority, and disbelief in the justice and sincerity of its administrators. He has been the subject, during his incarceration, of such numberless acts of gratuitous tyranny, outrage and cruelty, and has seen so much of "the way things go," in general, that though he may concede that honesty is the best policy, he can find no other recommendation for it, and is prone to the secret conviction that honesty itself is somehow only a cleverer way of cheating.

Such a state of mind is bred by prison experience — not otherwise. Prison obstructs or altogether closes every door to genuine moral reform in prisoners.

A few larger souls overcome the obstructions; for example, our John Ross, who more than thirty-three years ago, in the blindness of a drunken spree in Yokahoma, killed a shipmate who angered him. He died in jail last June (1913). He was sentenced to death, but got commutation to life imprisonment. He was a fine type of man, physically and mentally. His spirit was never broken by what he endured, and some years before being transferred to Atlanta, he became, in a simple, non-sensational, but profound way, religious. At Atlanta, in his cell, he was a center of good influence on his fellow convicts; truthful, hearty, faithful, manly, cheerful; his preaching was by personal example, and by support and help given at need to the weak and despairing. He was promised freedom on parole; the promise was not kept; but even this last betrayal failed to break his staunch heart. He died like a man, with composure and dignity.

With a few such exceptions, prisoners are unrepentant except for business reasons — that is, either because they recognize that crime does not pay, or in order to influence in their favor the pardoning power. Many of them, of course, employ their prison opportunities to devise new crimes and to train fresh recruits from the younger convicts. Men who have been imprisoned more than once lose hope of anything better than transient freedom; they know they will be prevented by the police from earning an honest livelihood, and that they must either starve or steal. They become in the end mere prison creatures, destitute of evil or of good, active or passive.

I repeat that the experience of associating with men without disguises is novel and refreshing. A tedious burden is lifted from the shoulders; the bones in the sepulcher are less revolting than the whitewash outside; it is pleasanter to know what a man is than to suspect him. It is certainly much wholesomer, on the other hand, to uncover your own deformity than to hide it, especially when you know, or fear, that the hiding is unsuccessful.

There is a sense of brotherhood, long since unfamiliar to human intercourse under usual conditions, but welcome even at the cost of conditions such as these. The truth gradually emerges to our consciousness — it is not the evil in us that kills brotherhood, but the vain, unending effort to make the evil seem good. Now our eyes meet one another's frankly; the skillfullest counterfeit was worse than the worst reality. There is nothing in us to be proud of, but something to be thankful for. Society has done its worst to us; but it could not take away from us our mutual kindliness, or the qualities that justify it. We are condemned as wicked, but we are comforted by one another's good.

Prison, in short, more convincingly than any abstract argument, demonstrates its own futility as a means of either taking revenge upon the prisoner, or of inducing him to hate crime and to turn to good. Revenge, of course, is officially discredited nowadays, though it is practiced as actively as ever under guises more or less civilized; but the pretense of moral reform by penal imprisonment is becoming too preposterous to be tolerated much longer. On the contrary, prison renders the great aggregate of prisoners collectively self-conscious; the goats find themselves, and are forced into antagonism with the sheep not only as individuals but as a body. They make common cause together, and in obscure ways achieve a degree of organization. They learn to regard the community not as better than themselves, but as more successful pensioners of fortune; they fear them because the advantage of numbers is on their side, but they hate them because they feel, either justly or unjustly, that they have suffered injustice at their hands, and they will prey upon them when opportunity serves not only from the original motive of physical need, but from the additional and more sinister one, bred in prison, of retaliation for the wrong done them.

When you sap a man's faith in plain justice, and terrify him with the threat of irresistible power, and torture him in mind and body through the exercise of that power, you drive him to the support and society of men similarly circumstanced, and thus create the precise analogue in the body politic of a cancer in the individual body. Prison attempts to segregate this cancer, but only promotes its increase. Its poison is in the blood and circulates everywhere.

As I passed out of the dining room after meals each day, I came to notice a young man who sat at a table near the door. He sat with folded arms, and with a set and gloomy countenance; his eyes were fixed on vacancy, and he did not speak with his companions. A crutch leaned against his shoulder; he had lost one leg.

I learned his story. In the settlement of a small estate of which he was an heir, a sister of his had obtained money that belonged to him, and when asked to restore it to him, had refused to do so. After some fruitless negotiation, he got angry, and sent her through the mails a message containing violent expressions of reproach and animosity. The young woman took this paper to a United States marshal, who brought it to the attention of the district attorney, with the result that the brother was indicted under some law of libel or of obscene matter, was arrested, tried, and convicted, and sentenced to Atlanta penitentiary for five years. After he had been lodged in his cell, his sister repented of her action, and sought to have him freed; but the law does not recognize such changes of heart, and the brother must serve out his time.

We all know how easily family quarrels arise, how bitter they may be while they last, and how readily, withal, they may be accommodated by tactful handling. The sister had done wrong; the brother had lost his temper; in what family has not such an outbreak occurred? But because the brother had happened to put his bad temper on paper, the law, being rashly invoked, seizes him, takes five years out of his life, and brands him with the shame of the jail bird. Upon what plea can such an act be construed as justice? But the district attorney shows the court that the statute has been violated; the judge charges the jury, the jury finds its verdict in accordance with the legal evidence, and the thing is done. It is a mechanical process — nothing human about it.

Review your own life, and discover whether you have ever stood in the shadow of a similar catastrophe. Were you ever angry with a relative or with any other person, and did you express your anger to him in words? Then you are as guilty as this one-legged boy, sitting there at his table with his life ruined. Only, he happened to write his anger, and the sister happened to show it to a lawyer, and the machine was set in motion which no repentance or forgiveness or remorse can stop. But the machine does not increase the culprit's fault, and for such a fault the legal penalty may be five years in jail. You are not so remote from the subterranean brotherhood as you may have supposed.

Will prison reform him? Is society protected? Is faith in human justice promoted by such things? His case is but one of scores in every jail that are as bad and worse. But — "throw him to the lions — serves him right!" is still the cry.

VII

THE MEN ABOVE

*T*he men below would like to feel respect for the men above, even if it be a respect married to fear. It is more humiliating to be dominated by worthless creatures, of no character or genuine manhood, whose authority is effective only because it happens to be the tool through which works the irresistible power of a government, than to obey men of native energy and force, captains as well of their own souls as of the bodies of their subjects. The despotism of a cur is revolting, and rouses the wild beast in the victims. Those responsible for its infliction insult human nature.

As far as I have had opportunity to observe, or have been informed, the despotism of the cur in our jails, and in those of other countries perhaps (though not to nearly the same extent as in ours) is the rule; and that of self-respecting and respected men is the rare exception. Hate inflamed with contempt is a dangerous and evil passion to stimulate. It awakens a thirst for savage retaliation which hate alone does not produce. Moreover, weak and cowardly tyrants are always more cruel than courageous and masculine ones, and they do not observe any consistent line of conduct; in the intervals of their debauches of brutality they are oily and ingratiating, make favorites, offer pusillanimous apologies, protest humane intentions, and allege absurd excuses for past outrages. A brute is bad enough, and we are all brutes at bottom; but a brute who covers his hyena snarl with the smug mask of a saint is monstrous and detestable.

The wardens of many of our jails are double men. Behind the imposing façade of their physical aspect we detect an uneasy, hurried, shrewdly contriving little creature, quite incommensurate with the material bodily structure built up for his concealment and protection. He will not come out in the open, but seeks some advantage, plans to get behind us and execute some cunning coup-de-theater, while our suspicions are lulled by the hospitable and comfortable glow of the exterior. In his dealings with the convicts as a body, he is apt to imitate Macbeth's witches, and keep the word of promise to the ear, but break it to the hope; he has vanity without self confidence, lacks the truthfulness of the strong, his voice does not resound and compel, he dances and fidgets, grins and is grave in the same instant. If the men's attitude be sullen, he tries to be bluff and hearty, "my-boys" them, claps them heartily on the shoulder, or lapses into whining and gushing. It is all of worse than no avail with these undeceivable readers of character. It is a curious effect of the working of esprit de corps in jails that the prisoners may feel ashamed of such unmanly antics in their warden, especially should strangers be within eyeshot.

Of course, in his encounters with prisoners singly, a man of this type may show more of his real nature, especially if the prisoner be one of the inoffensive sort. He will be bland, insolent, indifferent or cruel, as suits his mood of the moment. "For God's sake, won't you let me write her just one letter?" implored a prisoner who had just got news of the fatal illness of his wife. Picture the situation — two human beings face to face, one helpless and in agony, the other with absolute power! The official faced the man deliberately, with an amused smile. "I can," he said, slowly, "but — I won't!" How would you have felt in such a case? Could you ever forget it? and would you not be ready, for that official's sake, to hate mankind, and to curse God and die? But you perhaps believe that convicts have no human feelings, and that they are cheerful under such treatment.

The value of these remarks lies, of course, in their general character; the conduct of an individual, regarded by itself, would have small importance. And if I do not instance the conduct of those honest and manly officials who are to be found here and there, it is because the public is already informed concerning them; their deeds do not seek darkness, but are visible by their own light. It is the rascals that we do not hear about, or if we do, it is through reports of press agents in newspapers and otherwise, who are mere mouthpieces for the lying self-praise of the rascals themselves.

While I was in jail, I had access, by a fortunate circumstance, to the annual reports to the Department of several wardens of prisons in various states, and was able to compare their stories of themselves with the accounts given me by prisoners who had lived under them and with my own first hand knowledge of prison conditions, which, with a few shining exceptions, are so terribly and remorselessly alike the civilized world over. After making every allowance for the different point of view of master and slave, it was very plain that the author of the report was not merely prevaricating, or coloring his facts to render them acceptable to his superiors, but was lying outright often, both directly and by omissions. He would pose as a broad-minded and compassionate father to his inmates, when all the time he was subjecting them to cruel and needless severities and tortures. There was one man, who has lately resigned, I believe, full of years and honors, whose addresses at the meetings of federal wardens were almost angelic in tone and tenor, who was in fact notorious among persons who had actual knowledge of his official conduct as one of the most remorseless tyrants toward the men in contemporary prison annals. Many men of bad conduct may be excused on the plea that they are ignorant — know no better; but this man was an intelligent student of penology, and knew exactly how wicked and wanton he was. He was an innocent baby once upon a time, and might have grown up to be no worse a man than is the estimable person who now reads these lines; but he took up prison work, and the atmosphere of crime, and preoccupation with it, and the license to use arbitrary powers, made a devil of him. It is a common story.

Another series of reports showed a man who, beginning as a reactionary of an extreme type, advocating the most ruthless measures toward convicts, finally felt the pressure of the wave of prison reform which is gathering force just now, and adjusted his reports and addresses so as to make himself appear as a leading apostle of the new ideas. But though his public professions changed, the chief difference in his practices was that, from having been undisguised, they became secret, and so far as circumstances permitted, he acted, and permitted or encouraged his subordinates to act as cruelly as before. However, a new deputy warden was presently appointed, with more liberal ideas, and endowed with large powers, and for a while the condition of the prisoners improved; the warden, with his ear to the ground, and his eye on the handwriting on the wall, deftly adjusting himself to the situation, and industriously claiming for himself credit for all betterments introduced by the deputy — who, having no press agent, was forced to stand inactively by and see his honest credit filched away from him — in public opinion, at least. Of course, the prisoners knew perfectly well on which leg the boot was. But prisoners cannot make themselves heard outside the jail.

Accordingly, this warden, whose methods I know well, is now quoted as a signal champion of the new and more merciful dispensation, though only two or three years ago, according to his own personally written and signed reports, he was for keeping prisoners practically incommunicado — dead to the world; writing and receiving letters to be nearly or wholly done away with; newspapers withheld; visitors denied. Prisoners, he urged, were sent to prison for punishment, and punished, continually and thoroughly, let them be. Punish the man, kill his health, his hope, his spirit, his soul, his body too at need, and thus, and only thus, reform him. It was a simple plan, and likely to bring results — of a kind. Shall we believe that this man's professions of a change of heart are genuine? or feel surprise to discover that at the very moment he is receiving visitors in his commodious office upstairs, and purring out to them his fatherly affection for his prisoners, and denying that the old, bad methods of repression any longer are tolerated, there are miserable wretches being hung up by the wrists in dark and noisome cells under his feet?

Regarding the personnel of the officials at Atlanta I can for obvious reasons say little. They are a good deal like such officials anywhere. The warden is a Pennsylvania Dutchman; the deputy a young Kentuckian, gigantic and fresh faced; his first assistant is a stalwart man of middle age, a good deal of a martinet, but the men are inclined to like him because they see in him a solid, masculine creature, who stands pat, says what he means, and does what he says. Then there are the prison doctor, the steward of the commissary department, and the parole officer, and under them are the guards and the "snitches" — the latter not being officially recognized, although they wield an important influence, their reports against their fellow prisoners being seriously considered, and often made the basis of action by their superiors, which has no small effect upon the welfare of the jail. Yet these poor wretches — they are mostly Negroes — sell their brethren for a mess of pottage of secret favors and immunities; none save the most abject would accept such employment. Could any inspiration or procedure be more insecure? Yet it is an essential factor in the present principle of prison management.

The guards are, with some exceptions, such a body of men as might be expected from their salary — seventy dollars a month, with no raise for length of service or meritorious conduct. They cannot be rated as high as the average police officer, and the conditions amid which they live are so unfavorable to manly development that it is small wonder they grow worse as they grow older in service. They either dislike the men and use them accordingly, or they make secret compacts with them for surreptitious favors, which undermine discipline and corrupt such morals as prisoners may be supposed to possess. Often, however, they will solicit favors from prisoners, and, when the latter seek some accommodation in return, grin in their face, or austerely threaten to report them. Their brutality is sometimes quite whimsical and unexpected, — the outcome of some personal dislike, without bearing on the prisoner's conduct, — though they are voluble in assigning some alleged infraction of the rules, should a superior happen to call them to account. And the superior, I may almost say, never believes the prisoner against a guard, or rather, never acts upon such belief. That is the settled policy of the penitentiary; the warden himself has placed himself on record numerous times to the effect that under no circumstances would he take the word of a prisoner over that of a guard. To be reported means to be punished, be the report baseless or not. It follows naturally that guards never scruple to give full rein to any animosity they may privately feel against a man, knowing that they will be able to "put it across" with the higher official to whom complaint may be made.

I happened to be in the corridor one day when one of the guards, a tall, strapping fellow, was bringing downstairs a convict of stature much less than his own, a poor half demented youth, whose dementia was unfortunately wont to express itself in foul or abusive language, which came from him almost involuntarily, without any particular personal application. The two men were halfway down the final flight of steps, when, without any visible pretext, but, I presume, on account of some unlucky epithet or utterance let fall by the convict, the guard suddenly seized the youth violently by the throat, hammered his head against the wall, and dragged him headlong down the rest of the descent. They were now in the corridor; the man, bewildered and giddy, was whirled round and shoved to the head of another short flight of steps leading out to the yard; the door was open. The guard came behind him, caught him by the collar, and exerting his strength, hurled him through the door; he fell prone on the ground, and lay there.

Here, my own view of the incident was cut off; but ten minutes afterward I met a comrade, who, bristling with wrath, described the continuation of the affray, which he had just witnessed. He said that the guard, following the man, grasped him by the coat and jerked him off the ground and shoved him, staggering, toward the isolation building on the other side of the yard. There happened to be two visitors, a man and a woman, under convoy of another guard, passing at the moment; the first guard was by this time too much blinded by his own passion to notice them; the other laughed, and apparently reassured the visitors. Upon nearing the isolation building, a third guard, who was on duty at the gate, ran up, and struck the prisoner several times on the head with his club. The man put up his arms in an effort to ward off the blows, or to beg for mercy, but without effect; he was dragged between his two assailants to the deputy's office, as if he were a dangerous giant struggling to get away, though, in fact, he was quite helpless and partly insensible. From there, as we learned later, he was taken to a dark cell, charged with I know not what misdeeds, and nothing was ever done to either of the licensed ruffians who had mistreated him.

I recall such scenes with reluctance; they are ugly things to think of; but some illustrations are necessary in order to put in your mind some notion of what jails mean. An episode which, as it turned out, had elements of the ridiculous, but which came within a hair's breadth of having very fatal consequences, occurred a short time before I became an inmate; it is still spoken of with emotion by those who participated in it.

A large number of prisoners, some twenty or more, I think, were collected in one of the basement work-rooms, when a fire broke out there. The smoke soon became suffocating, and crept up into the ranges above, alarming the whole prison. But conditions in the room itself were immediately intolerable; the door had been locked, and the men were jammed together there, frantically shrieking for the door to be opened. Death for all of them would be a matter of only a few minutes. The guard in the corridor above, a huge, burly personage, with the brains, it would be flattery to say, of a calf, and exceedingly punctilious in his notions, came down the stairs to see what was the matter. One of the men shouted out to him, forgetting decorum in the desperate hurry of the moment, "Why don't you open the door, you — — —?" Now, it was not only against the rules that the door should be opened between certain hours, but it was altogether irregular and intolerable to miscall an official. The guard stopped short. "Who's that called me a —?" he demanded indignantly. But there was none to answer him, for the men were by that time strangling and fainting.

Down the stairs at this juncture came one of the higher officials, choking and gasping. "Open that door, why don't you?" he managed to call out, seeing the guard below him. "I'm trying to find out," replied the latter, "who it was called me a —." The higher official was understood to say something which penetrated the hide of his subordinate, and stirred him at last to action — not a moment too soon. The door was unlocked, and the captives tumbled and crawled out. The burly personage, who rated punctilio and seemly language above the lives of men, still retains his position in the corridor; but the prisoner who had insulted his dignity has never been identified.

But what can be expected of men in the position of guards of a prison? The function is abnormal, and unless it be undertaken from high motives and with an exceptional endowment of intelligence and humane feeling, it will steadily deteriorate a man; from being at the start to all practical purposes a social derelict, incompetent for productive employment, and often suffering from an incurable disease, he will sink lower and lower in the scale of manhood and morality. He has two chief aims in life — to requite himself upon defenseless convicts for the kicking-out bestowed upon himself by the community; and to get an increase of pay.

I had not been three days in the prison, when one of them came to me in my cell and asked me to write for him a letter to the Department urging a raise of salary. So be it by all means, if higher pay will get better men; but men who can command higher pay do not care to do such work.

Since my guard saw no impropriety in asking for it — though, of course, it was against the rules — I wrote his petition for him. The rules governing guards are explicit, but so far at least as they regard treatment of prisoners they are freely disregarded. For example, guards are forbidden by the rules to address prisoners insultingly, to apply names or epithets to them, to lay hands upon them or to strike them "upon whatever provocation" unless they believe their own lives are in danger. A rabbit has as much chance of throttling a bulldog as the ordinary prisoner of endangering the life of a guard; yet hardly a prisoner in the penitentiary has not repeatedly either undergone or witnessed, or both, insults and physical violence offered by guards to the men. As to the impropriety of asking favors of the men, the guards might plead distinguished precedent for it. One of the higher officials of the penitentiary summoned me to his office one morning. He informed me that he intended to devote his life to prison work, but that he was still a young man, and that advancement was slow and difficult. "When you were outside, you lived in society, and knew a lot of big men," he was kind enough to say; "you will be going out of here again before long. If you should find it in your way to speak a good word for me in quarters where it would be likely to do me good, I should appreciate it." I should perhaps have premised, lest he appear in the light of asking something for nothing, that he had opened the conversation by handing back to me the Ingersoll watch of which I had been deprived on entering the institution. I knew that my young friend and benefactor was deep in the darksome intricacies of prison politics, and was just then getting rather the worst of it; but I was unable to give him any positive assurance that my influence with the Department, or elsewhere, would suffice to give him a lift.

Favoritism rules in all parts of the prison administration; it and prison politics are, indeed, twin curses of our whole prison system. In spite of all the specious official promises of reward for good conduct in the form of parole and obedience to the rules, every prisoner knows that they are apples of Sodom; the most correct conduct, maintained for years, will gain a man nothing, while a worthless and heedless fellow, if he has a friend among the men above, will have his way smoothed for him. An official's pet snitch enjoys all manner of indulgences in the way of food and freedoms, and if he be an intelligent fellow, he can ride on his superior's neck and influence his conduct to a surprising degree. Again, certain guards, in the eyes of their superiors, can do no wrong whatever wrong they do; and others, who are apt to be men who retain some conscientious notions as to their duties, find their path difficult. Some guards, too, though they may be obnoxious to their officers, are not dismissed because they know too much, and might reveal uncomfortable facts were they cashiered. I could name an example of this — a young guard who, a few years ago, committed a cold blooded crime upon a convict, for which in the outside world he would have been liable to a hanging. But the prison authorities did not find it expedient to punish him, and he still saunters about the prison, with his cap tilted on his head, and his rifle. He is a good shot, and is employed a good deal on the towers, where quick marksmanship might be useful. He knows too much.

Evil conditions breed evil deeds and dangerous secrets. Conditions have improved somewhat during the last two or three years, but the improvement has been more outward than inward. One day, two or three years ago, suddenly appeared at the gates the Attorney-General from Washington. He had not been looked for so early. He walked straight into the dining room, where he noticed a number of convicts standing up with their noses against the wall. "What is this for?" he asked one of them. The convict couldn't exactly tell; he was waiting to be had up for examination. "How long are you kept there?" "From seven in the morning till seven at night." "Have you had anything to eat?" The man had not, nor any opportunity to discharge the functions of nature either.

This Attorney-General, in Washington, had never showed himself a friend of convicts; but when he saw — and smelt! — this comparatively slight instance of prison discipline, his gorge rose. He ordered all the culprits to the kitchen for a meal, and issued an edict against this punishment, and against some other things that he discovered. What he would have done had he seen the dark cells, and the condition of the men who had been kept there for a few months, may be conjectured. The public is indeed assured that the use of these cells has long been discontinued; but seven or eight hundred prisoners know that, as late as last October, a certain convict commonly referred to as "the old Englishman" was hung up by the wrists in one of them. And there were others.

Prison officials are political appointees, whose controlling aim must therefore be the security and prosperity of themselves, and only afterward (if at all) the welfare and just and decent treatment of the convicts. They have their salaries (niggardly enough if we regard the work they are supposed to do, but affluent in view of what they actually do), and they have the government appropriations for expenses and supplies for the penitentiary, which they are expected to handle economically. But economy, and decent and humane treatment of prisoners in a jail, are incompatible, even were the men kept steadily and productively at work under proper conditions, and paid for what they produced. A jail properly administered would be one of the most expensive investments in the world; but Congress, as at present advised, thinks only of cutting down the already miserably insufficient stipend; and that warden who can, at the end of his fiscal year, show a balance in favor of the government, may depend upon holding his position, and nobody considers the mortal tears, misery and outrage from which that favorable balance is derived. For not only if it be wisely and honestly expended is the supply of money insufficient, but much of it is wasted by mere ignorance, negligence and incompetence, and much more of it — as recent exposures in newspapers indicate — leaks away in the form of graft. For all this waste the convict must pay in privations and cruelties not authorized or contemplated by a government none too considerate at best; and men above grow fat and rosy gilled.

But nothing is so difficult to prove or so easy to conceal as graft; all the ingenuity and resources of the grafters are primarily and undeviatingly devoted to covering their tracks. So much is allowed for maintenance, subsistence, construction; the bills and receipts are shown; all seems right. And yet, somehow, buildings remain unfinished, grounds are a raw wilderness, men are clad in rags inherited from previous generations, and are starved and abused. Meanwhile, a warden on a four or five thousand dollar salary contrives to live at the rate of ten or twelve, and may own valuable real estate in the city.

Do miracles occur in jails, after having been so long discontinued elsewhere? Or must we at last realize that the comfort and soft living of a handful of rascals is obtained at the cost of the flesh and blood and despair of thousands of men — I believe there are five hundred thousand convicts in this country annually — gagged and helpless, to whom we give the name of convicts, but who, whatever their crimes, are still our own flesh and blood, brothers of ours, our own very selves but for special circumstances for which we can claim no merit; but for their souls and lives we are responsible, and to strive to redeem and succor them our own intelligent self-interest should prompt us to spend and labor lavishly. Instead of that, our habitual attitude toward them is that of indifference or even hostility. For why should we honest people waste our good money and precious sympathy on a convict? Has he not already robbed us enough?

It would be a shallow thing to hold up as monsters of hardheartedness and depravity the officials who have been entrusted with the conduct of our prisons. If they do wickedly and corruptly, it is not because they are to begin with preterhuman sinners, but because we summoned them to duties far above their capacity and training, which involve temptations and provocations which they lack will and power to resist, which give them power over fellow creatures which the most magnanimous and purest men might hesitate to assume, and which inevitably plunge men who are not magnanimous or pure into deeds of injustice, dishonor and inhumanity. In a sense, the officials are no less victims of the ignorance and frivolity of the community than are the prisoners themselves.

But, at any rate, the officials are few and the prisoners are many. If anything is to be done to make things better, there is more hope in dealing with the officials first. After they have been driven out, and their places filled with honorable and enlightened men, who will at least administer the law as it stands with integrity and judgment, we shall be in a better position to consider whether the law itself be beyond criticism, and its penalties justly and prudently devised. Crime as it exists is an enormous evil, and it costs us enormously; and cheap and pinchbeck methods will never rid us of it.

VIII

FOR LIFE

*W*hen a man hears rumors that his application for parole is likely to be acted upon favorably, a guard pauses at his cell door some morning, and tells him to go to the clothing shop at a certain hour. The prisoner, unless he has been forewarned, accepts this as proof positive that he will really be set at liberty, and presents himself before the head tailor with a smiling countenance. He is solemnly and specifically measured for a suit, looks over the material out of which it is to be made, perhaps ventures to mention some predilections as to the cut, and takes his departure with a light heart. The fact that the cloth is cheap, unshrunken goods, which will shrivel up at the first shower or severe humidity, and will, at all events, get wrinkled out of shape in a few days, does not dash the hopeful prisoner's jocundity; nor even the consideration that the "prison cut" will be instantly recognized all over the country, by every detective, private or federal, and acted upon as circumstances may indicate. It is not the clothes, good or bad, that makes his long-tried heart glad; it is the assurance of freedom. He would be more than content with a simple loin-cloth, if only freedom might go with it.

As a matter of fact, this measuring commonly means little, and guarantees nothing at all. Indeed, it has rather the appearance of a pleasant jest of the authorities — one of the cat-and-mouse plays with prisoners with which every old timer is familiar. One would say the authorities find amusement, amid the monotonous round of their avocations, in thus stimulating hopes which they know are not likely to be fulfilled. "Come, here is a heart not yet thoroughly broken; let us try another blow at it!" Days, weeks, months, drag tediously by, and nothing more is heard of the parole, or of the suit of new clothes. They have never been made up, or if they by chance have been, they are put away to gather dust on a shelf underground; they are old clothes now — years old, sometimes. And when at last they are brought out again, it is probable that they will be worn by some other, more fortunate man, who ignored the misfit for the sake of getting past the prison doors.

When this little drama was acted for my benefit, I noticed a man sitting in a certain chair amid the other tailor prisoners, stitching away perfunctorily at a piece of goods. I call him a man, but he looked, to my fancy, like an ancient frog, or the semblance of what had once been a frog, from which, however, all the impulses and juices that had made him alive had slowly leaked away, until nothing but the shell was left. He was a pithless automaton, in whom mind and emotions had long since become inert, and only enough sensibility was left to enable him to feel dimly miserable. Who was he — or, better, who had he been? I learned that for seven years he had sat in that same chair from morning till night, doing the same job of sewing on one suit after another of prison clothing. Seven years! But was he capable of no other employment? Might he not have been given the relief of a change? Maybe; but what would be the use? They couldn't be bothered finding him new stunts all the time, since he had learned how to do that one thing satisfactorily. He was a "lifer."

Life — your entire lifetime — means, perhaps, a good deal to you; even its sorrows, in the retrospect, were good in their way; they meant something. And you look forward to happier things in the future; it will be a long and on the whole a successful future perhaps. Think of the variety and the opportunity which this great, multiform, breathing world holds forth to a man; the friends, the activities, the changes of scene, the surprises, the conflicts, success and failure, hope and fear, triumph, defeat — life, in a word. It is a divine thing, a glorious thing, the God-given birthright of all men. It is the molding of character, the endless, stimulating struggle, the growing sense of human brotherhood, the faces and hands of our fellow creatures, the longer, deeper thoughts aroused by the slow revelations of experience as to the plan of human destiny, — and therefore are the words well chosen which condemn a man like yourself to penal servitude "for life?"

But human language has no word to convey the significance of lifelong imprisonment. It is surely not life: nor is it death — Oh, death would be welcome! For death means either (as you may imagine you believe) total extinction, or it means increased life, free from material trammels. But death in life is a monstrous thing; life, for example, spent in a chair in a squalid tailor's shop, doing over and over again the same piece of squalid, meaningless work, with ever another squalid year stretching out its length before you when the last one has been completed. Is life so endured *life* — the sacred Creative gift, imparted to all things, conscious or unconscious, without restriction? Life, the mystery, which we are impotent to bestow, and which even death, self-inflicted or inflicted by others, cannot take away; which one thing only can take away — the death-in-life of penal imprisonment; is it not a formidable thought that we have incurred the burden of this crime, which does not transfer life from one phase to another, but seeks to annihilate it absolutely?

Death would be welcome; the infliction of it can find forgiveness; but how can we forgive the infliction of death-in-life? How can God forgive it, this profane meddling with sacred and fathomless life? Will He accept the plea that we did it "for the protection of society? — for the man's own good? — or a warning to others?" In that day of questioning, I would rather take my chances with the man sitting in the chair in the prison tailor's shop for seven years, a "lifer!" Infinite mercy may find means to compensate him for what we robbed him of; but what can it do with us, the robbers?

In the Federal prison there were a score or more of lifers, with some of whom it was my fortune to become acquainted. I stood in a sort of awe of them; the thought of their fate was so overwhelming that my mind could not compass it, though my heart might approach some conception of it through obscure channels of intuition. Their treatment by the prison officials was not ordinarily severe; even a warden or a guard could feel that clubbing and dark-celling would be a kind of anticlimax for a man sentenced for life. Some of them — usually Negroes — would be given easy jobs, and not held too strictly to the petty regulations whose special object is to humiliate the ordinary prisoner, under guise of disciplining and reforming him. Nothing was to be gained by disciplining or reforming a "lifer." Others, however, in whom despair had taken the expression of obstinacy or savagery, were savagely handled; one of them bears terrible scars from a shooting by one of the guards, and he told me that, out of the twenty-two years he had already served, eight had been spent in the punishment cells. Others are maltreated for a while, experimentally, or to "put the fear of God in their hearts," and afterward let alone. But as a rule, there is not much fun to be got out of a "lifer" by the prison keepers, and they prefer to ignore him.

The introduction of the law allowing the privilege of applying for parole, did, to be sure, place in the hands of the authorities a weapon with which they could "get beneath the hide" (as they might term it) of these obdurate subjects. Needless to say, this measure, which provides that "lifers" may be paroled (at the discretion of the parole board) after having served fifteen years with a good prison record, did not contemplate introducing thereby a new element of misery into their lives. But the men to whose hands the "lifer" is entrusted found in it a means of making him more readily amenable to discipline by holding over him the threat of an adverse report should he prove intractable. They could keep him indefinitely in that state of torturing suspense as to his fate, which is perhaps the worst of all tortures, by withholding from him all information as to whether or not his appeal was likely to succeed.

Several cases of this kind came under my observation. In one, the release came before the man had collapsed; in others, too late. In only one or two that I know of was there any pretext that his conduct during imprisonment had been unsatisfactory. The delay was never explained; it was due to willful or careless neglect. Two men were carried out feet foremost in a deal box after they had endured suspense up to the extreme limit of mortal capacity. They died of broken hearts — gradually broken through long months of hope slowly fading into despair.

The warden sat serene in his office, attending to business as a good official should, writing reports to the Department which testified to his efficiency and economy, welcoming visitors with his genial smile, occasionally reading encomiums upon himself in a local newspaper, written and inserted there by somebody; the guards sauntered jauntily about, cocking their caps and making their clubs dance at the end of the cords; eight hundred unsightly felons, who had once been men like you and me, filed drearily in to their meals, and out again, the worse for the experience; and all the while, from morning till night, Dennis sat on the corner of his cot in the hospital room, waiting for the news of his release. He felt, and said, at first, that it was sure to come; it would come in a day or two, or at the end of the week anyway; or at the beginning of the week after. He knew his application had been accepted; of course, those big officials had lots to do, and could not be expected to attend to him at once; but they would not forget him.

For several weeks — a month or two — Dennis kept up his spirits well; he had been in prison many years, more than the number required for parole, and he had no bad marks against him. His wife and two daughters were still living, however, and he was full of plans for his future life with them; what he would do, where he would live, how happy they all would be together, after that separation. But one day as he sat on his cot, or paced slowly up and down the hospital chamber, news was brought to him, bad news, news that his wife had died unexpectedly.

He survived it; some men survive miraculously in prison, and some die easily. Dennis had his daughters left to him still; and the release was sure to come now — they would not surely delay it any longer. He had been a tall, powerful mulatto when he first came to prison; he was a gaunt, bent skeleton of a man now, with great, bony, strengthless hands, that closed round mine with a sort of appealing, lingering pressure when we met, as if he feared to let go his hold upon a man who was sorry for him. The doctor knew — any competent physician, at least, might have known — that he could not last much longer; but the doctor said nothing and did nothing. Then — for the stars in their courses seemed to fight against Dennie — came another piece of news for him; not news of parole, but news that his daughters, both of them, had followed their mother; they too were dead. Dennis, who had begun to plan out a life with them, to be father and mother both to them, to comfort them and work for them, and to die at last with their love and companionship comforting him, was now alone in the world, and still in prison.

Time had gone by; it was six months since he had begun to look for freedom. What would freedom mean for him now, with no one in the world to go to or to be with? Probably he gave up looking for it at this point; at any rate, he spoke of it no more. He spoke very little after that, and he very seldom rose from his seat on the corner of his cot, or took notice of anyone or of anything in the hospital room. He sat there, day after day, all day long, with his eyes fixed upon a certain point of vacancy; what he saw, what he thought, no one knew. His hands lay before him on his bony knees, lax and inert. Half a lifetime in prison, and now he was nearing the end, mute and motionless, making no complaint or protest — the power for that had gone by. He no longer spoke of parole; and no parole came. No doubt, the great officials were busy, and what was Dennis that they should remember him, and draw out that paper from its pigeonhole, and sign it, and send it to him? The world could get along without Dennis.

So, one day, Dennis died; and after his body had been laid in its box, the old market wagon, with the old mule between the shafts, was backed up to the door, and the box with the grey old corpse in it was shoved in and driven round to the prison burying ground and dumped into its red clay hole. There it lies; but I am not sure that that is the end of Dennis. A time may be coming, after this earthly show is over, when persons who were so much pressed for time that they could find no moment to sign a paper to save a fellow man's life, may see him again under awkward circumstances, and be asked to explain. Justice, after all, is an Immortal, and belongs to eternity. We should beware of measuring, by the apparent slowness of her movements on this lower plane, the likelihood of her final victory.

If you have some imagination to spare, put yourself in the place of a convict who finds himself, today, facing a sentence of imprisonment for life. The imagination of it, even, is so appalling that you will need more than common courage to picture it to yourself. What, then, must the reality of it be? It is hard to understand how any human heart and brain can withstand the prospect of it. If it has not stopped your heart at once — if your brain has not immediately collapsed under the shock — you will think of suicide. But, perhaps, before you can find means or resolution to seek that escape, you will become conscious, in the background of your mind, of a stirring of that almost ineradicable thing that we call hope. You cannot quite bring yourself to believe that your entire earthly future is to be passed in a prison cell. Some event will occur, some beneficent freak of destiny, some earthquake or lightning bolt, some national revolution or catastrophe, some belated sense of humanity in your brother man, some new law repealing the impious cruelty of the old law, that will break your bars before the end can come. You cannot believe that you will actually live and die in jail.

Thus you are tided over your first hours and days, and with each new day that you survive the chances of your surviving altogether increase. By and by, you fall into the prison routine, and your existence becomes mechanical and automatic. There will be occasional flamings-out of rage and despair, but they pass, and become progressively more infrequent. You have slipped down into a merely animal stratum of existence; you live today because you lived yesterday, and you do not forecast tomorrow. Perhaps you learn to assuage and deceive the hunger of your immortal soul by forcing your attention upon the petty ripple of daily events and duties, until you present, to the outsider, the appearance of a commonplace, non-tragic person, bearing no noticeable scars of the crime which society perpetrated on you. You perhaps lose, at last, the realization of your own inhuman plight, and are received, unawares, into the grey prison protoplasm, no longer really sensitive to impressions, though presenting the semblance of human reactions. You drift down the stream, passive, in a sort of ghastly contentment. You have forgotten that you ever were a man.

But I am merely speculating in the direction of truths that I do not know and cannot reach. The lifers themselves whom I knew could tell me nothing; they were less demonstrative than the men of five or ten years' sentence. We can never fathom the dealings of the Almighty with His creatures, and they, perhaps, can fathom them as little as we can. In ways inconceivable to us, they are supported.

There was a little old man known as Uncle Billy. If the parole board has kept faith with him, he should have been set free the 23rd of December. Uncle Billy's right arm had been amputated at the shoulder, the result of a shot through the arm from his own gun while he was getting out of a buggy. He lived in Oklahoma, Indian Territory, at the time of his story. Billy was married to a woman who must have had some attractiveness, for a journeying peddler, who periodically passed through the region, formed a liaison with her. There was at that time a daughter, who had just reached marriageable age. The peddler was wont practically to put Billy out of his own house during his sojourns, and usurped his place as master of the household. At one time he secured Billy's conviction on some minor offense, and had him jailed for six months. What Billy thought of the situation I don't know; he was a small, slight man, under five foot three, and of an intellectual cast. But he seems not to have attempted active measures, until one day he discovered that the peddler, not satisfied with the wife, was attempting the seduction of the daughter likewise.

Then, one night, Billy came to his house, and found that going on which his patience could not tolerate. He got hold of an ax, and, stealing into the room, struck the peddler, as he lay in bed, with his one arm, and split his head open. What passed then between him and his wife is not known. Billy, I believe, was for giving himself up to the authorities at once; but the woman prevailed upon him to conceal the deed. She tied the body to the tail of the horse, and dragged it across the fields to a ditch, where she covered it with dirt and rubbish. There it lay for some weeks, until a couple of men out hunting saw an end of a suspender sticking out of the ground, and pulling at it, discovered the murdered corpse. Billy confessed, and he and his wife were lodged in jail pending their trial. The woman died there; but Billy was tried and convicted, and in consideration of the peculiar circumstances, was "let off" with a life sentence. When I knew him, he had been in a cell nearly fifteen years.

The weather was chilly; some of the prisoners were let out in the yard every day at one o'clock, to pace round in a ring for forty minutes. I saw the little, bent, thin old man, with one arm, hobbling round and round with his cane. Conversation was not permitted under the rules, but the rule was often overlooked. After I had gained an outline of his story from some old timers, I spoke to him, and he looked up at me with a pair of singularly intelligent brown eyes, and with a kindly expression of his meager little face. We conversed a little on general subjects, and I found him well educated, observant, thoughtful, with a distinct vein of subdued humor. Afterward I saw him in his cell, though there was a rule against that, too; but the guard was tolerant.

He had a violin there which he had made himself, his tools being a knife made out of a nail hammered flat and the edge sharpened, and a piece of broken glass. It was admirably fashioned, and except that it was not varnished, would have been taken for such an instrument as you buy in a shop; its tone, too, was pleasing, and Billy could discourse excellent music on it. It was in the manufacture of these fiddles that his time was passed; the fact that he had but one hand to work with did not embarrass him. His contrivance for playing on the instrument was as remarkable as the instrument itself; he had rigged up a sort of jury arm of wood and metal, with an elbow to it, and a grip to lay hold of the bow. Persons who play on violins will doubtless be more puzzled than I was to conceive how he could do it; but he did it. And for aught I could see, he was content with his singular industry; it gave him constant occupation and enabled him, I suppose, to keep thoughts of other things out of the way. Otherwise, he was utterly unobtrusive, almost invisible, and the guards let him alone. But the government of the United States had kept him there for fifteen years, as a menace to society. You can see him in fancy, had he been set free for doing what most human beings must have done, ranging up and down the country, dealing out terror and slaughter. Such wild beasts must be restrained. They must be disciplined and reformed, and jail is the way to do it.

Just before I left the jail, I spoke to Billy about his parole. "You and

I will get out almost together," I said. "No, no," he replied, with his curious little humorous smile, "they can't get rid of me as easy as that; I've got three months yet, and I'm going to stick it out to the end." I have not heard the sequel; but I can hardly believe that the authorities mean to play the cat-and-mouse game with him.

I have perhaps mentioned John Ross, who died, under promise of parole, after thirty-three years behind the bars. And there was Thomas Bram, a prisoner hardly less remarkable, freed on parole after seventeen years' confinement. He had persistently asserted his innocence from the first, and nobody so far as I know doubted his assertion. The evidence against him was entirely circumstantial, and there was another man in the case who seemed, to judge by the reports of the trial, to have been at least as likely to be guilty. Bram's record in prison was wholly blameless, and though there was some opposition to freeing him, it sufficed only to obtain a delay of a few weeks beyond the date set for his release. But during those few weeks, his sufferings were trying to witness, and he was near collapse before the end came. He told me that the Attorney-General had personally promised him freedom two years before, but had done nothing toward keeping his promise. "It wasn't right, Mr. Hawthorne," was all the comment he allowed himself to make. Bram's self-control was great, and his manner always soft and ingratiating; he was politic and prudent, and had probably resolved from the outset of his prison career to obtain pardon or mitigation if good conduct and unfaltering adherence to his plea of innocence could compass it. He was given a job which procured him some indulgences, and was never punished. But if a life sentence for a guilty man be intolerable, what shall be said if he were guiltless? Think it over in your leisure moments.

I find my list is far too long to be dismissed in one chapter; and in cases where the men are still in confinement, discussion of them might prove injurious. There was a young fellow there who looked like a slender boy of seventeen; he was really over thirty years of age. But he had been imprisoned since his fifteenth year, and his face since then had not developed or taken the contours of manhood; and his manner was boyish. He was well educated in the grammar school sense, however, though I believe he had picked up most of what he knew in prison. He had a distinct, emphatic way of speaking, and believed, I fancy, that he was quite a man of the world, though, of course, he was almost totally devoid of other than prison experience. He would have been an interesting study, had not the pathos of his condition, of which he was himself unaware, made one shrink from probing it.

He had killed a man at the instigation of and under the influence of a step-father, who wished the man removed for ends of his own, and forced the child (he was nothing else) to take the job off his hands, and the law of Indian Territory, which was the scene of the affair, condemned him for life. After serving fifteen years, he applied for his parole under the law; there appeared to be no grounds so far as his prison record went for denying it; nevertheless, he was rejected. He asked the reason, and was told that it was not considered safe to set him at liberty; he had a "bad temper" — that was, I think, the explanation.

Psychological insight is a good thing in its way and place, but it may be carried too far, or employed amiss; and this looks like an illustration. The boy, in more than fifteen years, had never done anything in prison that called for discipline; but because some self-constituted and arbitrary psychologist chose to believe, or to say, that his temper was not under full control, he was doomed to spend the rest of his life in a cell. This prisoner knows, of course, that he has been wronged, but he does not know how much; he does not know what life in a world of free men is. But he, after being kept for half of his lifetime under duress, must submit to the caprice of a man to whom the country has entrusted absolute power. No man is qualified to exercise absolute power; no man is justified in accepting it; but we bestow it upon every chance political appointee, and what he does with it puts us to shame, whether or not we can as yet realize it.

There was at least one life prisoner in Atlanta who merits a chapter to himself; but I cannot speak of him now. He is one of the unreconciled, and his horoscope is still too cloudy to make it safe to tell his story. A desperate criminal, he would be termed by prison experts. In truth, he is a warm-hearted, generous, high minded man, sentenced to death in his boyhood for a deed which would have been properly punished by a few months in a reformatory, afterward obtaining a commutation to life imprisonment, and now a man of more than forty years, bearing upon his body terrible scars of severities practiced upon him for trying to resist wrongs which no manly man could tamely endure. A Balzac might find in him a more human and lovable *Vautrin*; a Victor Hugo could make him the hero of another *Les Miserables*; a Charles Reade could win new renown by summoning us to put ourselves in his place. But the best service I can do him now is to give him silence. He is not quite desperate yet; should he become so, the world will know his history.

IX

The Toil of Slavery

*B*efore the Civil War there were some millions of Negro slaves in the South, whom to set free we spent some billions of dollars and several hundred thousand lives. It was held that the result was worth the cost. But today we are creating some five hundred thousand slaves, white and black, each year — or that is about the number of made slaves each year in the United States; it costs us several millions to keep them in an enslaved condition, and their depredations upon society, before and after slavery, amount to several millions more. I have not the precise data, but the figures hazarded are not excessive. A sound statistician would make a more sensational showing; and when he proceeded to cast up his account for the aggregate of the years since the war, and of the estimated amounts for the coming fifty years, the bill would look large even with a hundred million paymasters to foot it.

In that bill, probably the smallest item would be the cost of crime itself — the actual loss caused to the community by the thieving of thieves, — of the thieves, that is, who have been convicted and condemned as such; for there is no way of figuring on how much the undetected thieves steal. Every time we shake the social body, in this or that spasm of probing and reform, hundreds drop out, like moths from an unprotected garment; so that at last we are prone to suspect that the thief, overt or covert, is more the rule than the exception, and that a good part of the cash in circulation was more or less dishonestly come by. But, leaving this aside, the money or values appropriated by thieves accredited as such and sent to jail, is an amount relatively inconsiderable, and by no means enough to pay the expenses of their apprehension, trial, and prison sojourn. It is, then, politically uneconomical to imprison them.

The reply to this is, of course, that penal slavery is preventive of crime; that if we did not prosecute malefactors, crime would multiply and abound, like weeds in a neglected garden. Perhaps it would; but the point is, that it multiplies and abounds even in the teeth of prosecutions; every year the number of convictions is greater, and the jails are already cracking their seams to contain the convicts. One might almost conclude that prisons, as now administered, stimulate crime instead of preventing it, and that we are in the predicament of Hercules in the fable, who, as fast as he cut off a head of the hydra, saw two others sprout in its place. At which rate, we might be led on to the surmise that it would be financially cheaper to let crime run on; the cost of our futile efforts to stop it would be saved, and might be set over against the loss from the increased annual depredations.

But finance is not the whole story; what about morality? and who can forecast the ruin of anarchy? The problem cannot be so crudely solved.

Crime must be prevented; doubtless nine-tenths even of the men in jail would agree to that proposition. The question is, can the jail system prevent it? and the answer is that, judged by long experience − the experience of thousands of years − it cannot. There are several reasons why it cannot, into some of which we may enquire later; but the objection to the jail system which I wish to emphasize just now is, that it not only makes slaves of convicts, but, unlike the more reasonable southern Negro slavery, it makes them unproductive slaves. Either it withholds this vast body of men from production altogether, or else it forces them to toil under conditions which bring forth results the smallest possible and the most unsatisfactory. The men are not paid for what they do. Whatever profit (in "contract" prisons) accrues from their toil goes into the pockets of the contractors, or, perhaps, is used to defray the cost of their keep to the community. Or, again, if it is made to appear to go into the prisoners' pockets, it is deftly taken out again the next moment by an ingenious system of fines, which no prisoner can escape.

In short, prison labor is slave labor, and slave labor of a worse kind than was ever practiced in Negro slavery times. For on southern plantations, though slaves were not paid wages, they got wages' worth in good food and lodging, and (uniformly) in humane treatment, including, above all, the companionship of their wives and families; and they were able, in many instances, to buy themselves into freedom. Most of the Negroes, moreover, had never known what it was to be free; their race, for generations unknown, had been slaves in their own country; they had never been free citizens of the United States, never had education, were unconscious of any disgrace in their condition, and were as happy as ever in their lives they had been or were capable of being — happier, indeed, than most Negroes are in the community today. In all respects their condition compares favorably with that of our half million annual prison slaves, manufactured deliberately out of our own flesh and blood.

I used to contemplate the population in the Atlanta Penitentiary — the eight hundred of us — and then look at the construction work, the gardening, the tailoring, the carpentering, the product of the forge, the farming in the prison grounds outside the walls, and the work of clearing and grading on the area which the walls enclosed, and I marveled at the disproportion. Eight hundred men, many of them skilled in this or that industrial employment, most of them physically capable of active labor, and almost all of them eager to work if given intelligent and useful work to do; not a few, too, intellectually and educationally equipped to plan and direct industrial operations; and yet, with all this great potential force at command, all that was actually accomplished might have been done as well or better by a corporal's guard of willing and well managed men. The mere economic waste of such material was criminal, without regard to the evil effect of inadequate or misapplied labor upon the men's moral and mental state. Can it be, I asked myself, that this extravagant idleness is forced upon the prisoners as part, and not the least evil part of their punishment? Or is it the result of ignorance, incompetence, or indifference on the part of those appointed and paid to take care of men sentenced to "hard labor?"

That the men suffer from it is beyond question. And I cannot find that the law provides or intends that their suffering shall be of this kind. Much of the insanity in the prison is due to the way they are made, or made not, to work. There is a legend of a warden who, being unable to keep his prisoners otherwise busy, set them to piling up paving stones on one side of the yard, and then taking down the pile and repiling it on the other side. After a week of this, most of them were maniacs. It was not the severity of the labor that destroyed their minds, but the uselessness and objectlessness of it. Sane men require reasonable employment; idleness, or irrational work disintegrates their minds. They want to see and to foresee intelligible results from their toil; mere toil without such results is maddening, or it rots men's minds as scurvy rots their bodies. The reason is, that the men are human; and if you have hitherto supposed that convicts are not human, the insanity which so constantly follows upon prison idleness or mis-employment should correct you.

Others may describe the horrors, almost indescribable, of contract labor in prisons; I saw nothing of that at Atlanta — type of another widespread system of prison work — though I heard enough about it from men who had undergone it in state prisons. But during the few first days of my imprisonment, I saw a building gang at work (to call it work) upon a new wing destined to contain dormitories for the inmates. It was to be a seemly structure of granite, massive and well proportioned. But after three days, work on it was stopped, and was not resumed until a week or so before I left this prison, six months later. Meanwhile, I read in the *Congressional Record* the report of a debate in the House, in which, on the authority of a Texas representative, charges of graft or waste were laid against persons concerned in the erection of this building which seemed incredible, but of which I was able to find no refutation. The hospital building is open to the same criticism, and another, which I believe is designed to be the laundry, had got no further, at the date of my arrival, than a square hole in the ground, and when I left had been furthered by a single course of stone or cement laid round the hole. A New York contractor, graft or no graft, would have had all three of them finished and in commission in the same time, and with no better material in the way of laborers than our prison could supply.

The thirty-four foot wall surrounding the buildings, a mile in circuit, built of cement, had been completed before my time. I read in a report of the warden's that its existence was due to his enterprise, and that he looked upon it as a worthy monument to his activity and intelligence. At every hundred yards or so of its length it was strengthened by a tower, containing accommodations for a guard, day and night, who watches with his rifle in hand, ready to shoot down any prisoner who seems to be acting suspiciously. No such shooting by a tower guard has as yet taken place to my knowledge, and none ever will on the pretext suggested; for the wall is absolutely unscalable; being five or six feet thick, it is impenetrable, and its foundations going down six or eight feet below ground, it cannot be beaten by tunneling; yet the towers and the guards are there.

But the point is that the wall itself is quite preposterous and unnecessary. Escape for prisoners was quite as difficult before it was built as after. There are a hundred guards in the penitentiary — one for every eight prisoners — all armed and eager for action; every article of a prisoner's clothing bears the prison mark; and the population outside the walls is penetrated with the idea that the apprehension of escaping prisoners is morally as well as financially profitable. Every prisoner knows that an attempt to escape would be suicide — "you might get hurt," as the prison rule book euphemistically phrases it — and they generally prefer suicide in some other form.

The wall, then, is superfluous; a fence of electrified wire would have served as good a purpose at about one-thousandth of one percent of the cost. And what did the wall cost? Let the prison archives declare. And then, perhaps, it would be interesting to investigate the discrepancy, if any exist, between the price which the United States paid for the work, and the actual cost of erecting it.

The wall was some time in the building, but it seems to have been the only thing built in the prison, work upon which was continuous and energetic. And it was a useless work, better left undone. The warden was proud of it, however, and there it stands.

As for the twenty-seven acre enclosure, in which the prison buildings are, which is — according to official prognostics — to be graded, leveled, drained, cultivated and planted till it looks like a private millionaire's park, it is a raw, rough unsightly waste of red clay and weeds, gouged out here and there with random and meaningless excavations, heaped up in other places with piles of earth; diversified in one quarter with some forlorn chicken coops and fences, made by the voluntary and unskilled labor of one of the convicts; and adjoining these, with the Tuberculosis Camp, a row of a dozen or more tents mounted on wooden platforms, with little flower beds in front and behind, and a pigeon house at one end. The only part of these grounds on which any visible thought and labor has been expended is the baseball diamond, adjoining the northeast corner of the wall. Here, the ground has been leveled and smoothed over a space sufficient to include the diamond itself, and a few yards on its south and north sides; beyond that is waste ground, and along the northern boundary is a parapet of earth five or six feet high, presumably made of the material scraped off the diamond. A ball vigorously struck by a batter either goes over this parapet into the swamp ground beyond, or sails away toward the Tuberculosis Camp, to be retrieved from the weeds and rubbish in that vicinity.

There are some forty score men behind the bars who would rejoice to be allowed to put these grounds in order, and who, under proper guidance, could do the job in a month. It would be a useful work, it would benefit the men both in the doing and in the accomplishment, and it would be an excellent advertisement of the penitentiary for the visitors who daily stroll about the enclosure; yet months and years go by and nothing whatever is changed.

One day, in midsummer, I saw a gang of Negroes digging a trench in front of the southern gate, and cutting out a heavy growth of weeds and underbrush on the slope above. Drain pipes were carted out and dumped in the vicinity of the trench, and three or four of them were laid down in it. This went on for three or four days, the whole gang of ten or a dozen men not achieving in that period more than one or two capable Irish or Italian navvies would have done in the same time. Then the gang disappeared; the open trench and the pipes remained in statu quo, and the weeds gradually resumed their ancient sway. So far as I know, work has not been resumed there since.

It is a typical example; even such work as is done, is done in such a discontinuous and futile way that it is impossible for anyone doing it to feel any interest in it, or stimulus to do it well. Time, toil and money are frittered away, with nothing definite or substantial to show for it. Intermittent and barren tasks are doubly onerous. The overseers may not be to blame; they may be incompetent; they may be hampered by the ignorance, incompetence or voluntary policy of the prison authorities; the consequences, at all events, are disastrous. If a handful of hearty, clever, driving men were given control of the various industrial operations in the prison, the results would seem magical.

There is dry rot or something worse everywhere; and it is difficult to believe that anything is gained by it either for the convict or for the country. It is to be sure punishment for the former, and a bad form of punishment, but it would be grotesque to assume that it is inflicted by design of our lawmakers. It cannot be that the government deliberately proposes to destroy convicts, mind and body; on the contrary, we must suppose that it wishes to reform them and render them again useful agents in the community. There is no way to do this better than to give them honest and productive work while in jail, so that they may acquire the habit of such work, and be encouraged to pursue it when they get out.

But in order to induce them to work economically, it is indispensable to give them continuous, intelligent, and manifestly useful work, and to pay them for doing it. It can be and it is done in some jails even now. Warden Fenton, of the Nebraska State Prison, has been putting his men on the honor system, and sending squads of them out to work on farms or for contractors, without guards or other precautions, sometimes for weeks at a time; all he asks of them is their promise to return when the job is done, which they uniformly do. And for this work, he causes them to be regularly paid; he retains their wages for them until the term of their imprisonment has expired, and then hands it back to them. The men are encouraged and inspirited by this treatment, and the neighbors among whom their work is done, seem disposed to take a helpful and cooperative view of the enterprise. If the neighbors — the community — loses nothing by this system, and if the convicts gain by it, why should it not be made the general practice? Convicts in Nebraska are the same sort of people as those in Atlanta.

Warden Fenton is progressive, but most other wardens are not, and there is no certainty that future wardens of Nebraska prisons will be; therefore he has not solved the problem for good and all; something more than the benevolent or wise ideas of any individual is needed for that. Mr. Fenton has absolute power – power, therefore, to give or withhold favors as he may choose. Enlightened legislation would deprive him and other wardens of absolute power, and make it mandatory to treat prisoners as he is doing it voluntarily.

Moreover, if men will go off and work without guards for three weeks at a stretch, and then return uncompelled to the prison, what is the use of making them return to the prison at all, or of having any prison for them to return to? Is not their conviction prison enough for most of them? And for such as prove incorrigible, or are criminal degenerates, ought not pathological care, instead of penal slavery, to be provided? Professor Marchiafava, physician to the Pope, said recently, "Eighty percent of youthful criminals are children of drunkards." That is a serious indictment of alcohol; but it indicts no less the policy which punishes victims of disease as if they were deliberate and freely choosing malefactors.

But leaving sick folk out of the argument, I say that, in view of Mr. Fenton's experiment, and others like it, conviction is prison enough for most persons who have slipped a cog in their moral machinery. Means could readily be found to make such persons recognizable at need, and they would have as great a stimulus to render themselves free from that stigma as they have now, and far better opportunities for doing it. They would have their families with them, or within touch, and they would no longer be slaves; and if they had been slaves to their own passions and propensities, the expediency of breaking such chains would become far more obvious than it ever can be when a guard and a warden is always round the corner waiting to club or dungeon them for infringement of a whimsical prison rule. It does not help a man to his manhood to see his keepers acting constantly the part of tyrants and torturers.

This is perhaps a novel doctrine, because, as the editorial writer in the *Saturday Evening Post* remarked the other day, "The truth is that, at least two times out of three, we send a man to jail because we do not know anything rational to do with him, and will not take the pains to find out." We lack imagination to devise more effective treatment, and we are wonderfully ignorant as to what prison treatment really means. And this indictment lies not only against the public at large, but against the Department of Justice and the Congress, who pass their judgments and inflict their penalties without in the least understanding what they are doing to human bodies and souls like their own.

Jail is the conventional and time-honored nostrum, which is administered with a glow of moral self-esteem, and no more thought about it. When a murderer is sent to jail for life, or a bank burglar or white slaver or financial crook for his specified term, do we not sit back in our chairs and clear our throats with a self-satisfied "hem!" and "There's one scoundrel has got his deserts, anyway!" Had it been your brother, father, son, or yourself, would you employ such language? Would you not rather say, "If the whole truth were known, this could not have happened?" But every case is a special case to the victim. And which of us who has not been a convict in prison has the right to declare that prison is the "desert" of any man? We do not know what we are talking about.

I was looking out of the window of the Isolation Building one day, with the runner, Ned, beside me; I did my writing there, and he was assigned for duty to the same building. Ned, to whom I have already referred, was a thoughtful young man, and often said a word that went to the center of the subject. We had no business, of course, to be conversing together, but the guard was absent for the moment. We were watching the convicts form in the yard for the march to their several places of occupation; there was a double row of them down there in front of us being marshaled to go to the stone-shed, about fifty yards away. There they would remain till evening, chipping away at blocks of granite, and breathing the dust created by their labor.

The stone-shed men were mostly recruited from the so-called hard cases among the convicts; the work was hard, and rapid-fire guards were generally picked to take care of them. A man had been shot to death there about five years before by a guard, on no better grounds than that the man had not moved quickly enough in response to an order. No action against the guard was taken, and he is still on duty in the prison; perhaps he knows too much. The stone-shed men prepare the stone used in the construction of the buildings already mentioned; and they are also employed at times, by no regulation to be found in any of the books, to do odd jobs for members of the prison force; as when, for example, they were required to turn out a monument for the wife or other relative of a guard who had died, and for whom he was unable to provide a suitable memorial at his own expense. For whatever purpose the stone work is done, legitimate or illegitimate, the workers are not enthusiastic about it, and probably not many of them will live long enough, at least in prison, to see their handiwork in practical use.

Arrayed near them was another file, destined to work on the grounds belonging to the prison outside the warden's famous wall, where turnips, potatoes, corn and other vegetables are grown. The vegetables grow — it can hardly be said that they are cultivated; I don't know what a New York market gardener would say to them. They grow, and in due season some of them appear on the prison table; others do not appear, but whether they are left to rot in the ground, or are put to a more remunerative use, I do not personally know. There is no great enthusiasm among the gardeners, either.

Suddenly, Ned groaned out, "Oh, the aimlessness of it! Why don't you write a piece in our paper about the aimlessness of prison work? Aimless — that's what it is! How can a fellow feel interested in what he's doing, when he never knows what he's doing it for, or what becomes of it when it's done — let alone that he isn't paid for it? Aimlessness — that's what we get here in prison, and that's all we learn here. Did you ever think what a prison would be if there was any common sense aim in anything? Those fellows could make this place the finest thing you could imagine, if they were taken hold of by somebody with common sense, and put on jobs that had any sense in them. But they are kept dawdling around, and never know where they're at. It kills 'em — that's what it does! You'd think a criminal would be taught anything but aimlessness; it was aimlessness that got him here in the first place, nine times out of ten.

"Why, take what goes on in the printing office that you were assigned to, for instance," he went on, with a sidelong grin at me. "You have a month to get out the paper, four to six pages large quarto. How long would it take to do that stunt in New York?"

"I suppose it could be done in twenty-four hours," I admitted.

"Yes, and there are six men down there, and they have thirty times twenty-four hours. They are in a cellar underground, with the air that hasn't been changed in years, and the heat-pipes making it worse. Their health can't stand it — you know that — but there they've got to stay every day from eight till half after four, pottering round with their types and proofs and stuff, and trying to drag it along till time's up — what's the good of it to anybody? It's the same everywhere; look at the tailorshop! Those fellows sit and fool around there, with the guard slinging language at 'em every few minutes, and taking an hour to sew a hem six inches long; and all the time here's you and me wearing clothes that were new maybe five or six years ago, as you may see by the numbers that have been stamped on your back and then blotted out, and were worn, since then, by some poor devil with tuberculous trouble or worse; but they'll be worn out for fair before we get any others. Why, look at your pants! They're split all down the leg, and there's your knee sticking out of the hole! The prison authorities call that economy, may be; what do you call it?"

I said that I was not competing for the glass of fashion just then. Ned offered to sew up the rent for me, but I said that the safety-pin now on duty would suffice. He still had some of his theme left in him, and he went on:

"Look at that power house, that's kept going night and day, the year round, with coal at government expense, running all sorts of machinery, and what do they get out of it? I was in the carpenter's shop the other day, and there was all kinds of machines going, lathes, and I don't know what; you'd think by the noise of them they was building the Ark at least. But I nosied round, and couldn't find anybody that seemed to be working much. At last I came to one of the big steam lathes, and there was a man that looked to be busy about something, so I went up to watch him. Well, what do you think he was doing? He was making one of these here little sticks that a fellow cleans his nails with! The power house was burning tons of coal, and everything humming, and that was what came out of it all. A nail stick! What do you think of that?"

No doubt there was rhetorical exaggeration about this; but Ned's arraignment was on the whole not devoid of justification. There are abundant means in the prison for carrying on useful and energetic work, but they are not properly employed. Neither the convicts nor the community benefits by it.

Not that it is wholly without benefit to anybody, either. Good clothes are made in the tailor shop, but they are not worn by convicts. At least one excellent dwelling house has been made by prisoners, but it is occupied by a high prison official. Unexceptionable meals are cooked in the convict kitchen, but convicts do not eat them. There is an admirable and productive kitchen garden attached to the prison, but its contents never appear on convict tables. There is a fine lawn, diversified with brilliant flower-beds, in front of the main prison building, and it is greatly admired by visitors and passers-by; but the convict sees it twice only during his term — once when he is brought into the prison, and again when he is led out. On neither occasion is he, perhaps, in the best mood to profit by it. Perhaps the prison officials do profit by it; but if so, the results are not seen in their intercourse with the prisoners. There is nothing flowerlike in that.

Idleness is an evil thing; purposeless work is idleness in another and worse form. Aimlessness, as my friend Ned said, is a miserable state for a man; it tortures him in prison, and the habit of it, acquired in prison, cripples and degrades him after he gets out. Contract labor is a crime which is getting recognized as such; it disgraces the nation or the state which tolerates it, and the shame of it, if not its immorality, may lead to its general suppression. Unpaid convict labor for the state, as on roads and so forth, is better than private contract labor, but is also a disgrace to the employer — a contemptible saving of pennies at the cost of human souls. Honest work is a manly thing, and those who do it should be treated like men, and as laborers worthy of their hire. Because we have rendered them helpless to demand their rights is no excuse for denying them. It is cheap, but shameful, and can only teach them that the community can be as dishonest as the veriest thief of them all.

But a system of work of which that at Atlanta is a type (and, alas! the type is far too numerous) is anomalous and abominable; it is aimless, and abhorrent to man, God and devil alike. It is difficult to absolve such a prison from the charge of being run at the expense of prisoners, for the benefit of its officials, since they alone appear to prosper by it.

X

Our Brother's Keeper

*T*igers love their cubs, hens their chickens, dogs love their masters and all these will fight and die in defense of what they love. Human mothers generally love their offspring. Love in the common sense is common or instinctive, and involves no moral quality. It is love of one's own, and contains a better form of self love.

But mercy is of higher birth. Animals know nothing of it; savages and the lower types of man ignore it. We ascribe a divine source to it when we pray God to have mercy on us; we do not ask Him to love us. All higher religions enjoin it. Mercy is love purified from self, or wholly altruistic. It is a man loving another not because of blood relationship, or because of expected benefits, or even because of benefits bestowed, but on the simple ground that he is his human brother, child of the same Divine Father. It is purer than the racial feeling, and it includes the animal creation outside humanity in its scope — as the Bible puts it, "the merciful man is merciful to his beast."

It is the Golden Rule in manifestation; we see in the one to whom we are merciful ourself in another form, under different conditions, and we do to him as we would have him do to us. It seems to require a certain maturity of mind, acquired or inherited; children below puberty seldom have it. It is easily forfeited, and indifference to the suffering of others is readily established. It is to be guarded and developed as a sacred possession of man at his highest, and constantly nourished by thought and deed. And no man is so high and strong but he may and does need the mercy of some being loftier and more powerful than himself, which he cannot claim if he have not himself done mercifully to those below him.

I have remarked heretofore that officials of prisons should be men of the highest character in the state — at least as high as what we would wish to ascribe to our judges of the criminal bench. Judges send men to prison; but prison guards and wardens have charge of them during their imprisonment, with powers practically unlimited.

Unlimited power is a trust too arduous for any mortal, for it should presuppose perfect knowledge, all-penetrating intelligence, boundless experience, and the mercy which is born of these — for there is a bastard brother of mercy which is of the parentage of ignorance and cowardice, which shrinks from the sight of suffering from mere pusillanimity of the nerves, and does not recognize that suffering may be mercifully inflicted or permitted and beneficently endured.

But the community does not select its prison officials on the basis above indicated; it is satisfied if they be competent to "handle men," have a sagacious familiarity with human depravity, will tolerate no nonsense, can indict plausible reports for the Department, and show a good balance at the end of the fiscal year, or, as guards and under-strappers, keep the men submissive and orderly and allow no outbreaks. As for knowledge, a public school education is ample, with such intelligence as may be supposed to go with it; and the experience of a ward heeler or a thug will ordinarily suffice to pass a candidate. As a matter of fact, the community never knows anything about its prison officials until some special scandal transpires under their administration, or unless some heaven-sent phoenix of a warden unaccountably manifests humane and enlightened tendencies. Their appointment is left to the political machine, which hands it out on the principle of what is he, or was he worth to us? As for justice and mercy — my good sir, you seem to forget we are talking of convicted criminals!

I affirm, however, that justice — which is intelligent mercy — is required nowhere so urgently as with convicts; that any punishment which aims at more than restraining convicts from practices calculated to injure their own best interests, is a crime; and that cruelty to persons imprisoned and helpless, be the plea in extenuation of it what it may, is damnable and unpardonable wickedness. Meanwhile, there is not and has never been in the United States a jail in which revengeful, malicious and unjustifiable punishments have not been inflicted, and in which cruelty does not stain the record of each year and day.

There have appeared lately in the newspapers stories of enormities perpetrated in Russian prisons. Terrible barbarians, those Russians! Yet, barring one feature of them only, they can be paralleled by what is currently done in prisons here. This one feature, is the absence in the Russian infernos of all hypocritical protestations to the public of humane treatment and of aversion from severities. The Russian cannot do more than beat, torture and kill his prisoners; but we do the same. It is done at Blackwell's Island, at Sing Sing, at Auburn, at Jefferson City, at Leavenworth (until the other day at least), in San Quentin, and countless others, including my own Atlanta: only, there, the policy of suppression of news and promulgation of falsehood is perhaps carried to a more nearly perfect extreme than in most other prisons.

A few years ago, but under the present régimen at Atlanta, the workers in the stone shed there were pursuing their occupation in the torrid heat of a summer day, when one of them, a young man named Ed Richmond, asked the guard on duty for leave to retire for a few moments. Such requests must of course often be made. But Richmond was a man who had not been lucky enough to win the favor of the higher officials in the prison, and this was known to the guards, who felt that they might with impunity treat him harshly. Richmond had been a good deal abused, and his mind had become somewhat unbalanced; he would sometimes talk incoherently and act oddly. It had been noticed that the stone shed guard "had it in for Ed," as the prisoners say; but nothing very serious was looked for.

Be that as it may, something serious was about to occur. Five or six years after this day, I was walking, under convoy of the Deputy Warden, in the prison grounds that lie outside the walls, when we stumbled upon the prison graveyard. It lay at the crest of some rising ground, partly overshadowed by second growth timber, and was merely an unenclosed clearing in the rough undergrowth with rows of headstones standing one behind the other, each with a name and date on it. But under all of them lay all that remained on earth of prison tragedies; for even if a prisoner die a natural death in prison, he dies with a broken heart and poisoned mind, abandoned, in grey despair, friendless, shut out from sky and freedom, hearing with dulled ears the clanging of steel gates, seeing the blank walls, deprived of the sympathetic words and glances of friends — a miserable, unknown death. Silence and obliteration close over him; and here he lies.

On one of the headstones I read the name of Ed Richmond, and the date of his end. He had not died a natural death, but there was nothing on his tombstone to show it. I already knew his story, having heard it from several eyewitnesses.

On the day above mentioned, the guard had granted his request; but after the man had been absent a few minutes, he called to him to come out. Richmond did not at once respond. The guard called to him again, more peremptorily, and advanced toward the place where he was, outside the stone shed building. Richmond, as the guard came nearer, mumbled something; the guard seemed angered, and stepped up to him, raising his club to strike. Richmond instinctively put up an arm to ward the blow, and as it descended he caught the end of the club in his hand. This was the head and front of his offending, and for this he was to die.

The guard dropped the club, drew his revolver, and shot Richmond four times in the body. He also fired another shot, the bullet going through a wooden partition into a part of the shed where some prisoners were working, barely missing one of them. Richmond slowly dropped where he stood and lay huddled on the ground; the guard stood looking coolly at him. One of the prisoners, a Negro, ran up and took the dying man's head on his knee; others looked on. After awhile an official came up and ordered the man taken to the hospital. But his hurts were mortal, and in a few minutes he was dead. The men in the stone shed continued their work.

An investigation within the walls was held, the guard was exonerated, and was still on duty when I was in the prison. The officials who had disliked Richmond were relieved of the annoyance of his presence. There were no inconvenient newspaper reporters about. If the dead man had friends outside, they never were able to do anything. It seems unlikely that the guard who killed him would have done it had he not felt confident that the higher officials would condone the deed. Perhaps, had he been arrested and indicted, he might have uttered some names; but he was exonerated, and he has kept his mouth shut. This happened before the date of Attorney-General Wickersham's visit to the prison, and therefore before the change in Warden Moyer's ideas as to the expediency of severe measures in the handling of convicts. Were the thing to be done again today, it would probably not occur out in the open air and sunshine, with persons looking on, but under circumstances of decent seclusion. The outside public is becoming a little squeamish about prison killing.

But in Russia there is no public opinion, or none that is audible, and the prison guards there are not hampered in their work by the necessity of doing it under cover, as they are here. It is a question which method is preferable. I believe some of our prisoners would vote for the open way of killing and torturing. It is exasperating to be "done up" in secret, in the dark, stifled and gagged, with no chance to die fighting. I have no comparative statistics as between us and Russia, but it would not be surprising if our record of men beaten, starved, poisoned, hung up in chains in dark cells, and killed by neglect and cruelties, were to size up fairly well against what Russia has to show. Considering the restrictions put upon them, our prison autocrats certainly do well.

Some doubt has been created in the public mind as to whether there really are dark cells in the Atlanta Penitentiary, or, if there be, whether their use has not been long discontinued. I never heard any categorical statement in denial of it from any of the officials, though I have read something to that effect in local newspapers. Visitors never see them, and I know of no prison inspectors who have done so; they are shown instead the light cells on an upper floor, which are habitable enough, with windows admitting daylight, and a cot bed. But the dark cells are another story altogether, and their existence can no more be denied successfully than that of the prison itself.

A man named H.B. Rich was employed in the prison for nine years as foreman of the blacksmith's shop; he says that he helped build two dark cells in the basement, and often riveted chains on convicts there. "They were chained to the door," he goes on, "hanging by their hands, sometimes for twenty-four hours. Often they were thus chained up during the day, but at night the chain attached to the frame of the door was loosened; the other chain was attached to a vertical rod, the ring sliding up and down, so that the man was able to lie on the bare cement floor. There were no cots. The food was generally one slice of bread and a cup of water a day, sometimes two or three. Men were often kept thus for weeks at a time, and would come out so pallid and weak that they could scarcely walk, and blinded from long confinement in darkness. A convict named S. was kept in the dark hole two weeks; I was often called to chain him, as he was a powerful man; but when he would come out, he was so weakened that he could scarcely move."

I may add here that I have often talked with the convict here mentioned, and he told me details of his experiences. I would print his name and story, but he is still in confinement — he has lived two and twenty continuous years in prison — and he might be made to suffer for his revelations. Among other things, he said that he had been in the punishment cells, in the aggregate, eight years! If he were not a lion of strength and courage, he would have been dead long since. The Atlanta penitentiary claims to be the most humane in the world. But eight years in chains and darkness seems a long time, even taken in installments.

A man lately released has this to say: "The administration of the penitentiary is a sham and pretense. 'Reform' is a show, for the benefit of government inspectors and visitors, with, underneath, a callous and brutal disregard for the welfare of the convicts moral and physical. No tortures? I was trussed up, face to wall, with arms outstretched, for ten hours. When loosed, I just dropped to the floor from exhaustion, and did not rise till the next morning. That was during the present administration. When visitors and newspaper reporters go through the prison, 'there isn't any hole'; but the prisoner who thoughtlessly infracts a rule knows that there is one!

"In the Isolation Building there is a number of three-cornered cells where men are chained to the doors; they have little cots; these cells are shown. But down beneath there is the real hole. These underground cells have no cots; when a man drops, he drops on the cement floor. If they wish severely to discipline a man, they can make these cells practically airtight, and then turn on the steam through the pipes."

Let us have more testimony as to the dark hole. "The hole," writes another inmate, "is not a hole in the wall or in the ground, but it is a place to turn a man's cheeks white and to make his knees shake and his lips tremble, when, for some infraction of very strict rules, he is ordered to the hole. It is a row of holes; far down in the bottom of the big bastile is a row of little cells, six feet wide, nine feet long, and perhaps ten feet high. Solid concrete, with iron grating in the narrow door. Absolutely dark. Furniture, one iron rod, one blanket. The man is handcuffed between the rod and the wall, hands apart as far as he can hold them; at night the wall fastening is loosed, and he can lie down sliding the ring of his handcuff down the rod. No mattress or bed – just floor. Food, three ounces of bread and a glass of water at noon. The rules are said to be less severe than formerly; but two half-breed Indians, former friends, recognizing each other in Sunday school, ventured to whisper a greeting; they were put in the hole two days and nights, and one of them, a stout hardy boy, came out trembling and shaking as with mortal illness."

A man who served as guard in the prison under the present warden, but left in 1907, affirms that barbarities were not the exception at that time, but the "horrible custom. The dark hole is a reality; men were kept there weeks at a time, to my certain knowledge, within stifling walls, chained standing for intolerable periods, with great suffering. The public understands 'solitary confinement' to mean a cell by one's self; but this cell is a dark dungeon below earth level. One convict had to be brought out on a litter, his legs swollen to a frightful size; he could not stand erect. I was reprimanded for entering his cell and helping him to sit up. A man named L. who had drawn back his hammer threateningly when a guard advanced upon him armed with a 'square,' but who ceased to resist when the guard drew his revolver, was sentenced to one hundred and forty-five days in the dungeon, with three slices of bread, with water, per day. Christian Endeavorers," this witness adds, "never have an opportunity to observe the real conditions. No outsider comes in contact with things as they are. No outsider in Atlanta has ever seen the dungeons."

G.W., formerly employed in the prison, says that "the hole near the plumber's shop was built while Morse, the banker, was in the prison, for I helped build it, and the warden, with another official, was down to see it at ten in the morning." Speaking of the statement that the dark hole was no longer in use, he adds, in his letter to me, "You know of the hanging up in the dark cell of the old Englishman, in October" — the month I left the penitentiary. I do know of it; the fight of this stubborn old fellow against the oppression of the prison authorities was the talk of the ranges just before my departure; he had done nothing worse than to use bad language; he would not give in; and I believe that it was found advisable at last to release him.

The case of poor little B. had a less agreeable sequel. He was dying of diabetes during the latter months of his confinement; he was an incorrigible little thief, a man of extraordinarily acute mind, and a sort of saturnine humorist withal. He had been repeatedly convicted and imprisoned, but "I can't let it alone," he would say. He was plump and flabby, ghastly pale, with protruding eyes, very clear and penetrating. He was ridiculously impudent, but being so soon to die, as he himself well knew, none of the prisoners bore him a grudge. The authorities, however, thought it well to discipline him, and he was so repeatedly maltreated by them, and put in the dark hole, that his disease was greatly inflamed and the end hastened. I said something designed to be encouraging to him shortly before I left; but he fixed me with those singular eyes, and said, "I am doomed!"

The last I heard of B. was in a letter from a lady who has done much to help and relieve the sufferings and wrongs of prisoners in the jail. "B. is in a dying condition," she writes; "he was severely punished while suffering from his disease. W.," she goes on, "died three days after a ten-days' punishment. He had to be lifted from the dark cell and carried to the hospital by attendants." Upon the whole, one has grounds for believing that the dark hole is not a fairy tale, and that it still exists and is at work in Atlanta Penitentiary, in spite of the impression to the contrary of the humane warden and his officials.

The geography of the places is, however, obscure, and is known to the elect only; it is said by inmates of old standing that underground passages connect the prison buildings and lead from one dungeon to another. This sounds romantic, but would be obviously useful in practice. A map of the premises, surface and subterranean, would be interesting, and may hereafter be achieved by some inspection which really inspects. I have not spoken of some features of the dark cells, as described by men who have experienced them, because they are so revolting that editors of newspapers would decline to print them. Human beings are compelled to endure many things which the fastidiousness of other human beings cannot tolerate even the hearing of.

A prisoner named Keegan was killed at Atlanta not long before I was released, not by a guard's bullet, but by means as sure though slower and more cruel. We were all conversant with his case at the time, but I will quote the man who knew him and his sufferings most intimately. Here is his crude narrative written to me on prison paper.

"William Keegan died in August of this year (1913) at the Pen. He was first taken sick with pains in the legs, hands and arms, and went to morning sick call, but could never get anything done, because he was a little deaf and could not hear what the doctor said, and so could explain no further, and he was in a very bad fix. They did nothing for him, and he was afraid to see the doctor, because he would have been impatient, and would have sent him to the hole, and then he would lose time. But he did go up to see him after the pains got into his back also, and he told him he would like to get out of the stone shed; and the doctor told him there was nothing the matter with him, but he was only faking and trying to get out of work — which I know and can swear to as being true.

"If ever there was a sick man, Keegan was him. He told M. the foreman about it one day, who told him to have the doctor look him over, and sent him up one afternoon; the doctor looked him over and told him he was only a crank — nothing at all the matter with him. Soon after he was taken very sick, and one night I called the prison nurse to his cell, and he had him taken to the hospital, where he stayed some time, but it did him no good, for he came back to the cell house in just as bad a fix as before. Then they put him to work in the paint-house, and after he had been there about a week, they said he was crazy, and put him in the hole. He was treated shamefully in the hole, for the prison nurse even told me so. Then he was taken again to the hospital, and he never came out of it, for he died there, and the prison nurse told me he suffered terribly before his death. This I will swear is true before God.

"Very near every man in the Pen had a bad stomach, and could get nothing for it, for if you went to the doctor, he would tell you you ate too much, and give you a big dose of salts, and if you did not take them, he would put you in the hole, and then you would lose good time. But if a man had a pull, he would get along right enough. There was A., a bank wrecker, he was clerk in the stone shed, and I have seen him have eggs right in the kitchen, when we had only rice to eat with cold water and bread which was sour. If he didn't want to work he didn't have to, for when I worked as runner for the plumber I have seen A. lying down and smoking and reading or pretty near anything he wanted to do; but if other men had done less than half the things he did, they would have been put in the hole and lost good time also. Things should be looked into, for it is sure run shamefully."

Readers would perhaps like to know more of the doctor, whose professional activities are so engagingly described in the above statement. He is a medical graduate of recent vintage, poor but aristocratic, engaged to attend four hours a day at the penitentiary at a salary of fifteen hundred dollars a year. "I need the money," he once admitted to a colleague in the prison. Keegan, as we have seen, was under his penetrating eye for months, and he died a few days after the young gentleman had assured him that there was nothing the matter with him. The doctor dresses well, and has an air; he has the use of an automobile, and sometimes escorts good looking young nurses, or other young ladies, about the prison grounds. He has a knack at surgical operations, and urges prisoners to be operated upon; they sometimes recover, and sometimes do not. His use of drugs in his practice seems to have been mainly restricted to prescribing salts, and the hole, both effective in their way, but not always happy in their application to the cases under consideration.

He was always civil to me, and put me under the obligation of saving my life, for he ordered me a milk diet when I was succumbing to the influences of prison hash and "hot dog." It was part of his duty to visit the dining room every day — or was it every other day? — and inspect the food served to the prisoners. During my six months' stay, he appeared twice in the doorway, where he exchanged amenities with the guard; and once he traversed the aisle between my row of tables and the next, accompanied by some very nice looking girls. He had other duties, which he discharged with similar punctuality and fervor. And all for fifteen hundred a year.

There was a hearty, full-blooded, good natured young fellow, with red hair, who worked in the blacksmith's shop, and worked well. His overseer was a Negro — this often happens in Atlanta Penitentiary. The heat in the forge room during summer was intense, and the red haired boy used to get rush of blood to the head, and finally asked a high official for leave to step out in the open air occasionally and cool off.

It was granted. But on one of these outings his Negro master ordered him to go back and do a job of work for him; the other quoted his official permission; there was a wrangle, ending in an appeal to a higher official still. The latter, in the face of the lower official's testimony that he had authorized the recess, supported the Negro, and the young blacksmith was sentenced to five days in the dark cell and thirty days' loss of good time. Discipline must be preserved.

Are such conditions as I have described general? The newspapers during my stay at Atlanta described a discussion in local prison circles as to the propriety or expediency of whipping female prisoners in the Georgia female prison (not connected with the federal penitentiary), and confining them in the dark hole. The warden of the prison, a gentleman named Mitchell, and his guards, said that women did not mind confinement in the dark hole, and got no harm from it — though it was shown that after being so confined for a day or two, they were scarce able to stand and wholly unfit for work. The guards declared that the women could not be effectively disciplined except by flogging, and threatened to quit in a body if the practice were disallowed. Dr. Mac-Donald, of the prison, testified that although some wardens might abuse the power of flogging, and had lashed women on the bare back instead of over covering of one garment, as prescribed by the rules, still he favored whipping for them; he said the use of the "leather" was really more humane than the dungeon. Secretary Yancey, of the Prison Commission, also favored the lash.

On the other hand, State Representative Blackburn said that it was "a dangerous policy to give such wide discretionary powers to wardens scattered about the state. It would give rise to terrible abuses and mistreatment. The sovereign power of the state should not be delegated to individuals only remotely accountable. The punitive system should be carefully guarded, and the line of punishment mapped out, otherwise evils will creep in; no corrective measures that border upon cruelty should be used." Representative Smith added that if we "put the power to use the whip on women in the hands of brutal and incompetent wardens, the same cruelties and atrocities which have shocked the civilized world will be repeated. Wardens, drunk with power, abuse their positions; they are appointees of a system, inexperienced and incompetent in many cases; chosen, not because of their fitness, but more likely to repay some political favor. When a good warden is found, it is more or less an accident. Give permission to whip, and the public would be horrified at the result, if ever they should learn the circumstances."

That is fine; but the concluding words mean more than they say. How is the public to know? If you had a mother or a sister or daughter in that jail, would you feel entirely reassured by the declamations in the legislature of these kindly gentlemen? Would it not occur to you that, when this little flurry had blown over, the warden and his guards might possibly, and as quietly as might be, revert to what they held to be the only effective means of keeping order? It is easy, in a prison, to gag a woman so that she cannot scream, and to take her down to a secluded place, and there to lay on the leather heartily, with or without first removing the inner garment. Who is to know, or to tell? We are not Russians, to boast of these things openly.

At the turpentine camp at Atmore, Alabama, thirty-five convicts whose contract had been annulled by Governor O'Neal, were brought to Mobile October 10th, 1913, and placed in the county jail. All but fourteen had been whipped with heavy straps loaded with lead, and affidavits were offered showing that two of them had been whipped to death. But Superintendent of Prisons Riley of New York, in a letter to Warden Rattigan of Auburn prison, writes: "I do not believe that anyone was ever reformed by physical torture." This was not the view taken, apparently, in Jefferson City (Mo.) prison, for there, a few weeks ago, a Negro was given a very hard task each day (says the *Post-Dispatch* of St. Louis), more than he could perform. At evening he would be taken out, strapped to a post and beaten with a heavy strap. There were cuts and sores all over his body. Favored prisoners were allowed to break rules, while others were severely punished for the same thing. The penitentiary there is described as a "small hell entirely surrounded by masonry and incompetent officials." Dozens of men were brutally whipped for minor offenses.

We have all heard about Blackwell's Island, New York City, where "beatings by officials, and much worse, resulted in the death of a man." Trustee Hurd found two men in dark cells, one stupefied, the other hysterical and sobbing. They had been punished for whispering. The dark cells had been ordered discontinued some weeks before. Warden Hayes, on being asked by the official why he had permitted them to be used, replied, "Well, the fact is, I've been so busy I haven't had time to get round to it!" What is his business?

In Atlanta we do not use the leather; we find the club handier, and some guards are skillful in so applying it to the bodies of their patients that, while the external evidences are negligible, it occasions internal troubles which can be ascribed to "natural" causes. And there are indications that we do use the dark cell, described by Dr. MacDonald, above, as more inhumane than the lash. If this expert be correct, he gives us a standard whereby to measure how inhumane they must be.

I cannot go on, though I have used only a fraction of my notebook.

Moreover, I am inclined to think that the physical punishments I have instanced are not the worst that are administered in Atlanta and perhaps in other prisons. Great ingenuity is shown in the application of mental tortures, which have their outcome in insanity, but which never can be investigated by commissions and inspectors. An insane man is as safe as a dead man — if he tells tales, no one will pay attention to him. The cat-and-mouse game is a favorite with the inhumane type of wardens. Give your man alternations of hope and despair, and the results will soon reward your pains. Then there are the insults, the gibes and threats, the obscure forms of tyranny and outrage, the degradation of manhood — there are a hundred subtle ways of destroying and corrupting the spirit of a man. To be compelled to occupy the same cell with certain types of criminals is a most successful form of inhumanity; and when, as often happens, one of the two is a comparatively innocent boy, the results are awful. "Insufficient number of cells" is the explanation given; and at Atlanta at least there are the unfinished cell houses, which might have been finished years ago, had the appropriations been properly applied.

"Lord, be merciful to me, a sinner!" we pray in our churches. But He says, "With what measure ye mete, it shall be measured unto you again." We do not set the Lord a good example of mercy in our prisons.

XI

THE GRASP OF THE TENTACLES

I have spoken of punishments inside the prison. When a man has served his time and is set free (as it is called) another punishment begins, which may be worse and more disheartening than the suffering endured inside the walls.

As I listened, on Saturday afternoons, or at other times, to the stories hurriedly and guardedly told me by my fellow convicts who had served more terms than one, I said to myself, "The wrong of prison is bad enough; but this of what happens to a man after prison is worse, and monstrous." The endless tentacles follow him, reach out after him, surround him, fasten upon him, and draw him back whence he came. And not that only, but they mark him and isolate him, disable him from free action, make honesty impossible for him. No citizen of whatever integrity and standing, if so pursued, maligned and undermined, would have any choice left him but either to perish or to break the laws. The spies of the government, with the prestige and power of the government behind them (however despicable and vicious they may be in themselves), can ruin any man; but ex-convicts are their staple food.

In the latter part of June, 1913, a federal judge named Emory Speer was accused of evil deeds on the bench, and a congressional investigation was announced. The judge was taken ill, and at this writing the investigation still hangs fire. Now, the evidence against him had been collected, it would appear, by the agency of government spies, and this fact caused great indignation in some quarters. Here was a man not convicted of felony, but a pillar of the state, being pursued by detectives just as if for all the world he were an ordinary person — an obscure private citizen, say, or an ex-convict! The judge himself was very indignant, and his friends on the local press were rasping in their comments. In a long editorial entitled "The Shadow of the Spy," one Atlanta paper denounced the proceedings root and branch. It affirmed that the governmental spy system had assumed such proportions during the past few years as to threaten one of the mainstays of free government.

All this interested my comrades, not because the spy system was news to them, but because no public notice had been taken of it until it began to wring the withers of persons who had hitherto supposed themselves to be in the position of promoters instead of victims of the practice. A federal judge had never protested against pursuing with spies men suspected of crimes, or men who, having served time upon conviction, had then gone out into the world and attempted to lead a new life. The spy system, so conducted, seemed to such persons proper and normal. But the moment they found their own acts investigated, their own footsteps dogged, they became indignant, and denounced the whole principle of the thing.

No man convicted in a federal or state court, or set free after having done his time in prison, but is abundantly conversant with the methods of the American spy.

As we all know, the first thing done with a new prisoner is to take his bertillons, and the record of these measurements and observations, together with two photographs of him, or with four, if he had a beard when convicted, is sent to every police office in the country, and is there studied by the detectives and police. The intention, of course, is to render easier the recognition of "old offenders," and to curtail their future industries. It is generally affirmed that bertillons cannot be mistaken; but in a Detroit court, on January both, 1914, an expert declared that "a difference of one-eighth of an inch in the laying on of the fingers made an entirely different impression"; and "judgment was awarded against the bank," which, relying upon the infallibility of the finger record, had brought the action. At any rate, the bertillon is still a potent weapon with the police, and when they want a man for a crime committed, or when they desire to drive out of any given place on the face of the earth a man who has been previously a convict, they have but to point to his bertillons, and the thing is done.

Let us see how this may work out in practice. A convict, having served his term, is presented by the United States (or a state, as the case may be) with a suit of new clothes, and with a five dollar bill. He also gets a ticket on the railway to the place of his destination, and, though he is in theory a free man from the moment that he passes the prison gates, as a matter of fact an official is assigned to take charge of him and put him on his train; he cannot remain in Atlanta (supposing for the once that Atlanta Penitentiary has been his abiding place during his sentence) on penalty, if he do, of forfeiting his ticket and having to pay his own way. This may be a provision of the law, or it may be simply a measure to prevent ex-convicts from talking to newspaper reporters or other enquiring persons. The thing is invariably done, unless the man's residence happens to be Atlanta itself.

In my own case (to cite an instance) the regular procedure was observed, with only one accidental modification. I received my suit of clothes, my five dollars, and my railway ticket — at least, the latter was given to the guard detailed to accompany me to the station, to be by him delivered to the conductor of my train. But I had previously made up my mind to say a few things to the reporter of a certain local newspaper, and I was ready, in case of necessity, to abandon my eleemosynary ticket and to pay my own way to New York on a later train. I had money of my own to do this with; most ex-prisoners, of course, have not. But the sacrifice was avoided by the circumstance that Mr. Moyer, the warden, was absent at the moment in Indianapolis, and the deputy incautiously let me out an hour or more before my train started. I lost no time in meeting my reporter, and during the next forty minutes, in an automobile provided for the occasion, we drove about the streets of Atlanta, while I imparted to his astonished ears my reasons for thinking that the penitentiary was not the paradise on earth that it had hitherto been believed to be. He brought me to the railway station in season for my train, and I got safely away, leaving mischief behind me.

That was my good luck. On the other hand, a friend of mine recently released told me that the warden had called him into his office at the last moment, and had extracted from him a promise not to talk to any reporter in the town before leaving. That is the usual way; but it is the exception, sometimes, that counts.

Let us return to our average convict, just out, and with the world before him, where to choose to display his prison-made garments and to spend his five dollars. It not seldom happens, to begin with, that he is not so much out as he had imagined. Our present method with convicts has peculiarities. Here is a common example.

A man was convicted and jailed for robbing a post office. The sentence was five years. The specific charge was of stealing postage stamps. Having done his bit in the federal penitentiary, he was given his outfit and the gates were opened. He was proceeding joyfully on his way, when a sheriff laid a hand on his shoulder, and informed him that he was his prisoner. What for? The sheriff smilingly explained that the sentence he had just served was for a federal offense; he was wanted now on a state charge of breaking into the grocery store in which the post office was housed. For this, the state prison accommodated him with lodging for five years more. The man outlived that, and fatuously imagined that his payment of that debt was fully discharged. He was awakened by the hand on his shoulder again. What was the matter now? Why, he had, while in the grocery store, and in addition to stealing the federal postage stamps, possessed himself unlawfully of a box of matches, thereby committing a second state crime, involving a further detention in the state prison of five years more.

This is an example of our cat-and-mouse way with convicts, and is, of course, much more destructive to the victim than an outright sentence of the same length would have been. But in what manner it tends to reform a man, or to protect a community, does not clearly appear.

Sometimes, the sheriff is dilatory in arriving to make the second or third arrest, and it would seem that the prisoner might have a chance to escape. But in such a case the warden himself would take a hand in the game. In an instance of which I heard a good deal, the man's sentence expired, we will say, on June 1st. The warden had been apprised that he was to be re-arrested, but the sheriff was not on hand — could not get there for two days. But the law, or prison regulations, or something, enables a warden to detain a prisoner beyond his fixed time, in the event of his committing some prison irregularity. The warden informed the man that he was reported to have broken a plate in the dining room, the penalty for which was three days more in his cell. Before the three days were up, the sheriff had arrived, the man was re-arrested, and justice was satisfied. We will suppose, however, that our man has no second or third or other indictments hanging over him, and that he really does get clean away. What will be his adventures?

If the weather be not rainy he reaches his train unscathed. But if that new suit, with "jail-bird" written all over it in characters which all detectives and police, at least, can read as they run, chance to get wet, the raw shoddy forthwith shrivels miserably up, and the wearer's ankles and wrists stick out so betrayingly that a mere child might recognize the sinister source of the garments. But, anyhow, a few days' wear will so wrinkle and crease and deform the suit that it becomes unwearable, and the man might as conveniently and more prudently go about in shirt and drawers. Should he present himself in it requesting a job from some virtuous citizen, the latter is less likely to grant it than to step to the 'phone and call up the police station. "There's a suspicious character here — better look him over!" The officer looks him over accordingly, and either advises him to betake himself promptly elsewhere, or, if a crime happen to have been committed recently in that neighborhood, the perpetrators of which are still at large, he takes the man into custody on suspicion.

That the man is utterly innocent makes small difference; his status as an old offender is readily established, and the rest follows almost automatically. "You did the job all right; but, if you didn't, you're a vagrant, without visible means of support, and they'll put you in the lockup for six months or a year. And let me tell you, our lockup is no joke! Likely you'll get on the chain gang, and then, God help you! If they don't take a fancy to you, they're liable to croak you anytime. Now, I'd like to see you get out of this easy, and here's what you'd better do. You own up to the crime, and I'll have a word with the judge, so he'll let you off with a short sentence in a place where they treat men right, and you'll get out in about three or four months. That's what you'd best do; and if you don't, I wash my hands of you! What do you say?"

What would you do? Stand on your rights, demand a full and fair trial, prove your innocence, and be acquitted without a stain on your character? That is the proper and righteous course for a free and independent American citizen.

But you are not a citizen, in the first place; your civic rights are gone for good, and instead of your innocence being assumed till your guilt is proved, it is the other way about. Your friend the detective is prepared, for one, to swear that to the "best of his knowledge and belief," you are the culprit; and there is commonly a number of other easy swearers hanging about the court room to support him. You have no friends; on the contrary, every eye you meet is hostile. You have no money to hire a lawyer, for that five dollars had gone before you had mustered courage to ask for the job that got you into this trouble. And above all, your spirit is cowed and prostrate from years in prison; you have known the long, sterile bitterness of penal servitude, and you have no stomach for a fight. No, you will not fight — you cannot. You will stand up in the dock and confess to something you never did, and throw yourself on the mercy of the court. Your friend the detective whispers to the judge — "He's an incorrigible — he ought to get the limit!" And His Honor gives you ten years. It is less than a week since you put off stripes, and went out into the world resolved to make good. If you outlive your undeserved sentence, will you ever resolve to make good again?

Can such things be? Indeed they can, and they are. There is poor C. in Atlanta now, the victim of such a deal; and S., and H., and many more. C., indeed, told me, and I believe him, that he never committed any crime at all, other than to get drunk and to sleep out on the road; he was apprehended for vagrancy, then charged with a post office robbery in another state (which he had never visited), advised by the detective who "took an interest" in him to confess, upon the promise of being let off with a light sentence; he got the limit, and will wear out his youth in jail, while the detective is complimented for his efficiency.

The Government is extravagant. What is the use of spending money on a shoddy suit of clothes for each one of thousands of convicts every year, and giving each of them a five dollar bill, with the certainty that, in a large majority of cases, they will be back in their cells in a few days or weeks, or months? Look up, if you please, the statistics as to the number of convicts who are second or third offenders. Nay, the Government is itself the prime and most effective cause of their getting back, since it is government spies that provide the evidence that sends them up.

But can we afford to trust ex-convicts? Must we not keep a strict eye on them? If the strict eye were also a friendly one, it might be of some avail. But our hand is against them, and we need not wonder that theirs is against us. Not only are we their enemies when they emerge from jail, but (as has been repeated interminably by every investigator who has been qualified to speak on the subject) jails are the best and only schools of crime. In other words, we first educate men to be criminals by putting them in places where they can learn nothing else, and then we keep them criminals by shutting against them, when freed, every opportunity to earn food and lodging in legitimate ways. And then we complain that they are not to be trusted.

Neither can men fed on poisons be trusted to be well. Jail life is poisonous; I think it was Judge McLeland who said, last summer, "Our million dollar reformatories offer university courses in bestiality and crime; it is as logical to send a man to jail to make him better as to shut him up in a garbage-can to improve his digestion. Forty percent of those who go to jail, go back again," he added; "one man went back one hundred and seventy-six times. Others are sent because they are poor and cannot pay a fine, and they are there made real criminals."

An instance of this occurred in a Georgia chain-gang while I was in Atlanta. A man was sentenced for playing cards for money. He could not pay the $45 fine demanded, and in default, was sent to the chain-gang for eight months. He wore stripes, night and day, and if contumacious, was whipped by the guards. His work was in a stone quarry, a deep hole, into which the summer sun poured an insufferable heat. He was forced to do his work with a 49-pound hammer in that funnel-shaped pit, at a hundred degrees in the shade — if he could find any shade. One day he told the guard he was sick, and could not work any longer. The guard shifted the quid in his mouth and remarked that he ought to have said so that morning. But the man meant what he said, and proved it by dying a day or two later. Probably you may have played cards for money at some time in your life. Did it ever occur to you that you merited torture and death for it?

Or do you think that, after such an experience (if you survived it), or after being twice arrested for the same crime and kept in jail five years three times over, or after doing time for a crime you never committed — that you would come out at the end of it all, smiling, full of energy and enterprise, loving your neighbor, eager for honest toil? Would you embrace Mr. Moyer (or whomever your jailer was) and tell him, with tears of gratitude, that you could never repay him for his warm-hearted, big-brained care of you — the starving, the dungeoning, the clubbing, and all the rest of the university course?

Would you feel like that? Or would you stare out upon the world into which you were contemptuously tossed with dull, hating, revengeful eyes, suspicious of all men, hopeless of good, but resolved to get even, so far as you might, by plying the evil trades which your life of slavery had taught you? Would you behave like Christ upon the Cross, or like an ordinary man? Convicts are ordinary men, except that they are often, to begin with, diseased men, or hemmed in by conditions so untoward as to make an honest life ten or a hundred times harder than it ever was for you.

But you did not scruple to put this diseased or unfortunate version of yourself into the jail cauldron, to stew there with others like or worse than himself, for doing what, in most cases, he actually could not help doing; and when at last he was ejected like stale refuse, you were indignant because his looks did not please you, because he bore upon him the stains and the stench which the cauldron had fastened on him, because he did not, in the teeth of the secret service, the post office inspectors, the detective bureaus and the police, at once begin to lead an honest life and support the commonwealth. Do you say that none of this was your doing? But it is your doing, in just so far as you have not striven in every way open to you to extirpate the doing of it by this representative government.

The wonderful thing — the unexpected and pathetic thing — is, that so many convicts come out of jail in a kindly and inoffensive state of mind. They are men who were born weak, humble and yielding, never esteemed themselves, were always ready to take a back seat and give precedence to others. They do not understand the rights of the matter, but suppose it must be all right, that penal servitude is the proper thing for them, that laws were made by wise men and must be enforced. They admit their stealings and their trickery, and blame themselves, observing regretfully that they didn't seem able to help it. Next time — if they get a next time — they will try very hard to be straight, and perhaps they will succeed after all!

There was little J., in the barbers' gang, a cheerful, smiling, sweet tempered fellow, who had served I know not how many terms for small larcenies and turpitudes. "I've always been such a damned little fool," he would say to me, as he smoothed off my chin. "The boys would get round me and rope me into some scheme, and I didn't seem able to keep clear of 'em. But I'm goin' to be let out again next July, and I've made up my mind I'll never be seen here again! No, sir! Oh, I've been talkin' with the chaplain, too, and I've been reading the Bible, and all that, and I'm going to be a good man. Yes, sir! I've had my fling, and I'm through with it; when the boys get round me and tell me of some easy job, I'll tell 'em, No! Not for J."

He was a man of forty, as naïve and "innocent" (in the unmoral sense) as a child; and he had been in jail off and on since he was ten years old. I happened to be in the front office at the moment when J. was signing receipts and receiving his property preparatory to leaving. He was dressed in a neat business suit of his own — not a prison-made monstrosity. He was clean and smooth and bright, and tremulous with excitement. He signed his papers with a shaking hand, he took up and put down again his well packed gripsack, he shook hands with a sort of clinging, appealing grasp, as if he were afraid of being left alone, he giggled and looked profoundly solemn by turns. The officials stood about, indifferent and contemptuous, the men who had been hard and cruel to him, and those who had not been so hard.

It was a bright, beautiful day, full of sunshine; J. picked up his grip and marched down the corridor and out into the free air. He wore a brave air of hope and determination, but one could detect underneath it symptoms of misgiving. He had vowed to be good, but could he keep the vow, when "the boys got round him?" I wished him good luck with all my heart. Six months have passed, and J. is not back in jail yet, so far as I have heard. But the spies are watching him, and he won't be safe till he is dead.

A man with whom chance brought me frequently in contact was H., a yegg, as the term is.

When a guard is escorting a batch of visitors about the prison, he speaks of the yeggs in an ominous tone, as if they were some deadly monster, hardly to be even looked at with impunity. But yeggs, as a body, are the best men in the prison; they have a code of honor, and strength of character. Outside, they blow open safes, and do other risky jobs; and they will shoot to kill on the occasions when it is their life or the other man's. They will do this, because they know what a prison is, and also what spies outside prison are. But they will spare your life, if possible; not because they care for you – they hate and despise you, as being a man who would be and have in the past been merciless to them, and as a hypocrite who is either a rascal on the sly or would be if you possessed the courage or were subjected to the temptation – they spare you not from mercy but a settled policy; killing is bad business, and means sooner or later a violent end for the killer.

Most yeggs are men of more than average intelligence, and sometimes of fair education; they were not born outlaws; but, if you can win them to speak of themselves, you will generally find that they have undergone things both in and out of prison enough to make an outlaw out of a saint. Most men succumb under such things, and either die, or become cowed in spirit; the yeggs have survived, and their spirit is unbroken. They hold the highest place in the estimation of their fellow prisoners; and the warden and the guards fear them. By that I mean that they fear to inflict severities upon them except upon some pretext at least plausible; for the yeggs know the rules, and though they will submit without a whimper to the crudest punishments if cause can be alleged for it, yet wanton liberties, such as prisoners less well informed or more pusillanimous submit to, cannot safely be taken with them.

The yeggs stand together; they have esprit de corps, and if, as happened last summer at Atlanta, the food supply drops actually to the starvation point in both quantity and quality, they stand forward – as they did then — as champions for the rest of the men; they protest openly, they will not be wheedled or terrorized, and they go to the hole as one man. Nor will they come out thence until the warden comes to them and promises improvement. The warden promises, not because he desires improvements, but because he fears the scandal of mutiny in the prison — an inconvenient thing when one is supposed to be conducting a model institution; and even an easy going public, which will tolerate other forms of cruelty to convicts, feels compunction about starving them, especially when it is taxed to provide them with wholesome and sufficient food.

About my friend H. — I have no space here to tell his story, nor to outline it even; it is a terrible one. I may be able, some time, in another place, to present it in full. I will say now only that he was once confined for three years in a contract labor jail which has the worst features conceivable in any prison of today or of a hundred years ago, and men are killed there by overwork and punishments as a matter of routine; few survive the treatment so long as H. did. Once during his three years he uttered three words aloud; for that he was punished so long and so savagely that the horror of it yet remains with him. Prisoners constantly maim their hands voluntarily in the machinery in order to be quit of the torture of the work; the bleeding stumps of their fingers or hands are roughly bound up, and they are driven back to their machines. The warden is an oily, comfortable rogue, who beams upon visitors and fools the prison commission to the top of its bent, and he bears an excellent reputation for the large amount of work he gets out of his prisoners; "They just love it, my boys do," he avers; "nothing like work to keep men happy, you know." And then, when the coast is clear, he turns upon his boys like a bloodthirsty tiger.

But what I wish to say here is, that when H. at last finished his term and was thrust forth into the crowded street of the city, his legs failed him, and he tottered along scared like a wild beast at the noise and bustle. A man addressed him, and he stared at him blankly, and could not command his tongue to speak words. He wandered on irregularly, starting at imaginary dangers, unnerved at the height of the sky, the noise, the movement. He sought the least frequented streets, but his aspect and bearing made people look suspiciously at him, and he found his way to the slums, where he got a room and shut himself in with a feeling of relief. It was several days before he could school himself to talk and act like an ordinary human being. His health was shattered, though he was naturally a strong and hearty man; eating made him sick, though he was faint for lack of right feeding.

He could find no steady employment, but helped himself along with odd jobs here and there. He was resolute to keep straight, but an old pal of his happened to meet him, did him some good turns, and finally proposed his joining two or three men in a promising burglary. H. asked time to think it over, and that night he left the city in a sort of panic, and traveled to a large town a hundred miles away. Here he succeeded in getting a good job; his spirits began to revive; he made some good acquaintances, and prospered beyond all expectation for nearly a year. One day he noticed a man in the street who stared hard at him; not long after he saw the same man standing in front of the house in which he lodged; the next morning his landlord came to him and, with some embarrassment, said that he would have to ask him for his room; a relative was about to visit him and he needed the accommodation.

It was as he had feared — the detectives had run him down. He put what he possessed in a trunk and left town that evening for a place nearly a thousand miles west. Here he was left undisturbed for fifteen months, and made a new start in business. Then the chief of the local police sent for him and said, "I don't want to be rough on you; but the best thing you can do is to skip; we're on to you — understand?" "But I'm doing a straight business," H. pleaded. "You may be; but you're a crook," was the reply.

We need not follow him further; he was driven from one place to another. At last he was caught with stolen goods on him, he having undertaken to help an old friend of his out of a tight place by carrying his gripsack from one place to another; it proved to contain some plunder from a recent burglary. He got off with a two year sentence; but it was the end of his attempt to reform. "Crooked or straight, I'll end in jail," he said to me, with that strange convict smile which means such unspeakable things. "I've got two years more here; if I last it out, they'll get me again."

I firmly believe that he would have been an honest and successful man if he had been let alone.

It sometimes happens that the manhood of a convict is so sapped by long sufferings that even his desire for freedom is lost. He is afraid to be free; he cannot live at ease outside of his cell walls. Perhaps you will say that goes to prove the gentleness and humanity of prison discipline. To me it seems a thing so appalling that I must be content with the bare statement of the fact. A man is afraid to be free, afraid of the great wonderful world, and of his fellow creatures, and can endure what he supposes to be life only in his steel cell. What has put that fear in him? But our laws provide no penalty for dehumanizing a fellow creature under the forms of law. If it be legal, it must be right.

I knew a man in our prison who had been thirty-five years in confinement, with short intervals of liberty. The best favor he could ask was to be allowed to stay all day and all night in his cell, doing nothing. Year after year, nothing else than this appeared to him worth while. He was well educated, as prisoners go, quiet and inoffensive. "I wish some doctor would examine me and tell me what is the matter with me," he remarked to me once. "Maybe I'm crazy!"

After all, the world, in its way, is as hard a place for ex-convicts as a jail; more cruel, perhaps, inasmuch as it seems to offer hopes that jails deny. But can a world be called civilized that is satisfied with that arraignment?

XII

The Prison Silence

*H*ow many convicts, during the past twenty years, have served their terms and been released? and yet what does the public know of the real inside of prisons? This used to perplex me at first. My fellow prisoners with whom I talked were bitter and voluble enough in denouncing the conditions; but no sooner had they passed the gates to freedom than they became strangely silent. Some of them even were quoted in the local papers as praising and upholding what they had just before condemned.

There was a Japanese prisoner, for example, the only man of his nation there, I think, who gained attention by copies of well-known pictures which he made, to be hung on the walls of the chapel, and by designing back and side scenes for the stage. I never talked personally with him, or saw him but at a distance, as he hastened along the corridor; but men who knew him said that he was especially savage in his diatribes against the prison and its keepers, and had promised, as soon as he was freed, to make numerous ugly disclosures to the world. But when we searched the local papers after his release, what we found was a hearty and explicit laudation of the prison and its officials. Had it been written by the warden himself, it could not have been more sunny and satisfied.

Again, there was a man with us who had been sentenced for life on a murder charge of a singularly revolting kind; he had been in confinement seventeen years when I first knew him, but had always consistently protested his innocence. He applied for parole, and his application was granted. At this time he occupied a large cell containing eleven other prisoners, of whom I was one; and he attached himself very closely to me, and upon coming in from his work each evening, would sit beside my cot and hold my hand and pour out his heart to me in lamentations, asseverations of his innocence, picturings of the horrors of his long confinement, forecastings of what he meant to do when he was freed — to address audiences from the pulpit and rostrum, and convince the world of the horrors of penal imprisonment. He was deeply religious, and had the moral courage to kneel down, before all the men in the cell, and spend five minutes or more in prayer every evening before going to bed. Everyone believed that he had been wrongly convicted, if for no better reason, because he had never once wavered from his claim of innocence during those seventeen years, and because his conduct and bearing in the prison had always been exemplary. He was a man of powerful body and strong, impressive mind; his speech was simple and convincing, and I told him that I thought he would succeed as an avatar of prison iniquities. He professed an ardent affection for me, and expressed enthusiastic anticipations as to the outcome of my own projects for calling public attention to the evils in question.

This man was tortured for five or six weeks by unexplained delay in fulfilling the promise of his parole, during which time it fell to my daily lot to comfort and encourage him; and I suffered no little emotional stress myself from this constant drain on my sympathies. Every evening, sitting beside my cot, he would repeat over and over again the same lamentations and speculations, interjecting at the end of each apostrophe, "It's terrible — terrible!" until at last I felt that I would gladly give up my own "good time" for the sake of seeing him freed without further procrastination. I was convinced, and so told him, that the delay could be due to nothing but neglect, inadvertent or criminal, on the part of LaDow, the President of the Parole Board, or of the Attorney-General himself; the papers had been thrust into a pigeonhole, and been forgotten or ignored.

What were the tortures of a man imprisoned for seventeen years, and now standing on the brink of salvation or despair, to a supercilious official up in Washington?

Finally, without explanation or apology, the order for release came;

and for me and his other friends, as well as for him, it was a day of rejoicing and thanksgiving. But, remembering that he was on parole, and therefore liable, on the least infringement of discipline, to be thrust back in his cell, none of us expected that he would venture to denounce the wrongs and expose the miseries of the imprisoned; we were glad to learn that he had secured a position paying him twenty or thirty dollars a month, with a chance of better things later, and that he had announced his purpose of running down the real perpetrator of the crime for which he had suffered, and forcing him to confess. For a few days, one or two local papers gave him half a column, and then there was silence.

I had been denied parole, and the restrictions thereof did not apply to me when my own day of freedom arrived; and I gave a short interview to a reporter, in which I said that the warden was unfit for his position, that the food was abominable, and that punishment in dark cells and otherwise was still practiced, though under cover.

The next day the newspapers printed an interview with my late friend, in which he was quoted as declaring that every statement I had made was a malicious lie, that the warden was in all respects the best, kindest and most lovable man he had ever met, and that the men in confinement had all the food they asked for, of the best quality, and that all tales of hardships and cruel punishments were false and wicked.

Is it conceivable that these statements were really given out by him? It seemed more likely that the words had been put into his mouth, under a threat, should he disavow them, of being sent back to prison. From such a threat the bravest man might shrink. But that statement of his still stands unmodified. And whether made spontaneously, or under the compulsion of a threat, its motive seems to have been fear of punishment for telling the truth. Such is the power of the System over its victims!

It is a state of things nothing less than nauseating. It is bad enough that men should be held in prison and maltreated; but that the truth should be imprisoned with them, gagged and terrified into silence, is a grave matter indeed. New York is complaining just now of the strength in corruption of its police system; but it seems almost trivial compared with this, for while the police ring profits by cooperating with the criminals they are paid to suppress, the prison ring profits by maiming or destroying human lives entrusted to their care to be restrained for a season from their own evil impulses, and thus if possible reformed; and, when they are released, it guards itself against exposure by the menace of revenge more formidable still. The parole and the indeterminate sentence, framed to open the way to reform of prisoners, is used by prison officials to intimidate and debase them; and if any ex-convict ventures to defy this fortified despotism, the immediate rejoinder is, "Who can believe a jail-bird? A man wicked enough to steal or murder is wicked enough to lie, and is not the malicious motive of the lie apparent?"

That rejoinder has been brought, and will continue to be brought against me. Among those who protested against the statements in my interview above mentioned was a lady whom I never spoke to – it is strictly against rules for a prisoner to speak with a visitor – and never knowingly saw, though I understand she was wont to sit on the stage during the Sunday exercises. She is thus quoted: "Julian Hawthorne is nothing more than an old grouch. A short time ago this old man told me himself that he was getting plenty to eat and had no complaint to make of his own or anybody else's treatment in the prison. . . . When he says such things as he is reported to have said, he should be made to prove them, or keep his mouth shut." Warden Moyer himself, less imaginative than this lady, contented himself with denying all charges and courting investigation, and added that he bore me no grudge, believed me to have been the dupe of malignant guards (since dismissed) and considers my motive to have been mainly the desire to make a little money. "The Department attaches little importance to these outbreaks," he remarked, "and I consider it unnecessary to place my word against that of convicts."

This may seem feeble; it is the mere instinctive stuttering of persons in a disturbed frame of mind. But the System will not depend for its defense upon persons of this kind. It has many strong forces at its command, of which the Secret Service, and the favorable prejudgments of the Government and of a large part of the public are but part. Anyone opposing it may expect to be kept under strict surveillance in all his movements, his mail will be violated, his words, written or overheard, will be scrutinized for material that can be used against him. Nor is the line drawn there. While I was in prison, I received the confidences of many prisoners as to their own experiences, among others that of a Maine boy who had been convicted of robbing a post office. He had been arrested in the first instance as a vagrant, and while in the local jail had been approached by a post office inspector who charged him with the post office crime. The boy had never been in the state in which the crime was committed; but he was told that, if he would plead guilty to it, he would be sent to Atlanta for a short term, whereas, should he refuse, he could be kept in jail awaiting trial for a year, and would then receive at least six months on the vagrancy charge. "Do as I tell you, and I will see that you get off easy," the inspector, who posed as a friend, told him. When he finally acquiesced, however, the judge imposed on him a sentence of five years, the inspector having testified that he was an old offender, implicated in many other crimes. The fact was, of course, that the real perpetrators of this post office robbery had not been caught, but it was expedient for the reputation and welfare of the detectives that a perpetrator should be produced — if not the real one, then one manufactured for the purpose. I learned of many cases similar to this — it is a common routine practice with the System. Moreover, when this innocent youth has completed his term, he will be thenceforth a marked man — "an habitual criminal," with a record against him; and he can be rearrested on general principles at any time. He will be given no opportunity to earn an honest livelihood, and it would be surprising indeed if his wrongs, not to speak of his empty stomach and hopeless circumstances did not make him a bona fide criminal ere long. Obviously, meanwhile, such a man is effectively gagged; if he be asked whether prison be a paradise, he will reply ardently in the affirmative, though his whole body and soul know it as a hell. For if, having blasphemed the Holy System, he is returned to the cell whence he came, every word of his rash revelation will be avenged upon him in torture and misery.

Am I attempting to retaliate upon the System for personal indignities and mishandling; or am I the dupe and tool of designing miscreants — convicts, guards or foremen — who plied me with false statements to wreak revenges of their own? I have already said that I was never harshly treated by any of the prison officials, and after the two first months indulgences were allowed me beyond the customary prison usage. During my two first months, to be sure, it seemed unlikely that I could live out my term, because I was kept at work in an underground place without ventilation or other than artificial light, and permeated with the hot-water pipes which supplied the buildings with heat and power. I was also unable to eat the prison fare, and was slowly perishing for lack of food. I never complained of this treatment, for it was in the ordinary prison course; but when the consequences of it became visible in my physical appearance, I was put on a diet of oatmeal and milk, morning and evening, and allowed to exercise in the open air. I voluntarily, during this period, went without dinner, being unwilling to poison myself with the rancid grease and garbage served under that name; but I made the most of the simple but nourishing milk diet, though it was insufficient in quantity; and I improved to the utmost the outdoor privileges, besides adhering resolutely to a régimen of daily callisthenic exercises; so that, when I was set at liberty at the end of six or seven months, I was in physical condition quite as good as when I went in. I was never denied leave to write "special letters," and my intercourse with the warden and his deputies, though always as seldom and brief as I could make it, was uniformly suave and smiling. The reasons for all which I shall have occasion to discuss later.

So much for the "grouch." As for being made the dupe of designing persons among the lower officials, and my fellow prisoners, — beyond replying tersely to questions put to me, I never had any communication with the former, and never heard or spoke a word with them reflecting upon the prison management. But what of my fellow prisoners?

They looked me over keenly and thoroughly to begin with; and no inquisitors have more sensitive intuitions or are quicker to suspect double-dealing than they. My aspect, my bearing, my speech, my affiliations, my treatment, all came under their scrutiny, and were debated in that secret court which prisoners hold. Not at first, nor lightly, did they give me the honor of their confidence. I might be a spy sent in from without, or a stool pigeon made within, or I might be indifferent or loose-mouthed. But when they did resolve to trust me — when I was elected a member of the "inner circle," as one of them phrased it, — they had no reservations. I was called on to make no protestations, to register no oaths, nor did I solicit any communications. They came to me freely, and either by laboriously penned or penciled letters written on surreptitious scraps of paper in ill-lighted cells, or by circumspect word of mouth mumbled into my ear on the baseball ground of a Saturday afternoon, they would disclose their long hoarded and grievous facts. "I wouldn't lie to you, Mr. Hawthorne — what would be the use? it would come back on me!" But I was listening to the break and tremor in their voices, the hurry and awkward indignation, the eager marshaling of insignificant details, the dreary, apathetic recital of sordid or callous outrages, the hopelessness striving once more to hope. "If they'd only send us an inspector who wouldn't be always dining with the warden, and junketing in his auto, and taking the screws' word against ours — a fellow who'd peel off his coat and size things up independent!" Their wish was not fulfilled in my time; the inspections were a farce and a scandal. There was a tradition of one inspector who had really effected something — who seemed to think of his duty, as well as of good dinners and joy rides — but that was long ago. That he never repeated his visit would seem to indicate that his report was found inconvenient.

Meantime, I did not need their asseverations of veracity; the truth shone through their uncouth stories. They were widely different from the glib patter that runs out of a crook's mouth in the presence of an official. Some of these men were seasoned criminals; often they did not themselves understand how iniquitous was the "deal" that had been given them, being too much inured to the tricks and treachery of the detectives' practices to feel special animosity regarding them; but more or less dimly they felt that wrong was being done them that was not contemplated or recognized by the law. The last thing to die in a man is his sense of justice; "I'm as bad a man as you like, and I'm willing to take my proper medicine; but they ought to give a man a square deal!" There was a young fellow there, well educated, with an intelligent, agreeable face and gentlemanly bearing; I got his story, not from him, but from the reminiscences of others. One time "Bob got nutty, and wouldn't come out of his cell, and started setting fire to his bedding. His cell got filled with the smoke and he was near choking to death, and fell down on the floor. A bunch of screws stood in front of his door making fun of him, and they held a blanket up so the smoke wouldn't get out. At last they opened the door and pulled him out, and they clubbed him good and plenty, and then they dragged him down the stairs — he was in an upper tier, understand — with his head bumping against every step. They threw him into a dark cell, and left him there." There he had leisure to recover from his "nuttiness." It was nothing much out of the usual, only the incident happened to offer spectacular features which served to keep the memory of it fresh. But does the Department of Justice countenance such diversions?

To return to my theme — I came to feel that whether or not I was handled softly, others as deserving as I, or less deserving, or more deserving, were not; and that if I had no personal grounds for complaint, they had. I could not adopt the point of view of one of the "better" class of convicts: "The warden has always treated me decently, and I don't mean to bite the hand that caressed me." I need not affirm, either, that my good fortune was due to an expectation that I would respond in kind; that would be an unverifiable inference. But it was plain that the officials took interest in the prison paper as a medium for advertising and gaining credit for the penitentiary; and that when I began to write for it, newspapers all over the country quoted the articles and commented kindly on them. My name was given a prominence, unwelcome, though well meant; accounts of my doings and condition, entirely apocryphal (for I never saw a newspaper man during my stay, or gave out any form of interview), were published and featured from time to time; I was kept more or less in the public eye. If, now, I were to be starved and clubbed, dungeoned and otherwise maltreated, not only would I be incapacitated from contributing to the paper, but some hint of the facts might leak out and impair the reputation of Atlanta Penitentiary as a Gentleman's Club and Humane Paradise. Accordingly, if I were found smoking out of hours, or were missing from count, — "Never mind — it's only Hawthorne!" It may be, of course, that my

personal charm was so irresistible that every official from the warden
down fell victim to it, and would rather prove recreant to their oath of
office than interfere with me; my vanity craves to believe so, yet I
hesitate. At any rate, with whatever sugar the gag was sweetened, or
whether the suggestion of it was inadvertent, I did not feel justified in
accepting it; and when I got out, the waiting reporters at last obtained
what they had so long awaited. But though my eight hundred comrades
seem to have been gratified with my words, I cannot think that they
were equally satisfactory to the officials; for I am informed that Hawthorne's writings are henceforth barred from the penitentiary. I must
have hurt their feelings in some way; no one can please everybody.

The naïve surprise expressed in some local quarters outside the
penitentiary went to show how unexpected and almost incredible my
statements appeared to be — or, from another point of view, how
successfully hitherto the truth had been suppressed. The truth being
once unshackled, I was anxious to get the widest possible circulation
for it, and therefore arranged for its publication in various newspapers
distributed over the country; but I was not altogether sanguine that my
plan of public enlightenment would prove an unqualified success. The
System, as I have indicated, had several guns which it might bring to
bear, and it was conceivable that some of the editors who had subscribed
to the syndicate might find reason to regard the articles as not adapted
to the taste of their readers, and decline to risk offending them any
further. If other guns of the System should prove inadequate, there was
always the great gun to be depended upon, known as the Law for Libel.
I took what precautions I could with respect to this formidable and
most respectable weapon; I stipulated that a competent lawyer should
read each article before it was offered for publication, and inform me
of any passage in any of them which might be obnoxious to the
provisions of this law, in order that such passages might be modified
or expunged. He carefully discharged his function; and if any reader
should detect a lack of continuity or explicitness in any of my statements, he may charitably ascribe it to the consequences of the lawyer's
advice; since, even in this free country, the proprieties must be observed.
If I were fortunate enough to escape the missiles of the Libel gun, I had
still to be on my guard against more obscure and personal weapons; I
am an ex-convict, and any lenity of treatment which I had hitherto
enjoyed is not to be looked for in the future. If I were sent back to
prison, my shrift was likely to be short; and I could only hope, in that
event, to have been able to say enough to afford my entertainers ample
provocation for giving me, as my comrades would say, the limit.

"You would have only yourself to blame!" — I hear that comment. If you are kicked, be like the puppy — roll over on your back and hold up your paws for mercy. But if canine models are in question, I feel more inclination to the thoroughbred bulldog, who does what he can and would do more if he could. I have undertaken a heavy responsibility, and must make the best showing I may with it. I no longer have a lifetime before me, but I have learned while I have been alive that the methods of the puppy are not remunerative in the end. Every natural instinct in me calls out for rest and peace, and to forget the valleys of grief and humiliation; but there is another voice which summons me to other issues. I am sensible of my lack of strength and fitness for the enterprise; but I believe that it was no idle circumstance that called me to it; I believe in a Divine government of the world, which chooses sometimes to use unlikely instruments to accomplish its will. The little I can do may inspire worthier deeds by more powerful hands. Emerson found simple words for a mighty thought —

"One accent of the Holy Ghost
  The heedless world hath never lost!"

The prophets of old had no dignity or weight in themselves, but they delivered messages which changed the world. "What! that old numskull be the mouthpiece of Jehovah?" his townsfolk might exclaim. But so it was. What is any one of us in himself?

However, I don't wish to bear too hard on this pedal. It is easier to look at things from the commonplace standpoint. One thing or another prevented any of my companions in the jail from doing what it was desirable to do, and circumstances quite unforeseen opened a way for me to do it. What I have said above was with a view of showing how difficult it may ordinarily be to bring prison facts to light; and if, by chance, some individual should find means to his hand to open a window, he would be a poltroon if he forbore to do it. I am under no illusions as to the obstacles in my way, nor do I anticipate that what I am trying to do will result in prompt or vital changes for the better in prison management. The facts I adduce may be discredited, but if they are true they will not be lost. My eight hundred inarticulate comrades are always present in my thoughts. I have left them in the body, but I see their faces wherever I turn. It is a crime that any human beings should be arbitrarily kept in the conditions which surround them, and if I can loosen one stone of the Bastille which, at Atlanta and elsewhere, annually engulfs and destroys so many of them, I shall be content.

XIII

THE BANQUETS OF THE DAMNED

*T*he walls of jails are good non-conductors of what goes on behind them, and this applies to other prisons as well as to that at Atlanta. Yet once in a while a groan or protest, or a partial account of some outbreak, finds its way through; and in many cases the gist of the story is to the effect that the food is bad or scanty. Other things the men behind the bars suffer stoically, or not so stoically; but lack of food arouses them to despair and frenzy. We have lately heard reports from Sing Sing illustrative of this condition there; and many another jail could echo the complaints of the unfortunates in that gloomy hell-chamber.

Convicts know that they are to be punished, that the government has sentenced them, that it is the law; and though they may find cause to disagree with the decree that consigns them to hopeless and useless servitude, they accept it as at least legal and incident to the game as played. But they do not believe that the government has condemned them to starvation, or to poisoning (and the condition in which food often comes to the convicts' table is practically poisonous). They know that no such punishment is included in the statutes; and they can only conclude, therefore, that it is an arbitrary and illegal piece of cruelty or neglect on the part of the warden or commissary officer. They are prone to think that these persons profit financially by cutting down their supplies; and that they are careful to conceal the fact in their reports to the Department, or to disguise it as a meritorious economy. At the same time, they are conscious that there is no regular channel through which they can make their injury known to the authorities, and that nothing is more readily denied, or more easily concealed from inspectors, than is this very abuse.

But the suffering which it occasions is constant and cumulative. They are still required to perform their labor, as if in full physical vigor. They are punished if physical weakness causes them to fall short in their tasks.

They feel their vitality ebbing, they find themselves ever less able to resist the inroads of disease, their appeals to the doctors are often met with sneers and even animosity; and what marvel is it that stoicism and patience at last give way, and they break out in some wild and savage excess which justifies the resort by their masters to the dungeon and the bullet? But death may well seem to the rebels preferable to the lingering pains of the alternative fate.

The under nourishment and malnourishment of convicts is, in fact, one of the worst crimes of the many which their despots perpetrate upon them. From any point of view, it is barbarous and wicked — the crime of a Weyler upon the defenseless Cuban revolutionists, which, as much as the destruction of the Maine, impelled this country to declare war. Yet, knowing as we do that it is perpetrated upon the human beings in our prisons, we sit supine and acquiescent, and thereby make the crime our own.

Have you not imagination enough to put yourself for a moment in the predicament of the prisoner? There you sit in the narrow gloom of your cell, or you toil in the stifling confinement of your work room, and such is not only your state today, but for years to come it will be unchanged. You are isolated from sight of and association with every man and woman in the world who cares for you or thinks kindly of you; silence and rigid obedience are imposed upon you; you meet no looks that are not harsh, and hear no words but sharp commands or angry menaces. Your very toil is idle and unpaid, and its diligent performance brings you no credit or hope, except treacherous promises of a good constantly delayed. And then picture yourself when, after wearisome hours, the whistle blows that means intermission of labor and the renewal of strength by food. Yet that summons, instead of cheering you, does but make the burden of your misery heavier.

Sullenly and heavily, in the endless line, you tramp into the huge, comfortless hall, with its hideous tables and benches, and as you pass up the aisles you glance abhorrently at the dirty scraps and masses of provender dumped carelessly out of noisome buckets by the filthy hands of the servers upon plates still rough and foul with the hardened grease of foregoing meals. You are faint for lack of nourishment, yet the sight of what is provided, and the unclean smell of it, nauseate instead of inviting you. Eat you must, if you would live and have strength to work, yet if you eat you invite sickness and suffering, and if you could eat all, and assimilate it, you would still leave the table but half fed.

Every tyro in physiology knows the effect upon the general organism of dejection and resentment at meals. Prisoners more than men in any other condition need abundance to eat and good cheer while eating;

but the food they get, and the circumstances in which they get it, causes them to degenerate physically, and the body affects the mind. Physical disease breeds the disease of evil thoughts and impulses. Criminals might be generated by prison food alone, without taking account of their previous records and future prospects.

We of Atlanta penitentiary used to hear occasionally of the bills-of-fare of our repasts in the prison that were daily forwarded to Washington, by way of reassuring the Department of Justice, and whom else it might concern, as to the substance and excellence of our nourishment. These alimentary documents might be compared with like lists at Delmonico's and the Waldorf, and the names of the viands would be found to be identical. The inference, to the legal mind, not to speak of the penological one, was plain: the convicts at the penitentiary fared as sumptuously as do the banqueters of the Four Hundred — at no cost, moreover, to themselves, not even waiters' tips.

For here were rich soups and gravies, substantial roast beef, succulent steaks and chops, the renowned baked beans of legend, comforting hashes, pies and puddings, fresh vegetables, including the famous sweet potato of the South in its pride; and long drafts of milk from the tranquil cows of the pasture, together with tea and coffee from the Orient, sugar, mustard, salt and pepper and vinegar, enough to beguile the most squeamish appetite, and, to top off with, fruits in their season, led by the incomparable Georgia watermelon. I may have inadvertently omitted some items from this toothsome list, but it is enough as it stands to make an epicure's mouth water. And if any skeptic were still unconvinced, a photographer would be admitted with his undeniable camera at certain seasons — Christmas and Fourth of July, for example — who would place a picture of the revelry and the revelers on the everlasting records, with garlands and festive decorations, and actual dishes of some sort on the groaning boards, and serried rows of plump felons ready to fall to.

The fame of all this went forth into the world, and Atlanta Penitentiary, its warden, its guards, and its cooks shine in penal annals as the acme and ideal of modern humanitarian ideas upon the reclamation of convicts through gentleness and love, and a full stomach.

I found opportunity to study some of these historic scrolls, and was so much impressed by them that I caused a suggestion to be conveyed to the warden. Instead of sending all the menus to Washington, and to admiring friends in the Atlanta neighborhood, let one or two of them be placed at each meal upon the tables of the diners, to the end that they might be stimulated, by the perusal of these literary masterpieces, to choke down their gullets the actual garbage which was furnished in the name thereof. But the warden's views seem not to have been in harmony with mine on this occasion. I am glad to learn, however, from certain graduates of the institution since my own departure from it, that the food has greatly improved in quantity and somewhat even in quality, since these chapters began to appear in newspapers.

I need not attempt to fathom the reason. If it were incomparable before, why or how better it?

It could hardly have been done at the instance of the old and warm personal friend of the warden and the Attorney-General who was sent to Atlanta recently in the guise of a Spartan inspector of the alleged abuses; because, for one thing, the improvement had set in long before he made his investigation, and the investigator, in his report, appears to have discovered no room for improvement anywhere. It must have just happened — one of those miracles in the way of gilding refined gold and painting the lily which are so common nowhere else as in our model penal institutions.

I had ample opportunity to study the subject personally while a guest at the prison table, and to compare my impressions with those of my fellow prisoners, as well as to enlarge them by conferences with persons employed in the kitchen and commissary department. Men who had served in other prisons — and their combined experiences covered a great many — were unanimous and emphatic in declaring that the table at Atlanta was the worst they had ever known, not only as to scantness of supply, but as to the unwholesomeness or positively poisonous quality of the food furnished. But let me tell a little of what I saw and knew myself.

When the change was made from long tables and benches to tables seating eight and chairs, it was announced that table cloths would also be supplied, and napkins. That was two or three years ago, but table cloths have not yet appeared, and the eaters still wipe their mouths on the backs of their hands in the good old way. Pepper and salt were on the table, and a bottle of something that looked like beer and was supposed to be vinegar, but was sampled only by the more reckless or inexperienced convicts. Sugar was not provided except on rare occasions, and to "diet" prisoners — men who were restricted to bread and milk and oatmeal. Some beverage that dishonored the name of tea was served about once a fortnight; a brown, semi-transparent rinsing of dirty kettles, sugarless, thin and bitter, called coffee, came every day; but if your stomach rejected either of these, you could fill up on plain water.

The latter, however, like the "diet" milk and oatmeal and the drinkables generally, had to be taken out of metal mugs covered with white enamel, minute particles of which chipped off and mingled with what you drank. These particles were hard and sharp, like pure glass, and they cut and lodged in the intestines, causing, with other things, an excessive predisposition to appendicitis — a frequent disease in the penitentiary. This was also promoted by the bread, which was made of the poorest grade of white flour, without nourishing quality, the value per loaf being about two cents; the flour was ground in steel mills, and microscopic particles of steel were rubbed off into it — this fact I had from a physician who had examined it. The flour, when received at the prison, was frequently full of weevils, most of which but not all were sifted out before it was used. The bread was tasteless and light; it was baked in large quantities, and what was not consumed by the prisoners was sold outside.

It is not provided in the prison regulations that officials shall be fed at the expense of the prisoners. Nevertheless, a separate and superior grade of flour is purchased at government expense, and is used to make bread which is given to the officials; the loaves are placed in the outer corridor, and are taken away by guards and others every day. Separate cooks are also assigned to prepare the officials' food on the prison ranges; the meats and vegetables are of a grade much better than is supplied to prisoners; but some favored prisoners participate in their consumption. The higher officials have the best food the market affords and in such ample abundance that certain prison pets, usually Negroes, get their main subsistence from the surplus.

The beef given to prisoners was of the third grade — the worst on the market — it is cow or bull beef, never heifer or steer, and often it is rotten, and must be treated chemically before being offered even to prisoners. It used to come on the table in gristly and bony gobbets, after having lain on the kitchen ranges for hours, until it was reduced to a hardness which resisted all but the most efficient and vigorous teeth (which, except with Negroes, are rare in prison). I used to compare these "steaks" and other pieces with old blackened boot heels; they were hardly less eatable and nourishing. Often it smelt so that nature rebelled against it; but complaints were liable to be met by committal to the solitary cells.

But groups of visitors used to appear in the dining room occasionally; they were lined up along the wall adjoining the door, and were not allowed to walk between the tables, so that the only food they could see was what was put on the tables nearest the door; and this was always of a quality superior to the rest, and there was more of it per man. It was one of the little tricks employed to maintain the entente cordiale, by which the prisoners who sat at those tables benefited, and the visitors went forth to sing the praises of our warm hearted warden. On the days when the bread was sour or the meat stank, visitors were headed away from the dining room, and their attention directed to more important matters.

The hash, which often made the breakfast, was composed of fragments of gristle and refuse left on the prisoners' plates after dinner, mixed with potatoes and rancid grease; this, and the soups and gravies, which had a similar origin, gave out a most nauseating smell. The men would gulp it down — it was that, or starve — trying to help it on its way with all the condiments they could lay hands on; but the effect of it, and of the food generally, upon the digestive tract was so disastrous in most cases that they might better have left it alone. I myself retired from the enterprise in my second or third week, and would have literally died of inanition had not the doctor, moved by I know not what suggestion (not mine), put me on the milk and oatmeal diet during the remainder of my sojourn. This applied for breakfast and supper; I sat at dinner, but satisfied myself with nibbling bread crusts, and witnessing the forlorn and perilous efforts of my friends to walk the line between starvation and acute indigestion. Not many were successful.

For vegetables we had Irish and sweet potatoes, turnip tops (uneatable), black-eyed beans, bitter and greasy, and once a month, perhaps, a tomato. The butter was made of an inferior quality of lard, and cottonseed oil — a substance which entered into many other of our viands, and of which, with grease, it was calculated by an expert in the kitchen, we were offered as much as one pound per man every day. It produced a calamitous effect upon the digestive tract, inasmuch as there was hardly a white man in the prison who did not suffer chronically from stomach troubles — constant suffering, often becoming acute. The strongest digestions would resist for a while, but finally succumb.

There was a poultry farm on the grounds, donated by outside benefactors specifically and exclusively for the benefit of prisoners, beginning with the tuberculous patients. After it got going, there may have been an average of six hundred fowls on the place. Of these, not one ever appeared on the prison tables. With the exception of a possible few that were stolen by prisoners having access to the yard, all were appropriated by higher officials, and the eggs as well.

One official gave frequent dinner parties to his friends, and was said to use as many as five or six chickens a day, though I cannot vouch for that — it seems excessive. He certainly, sometimes, commandeered as many as fourteen or more at one time. There was a story of a great cake which he had made for some festival, into the composition of which entered one hundred and four eggs from our farm. To neither chickens nor eggs had he, of course, any title more legitimate than have you who read these lines. He had a large and hungry household, and many guests — among them, commonly, such government inspectors as were sent down from Washington, to see whether he and his fellow officials were honestly discharging their functions.

As for the tuberculous patients, I was never able to find any of them who had eaten chicken from the farm, or any part of one. Some chicken soup was at one time ordered for a patient by the doctor; a prisoner (a famous physician), a deputy of the doctor, happened to be at the tuberculosis camp when the soup arrived from the kitchen. It consisted of some warm water with the shank — not the drumstick, but the shank and foot — of a fowl in it. This aroused his interest, and twice again he was present when a chicken soup prescribed appeared at the camp. On both occasions — he stands ready so to testify under oath — he found the same foot and shank in it, but nothing else recalling chicken. The foot was identified by an imperfection in one of its toes.

Eggs were indeed provided for the hospital prisoners (never for the general mass), but they were cold storage eggs, the cheapest grade that could be bought in the market, and that is saying much for this sort of product nowadays. Out of one mess of eight that were served in the hospital, and of which I gained authentic news from the prisoner physician already referred to, six were bad. I am informed that these notes and comments of mine are not permitted to be read by the prisoners; but perhaps the original donors of the poultry farm may see them, and be prompted to inquire into their accuracy. Let us return to the dining room.

Sweet potatoes abound in the South, and subsistence upon them exclusively would reduce the cost of living; the only trouble is that the human stomach refuses to cooperate in this economy. Sweet potatoes were served at Atlanta during the season three times a day, baked, boiled and in pies; the men were hungry enough, and the supply of potatoes was adequate; but had they been of the finest instead of the worst quality in the market, the experiment would have failed; starvation proved preferable; we could not get them down. That soft, slimy sweetness, foul with dirt and often tainted with decay, reappearing day after day at every meal for weeks on end, outdid endurance, nor could we be stimulated by the argument that the Government was saving money by it. Had the sweet potato season lasted the year round, the warden would have lost his job from mere dearth of prisoners to earn his salary on.

I do not forget the corn, either; it was of the brand fed to farm animals; but this enumeration becomes monotonous. We had apple pies once a week or so; and I was told by an employee in the kitchen, who had been a farmer in his time, that the apples were such as could be bought at a dollar a barrel, and that the charge appearing in bills submitted to the Government was five dollars. The quality of the apples in the pies supports my informant's contention. As for the watermelons — a benefactor of the prisoners bought a consignment of them sufficient for the prison population, to be eaten on the Fourth of July, 1913. The contract was for the best melons obtainable; and Georgia is famous for good melons. A day or two before the Fourth, the benefactor called at the prison, and asked to see the melons, which had been delivered some time before. Examination showed them to be of an inferior grade, such as farmers used for cattle and poultry. It was too late, however, to get a fresh supply, and the benefactor had the mortification of seeing the kindly meant gift dishonored. It is pertinent, here, that there is said to be an individual in Atlanta not officially connected with the penitentiary who is commissioned to make all purchases for the prison — food, tobacco, and other supplies. He buys the stuff, and hands in his bills; but the bills he pays are not submitted. It is conceivable that there may be a discrepancy between the two amounts, and it might be interesting to learn whether he alone benefits by it.

Guards walk up and down the aisles between the tables, during meals, to keep order and also to attend to complaints or requests from prisoners. There is also the man in the window with the loaded magazine rifle, ready to settle any complaints that become too insistent. The common protest is against the badness of a specific piece of food, or against some example of dirt. The former seldom get relief; in the latter case, the dish or cup is sometimes changed.

A prisoner at my table called the guard's attention to a quid of tobacco which had got into his soup. The guard, who was of a humorous turn, replied, smiling, "Well, you use tobacco, don't you?" and passed on. This was the same guard who assaulted and clubbed a prisoner whom he was taking downstairs, as described in a previous chapter. On another occasion, a prisoner complained that there was a beetle in his hash. An examination was made; but whether the beetle was alive and got away, or whether the prisoner himself had "bugs," as the slang is, at any rate the examiners reported no beetle. The matter was then brought before the authorities, who ordered the complainant to the dark hole.

Another day, following some months of constant deterioration in the food, and diminution in the quantity of it, a dinner of hash and bread was served, and both bread and hash were sour. The air of the room was full of the sour smell; the captain came down the aisle near mine, and a prisoner had the boldness to stop him and hold up his plate. "It's sour, Captain!" said he. The captain looked the man in the eye and replied sternly, "It is not sour!" "But, Captain —" "I say it is not sour!" the other repeated with a threatening look. It was either submit, or the hole; the man sat down.

But a few minutes later, someone hissed; before he could be identified, hisses came from every part of the room. It was a critical juncture. The captain ordered the band to play, and play it did at the top of its compass; but the hissing was audible and continued through the playing. Presently the men got up and began to march out; it was then that a group of guards from the smoking room below came running up the stairs armed with clubs and revolvers and tried to get through the barred door at the stair head, but were checked by the captain, who was a wise tactician. The men went to their cells, and there began to howl and screech like a crazy menagerie, and kept it up for hours. Twenty or thirty of the supposed ringleaders were sent to the dark holes; but the revolt was not checked until the warden personally promised reforms, and gave his word that no further punishments should be inflicted — fair promises, made to be broken.

The dining room windows were protected by wire netting; but there were many holes in it, as large as a man's head, through which the flies, in summer, entered in swarms; and there was no provision for keeping them out of the kitchen, which opened into the dining room. Complaints were constantly made, but the holes were never mended, and no means were taken to kill the flies. Food sometimes was placed on the tables hours before the men sat down to their meals, and the flies, not having the same delicacy of appetite as the men, feasted freely in the meanwhile. There was also frequent protest against the bits of loose enamel in the bowls; many of these were made direct to the doctor; but he did nothing. If a man whose digestion had given way called on him for help, a dose of salts was the only reply, and several deaths, while I was there, unquestionably had their beginning in this neglect. Upon the whole, contentment with starvation was the most prudent policy in Atlanta Penitentiary.

I am not a sybarite or an epicure. For fifteen years before I was sent to prison I lived on the hardest and most Spartan diet, eating as little food as possible and that of the simplest kind. Wheat, milk, a few green vegetables, and fruit made my menus. I was therefore better fortified against hardships than the majority of prisoners; I could hold out against starvation longer; but against the poison of rotten or bad food I had no protection.

The wardens and the chief clerks of prisons often wish, for motives of their own, to make an economical showing, and perhaps do not much care if it is made at the expense of the health or lives of prisoners. Some friends of mine in Atlanta prison and myself made an attempt to determine just what was paid out per man in the prison for subsistence; we quietly obtained statements from men in the kitchen and commissary departments, and made our calculations. After careful revision, the figures showed that we were being fed at the rate of from eight to eleven cents per head, a day.

About that time, a great scientific discovery was announced by the chief steward. Food, he had been informed, contained a certain amount of heat and power; and these heat units, called calories, could be estimated for any given article of diet. (As I write this, an editorial on the subject in a recent issue of a New York newspaper states the matter in terms which I am happy to reproduce.) "Physiologists have determined by repeated experiments that a definite quantity of certain foods furnishes a definite number of calories or heat units, which produce a certain quantity of energy in the animal or human body. . . . In twenty-four hours a normal man of about one hundred and thirty pounds at rest, needs 1680 calories or heat units, while a man doing severe physical labor would require sufficient food to produce 3000 calories. . . . Since the efficiency of labor depends upon the energy of the body and this energy or power is produced by the food, it is not difficult to calculate the actual outlay required for this purpose. . . . The household requirements of a family where two servants are kept would at this rate be from $1.00 to $1.40 a day, a sum sufficient to furnish all the energy for all purposes of normal maintenance."

Such being the case, our steward figured that the convicts could be well enough supported by about 2500 calories apiece; and upon making a scientific estimate of the calories in our average bill-of-fare, he found that we were being overfed rather than the contrary. Meat, so many calories; soup, so many; sweet potatoes, so many; bread, so many; and so on. It was found possible, on this basis, to retrench here and there; the bills were reduced — it was hoped that we might ultimately beat even eight cents. The sole difficulty appeared to be that the men, the subjects of the experiment, began incomprehensibly and perhaps maliciously to starve.

I was fortunate enough to have access to a physician (a fellow prisoner), of forty years' eminence in his profession, who solved the enigma for me. The sum of his comment was this: "Put a Delmonico dinner in one bucket, and an equal bulk of swill or garbage in another; the number of calories may be the same in both. The steward, in his calculation, has forgotten to consider the condition in which the food is served — its eatableness, in short. If men could devour swill, it would be all right; but if they cannot, they will starve in spite of calories."

So the steward's calories became a byword and a mockery in the prison for many weeks afterward.

Similar conditions, perhaps due to the same cause, seem to have obtained at Sing Sing and elsewhere. It is not enough that prison food should be sufficient in amount; it must also be of a quality such that the men are able to get it down their throats. Nor are the doctor's salts a remedy; their violent and abnormal action finally paralyze the excretory and digestive powers of the organism, and the man dies from poisons generated by indigestible food in his own system. Even keeping him in the dark hole fails to recuperate him, though it has been constantly tried at Atlanta, and very likely in other reformatory institutions.

Plenty of vigorous and hearty outdoor exercise would help much; not the exercise of prison toil, which but deepens the darkness of the heart; but exercise for its own sake, for the cheer and excitement of it. Much has been said of the baseball at Atlanta Penitentiary; and doubtless it has been of benefit. But only a handful of the prisoners, and nine-tenths of them Negroes, play the game; the others can only stand and look on. The games occur, weather permitting, once a week, on Saturdays. From Saturday at half past three until Monday morning at half past seven, the men are locked in their cells, absolutely inactive in body, and abandoned to such mental activities as, for the most part, breed no good either for themselves or others. The only outlet is the Sunday church service hour — a crowded session in a blank hall, with rifles ready to subdue any disorder. A very apostle might fail in his efforts under such circumstances; and very apostles are few.

A man who is sick and sad day after day and year after year, and conscious of his impotence to amend his state, is in no mood for moral reform. Much of the sickness might be averted if the medical treatment at the outset of disease were such as to encourage the patients to avail themselves of advice. But each man, as he comes up in the sick line every morning, is met with indifference or insults; he is presumed to be a malingerer unless he can prove himself genuine on the instant; the only other recourse is to become so sick as to be beyond help of medicine, and then, taken belated to the hospital, to die outright. The consequence is that the men will suffer silently in their cells rather than appeal to the doctor; and many diseases become ineradicable from this cause.

Even a convict, when he is miserable and weak from illness, shrinks from facing rough and unsympathetic handling and words in the doctor's room, with a good chance of being sent to the hole if he remonstrates. The doctor of a prison could be its good angel, if he would.

XIV

THE POLICY OF FALSEHOOD

*T*he subterranean brotherhood waxes curiously indignant over being lied to by prison officials. For why should criminals, whose success in their trade must depend largely on lies either spoken or acted, be resentful when they are paid back in their own base coin? I am inclined to think that the anomaly may be due to some survival in prisoners of the old belief, that honor and fair play do, or should, exist in officers of justice; although their own experience should admonish them that officers of prisons, at least, cultivate the art and practice of fighting the devil with fire (as we say), and so far from ever thinking of keeping faith with a convict, study the art of deceiving and hoodwinking him, and appear to derive no small amusement from their results. Indeed, any tendency on the part of a guard or other official in a prison to deal honestly and above board with their charges would at once awaken suspicion of his loyalty to the "system," and his superiors would be apt to improve the first opportunity of getting rid of him.

The lies told to prisoners are sometimes told for art's sake merely — for the delight of the artist in his fabrication. There is fun in overcoming the suspicions and skepticism of some old timer, and beguiling him into the belief that for once, and at last, he really is getting trustworthy information — that he has finally succeeded in touching the elusive hem of the robe of Truth. But commonly the official liar has some practical object in view. This object is usually the tightening of the prison's grip upon the convict; not only to strengthen the bonds which confine his body, but to bring his spirit or soul under more complete subjection and to make him feel that so far from moral reform being the end sought in his incarceration, he will best consult his private interests by abandoning all thoughts of decency and honor, and acting, with the officials, against the welfare and hopes of his own fellows.

The consequence of the falsehood policy in prisons is, for one thing, that the men most worthless morally are uniformly those who get most favors. Men of unbroken spirit are handled in a hostile manner, and are subjected to a régimen calculated either to kill or cure their obstinacy and themselves. "You have no right to do this — there is no law for it!" the convict may protest. The reply is a sneer: "What are you going to do about it?" What do you think you would do in such circumstances? — write to the President, or to some Senator or Congressman? awaken the country to these iniquities? The warden and the clerk will smile over your letter, and drop it in the waste-basket, or will make it the basis of an adverse report against you to the Department, — insubordination, incorrigibility, insanity perhaps.

Or, if you reserve your protest till after you get out, and can then find any medium for ventilating it, the prison authorities will promptly and smilingly "welcome an investigation"; and the Department will eagerly send down some old friend and boon companion of the officials, to make a "strict investigation," "without fear or favor." Now, at last, the truth shall be known, let it hurt whom it may! So the severe and incorruptible inspector comes down; and after snubbing and insulting a few prisoners, and taking notes of the information of a few snitches, and dining and wining with the officials, and inspecting the country in the government automobile, he goes back to Washington with the reassuring news that the reports of abuses, where they were not absolute fabrications, were gross exaggerations.

Is this an imaginative sketch — or colored a little — or a good deal? How shall it be determined? — for I am only an ex-convict, and we all know what an ex-convict's word is worth. I can only suggest that, for your own individual satisfaction at any rate, you commit a bona fide crime and get sentenced to prison for it. If you survive, we can converse further on the subject. Or — to offer a bolder suggestion yet — perhaps the head of the Department himself might take a hand; perhaps he would oblige us by breaking a law. Let him be handcuffed and brought to Atlanta or elsewhere — we are not particular — and there be numbered and U.S.P.'d and set to work. After a ten years' experience, or, if his time be valuable, a year and a day might do, let him write his report, and I for one will abide by it.

The prison policy of falsehood may be illustrated by the uses to which the parole law is put. This unfortunate measure was no doubt conceived by its parents in love and charity, to supply prisoners with a stimulus to reform by rewarding them for it with early release from imprisonment. If a man's conduct while serving his sentence had been orderly and obedient to rules, he was to be freed after serving about one-third of his appointed time; but he was required, for a reasonable period thereafter, to make monthly reports to the prison, and to show that he was usefully employed and was not frequenting drinking saloons or otherwise going astray. A parole board was appointed to carry out the law and to look after the paroled prisoner, helping him if necessary to get employment. Meetings of the board were to be held at stated times, to pass upon applications for parole; it was to consist of the warden and the doctor of the prison, together with the president of the parole board, who officiated at all Federal prisons, and who would, naturally, be the superior official of the three. But two members of the board would form a quorum; and meetings of the board at times other than those regularly required could be held if thought desirable.

This looked humane and innocent, and raised great hopes in prisoners; and an improvement in their general demeanor was soon observable. Question soon arising as to whether life prisoners could be brought under the new law, it was decided that lifers who had served fifteen years were eligible, if of good record, — not an extravagant act of mercy, — and in obtaining this concession it was made known that the warden of Atlanta Penitentiary was instrumental. Of course the reputation of Atlanta as a model and humane prison was greatly enhanced thereby.

But the prisoners, and perhaps the framers of the law also, had overlooked one little word in the language of the law, which grew to have a large significance afterward. The language is, that if the prisoner's conduct has been correct, etc., he may be granted parole. If, for that harmless looking "may," had been substituted "shall," or "must," the secret annals of federal prisons since then would have been spared much rascality, corruption, cruelty, torture and death; and prisoners would not have hated and distrusted their keepers as they do now, and subordination on one side and humanity on the other would have received an impetus.

That "may" rendered it optional with the board to grant or to refuse parole in any given case; they might not only determine whether or not the conduct of the applicant had been, while serving his sentence, good enough to justify clemency; but also whether, even then, it were expedient to exercise it. No matter how unexceptionable the behavior of a prisoner were shown to be, it was open to the board to say to him, "We hold that your liberation would be inimical to the welfare of society, and we cannot therefore recommend it to the Department."

The prisoner, going before the board unsupported by the advice of counsel, had no further recourse; he must go back to his cell feeling that all his efforts to be obedient (persisted in through what discouragements only prisoners know) had been futile; that he was not a whit better off than was a man who had defied every regulation, and was worse off in so far as he had taken all his pains and indulged all his hopes for nothing. He must serve out his time; for if he renewed his application at the next meeting of the board, he was told that nothing could be done in his case except upon the presentation of "new evidence."

New evidence of what? The obstacle he had to meet was the arbitrary opinion, or fiat, of the board that it would not be a good thing to set him free; with what argument, except his good conduct, which had already proved unavailing, could he hope to reverse it? The decision left him helpless and hopeless, and with a sense of despotic injustice on the part of the authorities which was anything but conducive to good discipline in him or in his comrades who were conversant with his fate.

Obviously, however, there was a weak point in this kind of arbitrary rulings of the board; it was conceivable that some enterprising Attorney-General might want to know why the board had not held the good conduct specified in the law to be sufficient ground for freeing the man. To guard against this, the services of a subordinate called the parole officer were called in. This person's normal functions as indicated in the law were to help paroled men to procure employment, to aid them in general in their efforts toward a better life, and to stand by them as an authoritative and kindly friend. But he was now required to play a very different part.

As soon as a man applied for parole, the parole officer betook himself to the place where the applicant had formerly lived or been known, and there busied himself in unearthing whatever gossip and scandal of a hostile nature any enemy might be willing to supply. There was no time limit on these revelations, nor were any apparent precautions taken to determine whether the evil reports were founded in fact; the tale bearer was not compelled to testify under oath, and his story might refer to incidents which had happened years before, and which had nothing to do with the crime for which the prisoner was now undergoing sentence. With this budget of information the parole officer returned to his superiors, who were now prepared for any contingency.

When the prisoner comes up for examination, and has handed in his report of good conduct while incarcerated, the president of the board fixes a distrustful eye upon him, and says in effect, "Your behavior here seems to have been unobjectionable; but the board cannot take the responsibility of granting parole on that ground alone. It desires to be informed what you were doing in such and such a place, in such and such a year? Is it not true that you were arrested in this or that year for this or that offense? Has your career, in short, been absolutely blameless during the whole course of your life? Because, unless you can prove such to be the case, it will indicate a predisposition to law-breaking on your part which will render it imprudent for the board to recommend you for parole to the Department."

The president has a sheaf of papers in his hand, which he glances over significantly while the mind of the prisoner goes groping back over the past, asking himself what he has done amiss in forgotten years, and who can be his accusers. He has no counsel beside him to tell him that he is being tried before an unauthorized tribunal, on unsupported testimony, on charges irrelevant to that for which he is now undergoing punishment; or to remind him that the judge who passed sentence on him had specified that if his behavior were good while serving that sentence, he would be eligible for parole — that he had, perhaps, given him a longer sentence than he would otherwise have done, upon this very understanding; and that, consequently, the parole board was now arrogating the power to override the purpose of the federal court, and to inflict additional and unwarranted punishment upon him for something which he may or may not have done in the past, or for which, if he had done it and been convicted, he may already have served sentence. He has no one to argue thus for him; he feels that he is alone and among enemies; and he can make no effective defense. And the parole officer stands by with a sad countenance, as of one who had done the best he could for a protégé, but was powerless to stem the tide of justice.

It can't be done, legally or justly; but it is done; that is the gist of the matter. There is no one to know the wrong and to insist upon the right; and the wrong is perpetrated. Unnumbered victims of it, in every federal prison of the country, substantiate this fact. The parole board — which means, in practice, its president — exercises more power than the federal court, and there is no appeal from his decision. At his will, a man may be tried twice for the same offense, behind closed doors, without aid of counsel. He may be condemned, though the offense was never committed except in the imagination of an enemy. We tell our convicts that they have no civic rights; but it is not generally understood, I think, that the Spanish Inquisition of the Middle Ages can properly be reproduced in Twentieth Century America even with men behind the bars.

But let that pass. Things are done under the parole law worse than this. If it were used merely as a means to induce unruly men to be docile, no one could complain; if men thus induced should after all be deprived of the reward they had earned, we might condone it. But what if we find the parole board turned into an accessory of the secret service or spy system, and learn that an applicant for parole, whether or not he have maintained good conduct during his term, may yet hope for a favorable report on his case if he will consent to betray some man on whom the police have not yet been able to lay their hand?

Here comes a post office thief, for example. He was known to have had confederates, but they escaped. He is up for parole, with only an indifferent prison record to plead for him. "We do not find your case meritorious," says the president to him (in substance), "but there were two or three others concerned in your crime. If you are able to furnish their names to the board, with such other information as may lead to their arrest and conviction, we might see our way to recommend leniency in your matter." I will not guarantee that the president expresses himself in terms quite so explicit, but he makes himself perfectly understood, and the prisoner perfectly understands that his liberty is purchasable at the price of treachery.

I don't know what percentage of the miserable creatures accept the ignoble offer; but I know personally of many who refused it. And I do not need to ask what are the prospects of an honest and worthy career for those who chose to be traitors. If they go to ruin, is not the parole board responsible? On the other hand, who shall blame the convict if he accedes to the bargain? The alternative presented to him is one which might cause even virtue to waver, and convicts are not supposed to be virtuous, especially when such an example as this action of the board is set them. The alternative is liberty, or continued incarceration with the strong probability of increased severity of treatment, and always the off chance of death.

Meanwhile, is there not something humiliating in the reflection that a tribunal authorized and appointed by the Government of the United States should descend to such practices? Or are we content to accept the spy system in toto, cost what it may? Perhaps, however, the president of the parole board is prepared to deny that he ever entered into any such compact with a prisoner; and perhaps the Department of Justice will be astonished to hear that he ever did. Is the thing true, or not true? I think men exist who have excellent reasons to believe, and who may be willing to testify, that it is.

But take the case of a prisoner who had no confederates – how does the board deal with him? According to my information, which includes my personal experience, question is put to the applicant whether or not he admits himself guilty of the crime for which he is undergoing sentence? My own reply was, "Not guilty"; and though the president was very courteous to me, and gave me every assurance that I might expect favorable action on my application, as a matter of fact and of record the recommendation made to the Attorney-General was that my application be denied, and denied it accordingly was. But in other cases nearly contemporary with mine, which came to my knowledge, the reply of "not guilty" called forth the rejoinder that in that case the matter was not one for the board to pass on, but should be referred to executive action — that is, that the President of the United States should be petitioned for a pardon. Some men are so persistent or so infatuated as to take the suggestion seriously; but their petition does not bear fruit; probably its path to the President is by way of the Department of Justice, where it is either pigeonholed, or reaches him with an endorsement to the effect that it is not a case for clemency. But in such cases as came to my knowledge, the President never saw the petition at all.

And what happens if our man pleads guilty? Why, in that event he is told that such a person as he should not have made application for parole — that he has not been sufficiently punished — that the best he should hope for is to serve out his sentence, less the regular allowance for good time. It is a case, in short, of heads the board wins, tails the convict loses; and he withdraws, wondering, perhaps, what the board is for. But let him beware of becoming restive under his disappointment, or he may forfeit his good time too.

That the parole law is interpreted, under all conditions, as being a favor or privilege and not a right earned by good conduct, is perhaps no more than one might expect; but no prisoner who lacks powerful friends, or whose parole does not in some way inure to the advantage of the prison quite as much as to his own, can make his application with assured hope of success. Upon the whole, prisoners feel that parole will not be granted if any means can be found or devised to prevent it; the good report of an entire county where a man formerly lived will not prevail against the adverse report of some inspector — one enemy of a prisoner outweighs, in the board's estimation, the favorable words of many friends.

Moreover, men released on parole live in constant dread of the secret service, for they know that unjust and trivial pretexts are often made the occasion of their re-arrest; and a paroled man re-arrested must serve out his whole time without rebate, and not including the period during which he was at liberty. Some supervision by the Government is of course proper; but the men feel it to be hostile, not friendly or helpful; that any error they fall into or mishap they meet with will be construed against them, not in their favor. In short, under the outward forms of liberty, they are still in prison, and are often discouraged from doing their best by this sleepless fear of the prowling spy.

Atlanta prison records show that out of one thousand prisoners who applied for parole up to June 30th, 1913, two hundred and seventy were successful. These applicants were serving terms of from one year and a day to twenty-one years. The two hundred and seventy who were paroled had served an aggregate of eighty-three years beyond the period when they were eligible for parole (that is, after one-third of their original sentence), or an average of about 112 days each, and with an average of from twenty-five to forty percent, of the time contemplated for them to reestablish and rehabilitate themselves.

The one-year-one-day men lost about thirty-three percent of their time during which they might have labored to reform themselves; and there were about one hundred of the two hundred and seventy whose sentences ran for a year and a day. Some sixty-five of the two hundred and seventy had sentences of more than a year and a day and less than two years; about thirty-five had over two years and under three years; from which it would appear that short term men, convicted of minor offenses, were given preference for parole over long term men. Yet it would seem to the ordinary intelligence that it should be the long term men who most needed parole and, if their conduct had been good, best deserved it. It often happened that men would be paroled when they had but a few weeks or even days yet to serve of their full sentence. In such cases, the prison got whatever credit may belong to granting parole, but the men got rather less than nothing, for they stood the risk of re-arrest and further confinement.

When an applicant goes before the board for examination, he is sometimes turned down summarily; but more often he goes out ignorant whether or not he will succeed, and, as I have already shown, he is not seldom kept in this torturing uncertainty until the day when he is either turned loose or told that he has been rejected. This seems unnecessary, and often appears to be due to sheer carelessness; the papers are not promptly submitted to the Attorney-General, or they are pigeonholed and forgotten. It may be true that the law does not categorically demand that a prisoner shall be released immediately upon a favorable report; but there is no obvious reason why he should not be, and it is cruel to keep him in suspense.

There was a young fellow while I was there, a well educated and agreeable man, whose conduct had always been unexceptionable; he applied when eligible for parole, and was informed that he would be released. Every morning thereafter for three weeks he arose with the hope that the release would come that day; every night he went to bed with a heart heavy with disappointment. He could not eat or sleep, he could not talk connectedly, he trembled and turned pale, and was on the way to becoming a nervous wreck; but no explanation was vouchsafed him. At last he was suddenly told that he might go. The sole reason that I ever heard for the delay was that the papers had been overlooked. There are a great many government employees at Washington; it might be worth while to appoint one more, charged with the duty of seeing that the overlooking of parole papers be henceforth avoided. This was a very mild instance; I have related how poor Dennis lingered for six months and finally died from the same inattention or indifference.

There was a friend of mine, M., a highly intelligent, good natured fellow, active and efficient in his prison duties, always courteous and obliging; he was serving a sentence of five years, I think, for some theft or confidence game. He had "done time" some six or seven years previously, but during the interval had lived straight. At the time of his last arrest he had been kept in the local jail, somewhere in New England, after conviction, for four months before being transferred to Atlanta. Time spent in a local jail before conviction is not counted in the prisoner's favor; for example, I was arrested several months before my conviction, and the trial itself lasted four months, and after the trial I spent ten days in the Tombs.

With the exception of the last ten days, however, I was lucky enough to be out on bail; but none of this time was applied to the lessening of my sojourn in Atlanta, although the judge specified in his sentence that my imprisonment there was to count from the time when the trial began; an injunction which, had it been observed, would have caused my release on parole a few days after my arrival at the penitentiary. But it appears that such rulings by a trial judge have no weight with the Department of Justice; and I am willing to admit that the judge's ruling in my case seemed rather like whipping the devil round the stump — an evasion of the manifest intent of the law, which, if I were guilty, I had no right to expect. At all events, the Attorney-General made a decision, based upon my case, that hereafter no such evasions were to be allowed; and I presume his authority must be superior to that of any federal judge.

But my friend's case did not come under this category. His four months in jail came after, not before, his conviction; and yet, when he arrived at Atlanta, he was told that this four months would not be deducted from his penitentiary time. Turn this which way you will, you cannot escape the conclusion that this man is getting four months more than the sentence of the judge required. Well, M. applied for parole on the plea of perfect conduct during his imprisonment; no denial of that was offered; but he was informed that his conviction seven years before, for which he had been duly punished at that time, prevented the board from giving favorable attention to his application.

This looks to me like trying a man twice for the same offense, and twice condemning him; and I can find nothing to warrant it in the wording of the parole law. If every actual or alleged misstep of a man's whole life can be quoted against him as ground for refusing parole, it would seem tantamount to stultifying the law for parole.

This is not done in every case; but the point is that it may be done in any case, and thus the fate of the applicant is at the arbitrary and absolute disposal of the board, whether or not he have complied with the stated provisions of the law.

The president of the parole board, in my time, was a Mr. Robert LaDow. A former deputy warden of the Leavenworth Penitentiary, one W.H. Mackay, wrote a letter to the Attorney-General on the 6th of November, 1913, parts of which were published in newspapers about that time. In this letter he said that Mr. LaDow was egotistical, arrogant, negligent, extravagant, visionary and impractical, showed favoritism to prisoners, and was totally unfit for the position he held. He goes on as follows:

"Personally, he knows nothing of Leavenworth Federal Prison; he is too cowardly to go among the prisoners in the yards to make a personal investigation of conditions; he has dealt unfairly and hastily with so many at the parole meetings that he is afraid to meet prisoners face to face. . . . Prisoners will stand punishment without a murmur if there is a just reason for it, and they will permit you to be the judge; but when men under the law are entitled to parole, and the flimsy excuse to hold them in confinement is made that they will be a menace to society, they cannot see it in that way. The parole board at this time is arrogantly dominated by LaDow; it is practically a one-man board. . . .

"When the board meets here, the men do not know sometimes for weeks and months afterwards what their fate is. . . . Instances occur here where the board acts unanimously upon a parole. Mr. LaDow takes these cases to Washington and holds them thirty, sixty, and even ninety days on some flimsy pretext or other. He often claims press of business, until finally some senator or congressman or influential politician calls on him, and then he gets busy very suddenly. . . .

"When he comes to a parole meeting he begins work generally with a rush and a flurry. . . . Usually has about 180 cases; he rushes them at the rate of 60 to 80 a day, without getting at the merits or giving them serious deliberation. He brings a stenographer, his private secretary, from Washington at a heavy expense. . . . Then, when they return to Washington, the stenographer writes up the result of the meeting, while LaDow will take a junketing trip at Government expense . . . as a sort of recreation from his arduous duties."

I had not been long in Atlanta before a guard informed me that LaDow was the best hated man in the prison, by officials and convicts alike. Nor did I find any prisoner there, afterward, who did not speak to the same tune. If he be really an efficient and trustworthy official, this is singular and unfortunate. Mr. Mackay's charges against him at

Leavenworth are almost identically the same as what may be heard against him any day in Atlanta. If there be any basis for them, perhaps it would be expedient for the Government to supersede him. The parole law, at its best, seems to be rather a weak-kneed and perverse institution, and it would be a pity to deprive it of what value it may have by committing its dispensation to the hands of a man not peculiarly fitted by nature and temperament to carry out its provisions. It was Napoleon's opinion that a blunder is worse than a crime.

XV

THE FRUIT OF PRISONS

*A*fter weathering Cape Parole, I laid my course for the Port of Good Time. Men whose prison records are clear are liberated after serving two-thirds of their original sentences. This new posture of my mind invited a review of the experience through which I had been passing, and of the conditions with which I had become conversant, and their significance in connection with the policy of penal imprisonment in general. I will introduce some of these reflections in this place.

As I have just said, men whose prison records are clear are liberated after serving two-thirds of their original sentences. But part or all of this abridgment may be lost by imperfect conduct. One man, at least, within my knowledge, was punished by the dark hole several months before the expiration of his original sentence, and was kept there until that sentence had expired. Then, out of that filthy dungeon he was thrust abruptly forth into broad daylight and the crowded world. It was a miracle if he survived. What have most convicts to live for? Perhaps those who have most to live for are unlikeliest to survive — their anxiety is greater.

On the other hand, severity itself may stimulate a convict. His human mind cannot comprehend despair. Instinct forces him to hope. So weeks, months, years go by, and hope seems to him more instead of less justifiable, till at last, perhaps, he dies with the illusion still strong in him. Real despair is un-human and possibly rare. Otherwise prison mutinies and killings would be more frequent. The argument of despair is, "Since I must die here anyway, I'll take two or three of those devils with me!" But few men believe they will die in jail, therefore the guard or other official escapes.

Not ten percent of men in jail would regard such a killing as unjustifiable. We were taught in school that resistance to tyrants is obedience to God, and many who had disobeyed God in other ways would gladly obey Him in this. I speak not merely of "ignorant and brutal" convicts, but of educated and intelligent men like you and me. Even a sensitive conscience may condone the killing of a tyrant who is slowly and surely destroying you, body and soul, under sanction of law. But we punish convicts who fight for revenge or liberty, and protect the officials who taunt and torture them into doing it.

What a hideous and almost unbelievable situation! Historians wonder that the Aztecs of Cortez' time, with their comparatively high civilization, tolerated human sacrifices. But their human sacrifices were merciful compared with ours. What is cutting out a man's heart on an altar to propitiate a god, to hounding him to death through miserable years in a prison to placate the spite of an accuser, the justice of a court, or the grudge of a warden or guard?

And what is the fruit of it? For pure, carefree, smiling, remorseless wickedness nothing in human annals surpasses the young criminals — black-mailers, bomb-throwers, gunmen — now infesting our cities. "I think no more of killing a houseful of human beings, men, women and children," one of them was quoted as saying the other day, "than of crushing so many beetles." How came such a monster to exist? Why, we bred him, supplied him with the poisonous conditions that generate such beings and can generate nothing else. He had intelligence enough to understand that the established order made earning an honest living hard work; saw thousands living well without labor apparently, other thousands robbing under cover of legal technicalities; a legal profession living by devising statutes to punish crimes and prosecuting the criminals thus manufactured; often living better yet by teaching criminals to escape the penalties which their law imposed. He saw reform schools which instructed such children as he had been to become such men as he was; prisons and penitentiaries which graduated such as he in the latest devices of crime — and he made up his mind that goodness was at bottom humbug, that only a fool would be honest or merciful when money could be got by theft and murder.

We breed poisonous snakes and scorpions, give them no chance to be anything but that, and then wonder they are not doves and butterflies. Things like this gangster are infernal spirits, irreclaimable; but we gain nothing by extirpating the individuals; the black stream which carries them must be dammed at its source. Of the conditions which generate them, a part is the prisons and their keepers. But we are not yet at the root of the matter — the keepers are not primarily to blame. It is the principle which prisons illustrate which attracts and molds keepers till they become often as bad as the men they have charge of, and often much worse.

Prisons mean social selfishness, the disowning of our own flesh and blood. They segregate visible consequences of social disease; but the disease is invisibly present in all parts of the body corporate, and can no more be healed by cutting off the visible part than we can heal small pox by cutting out the pustules. Prisons are not the right remedy; they inflame and disseminate the poison we would be rid of and prevent any chance of cure. The soul of all crime is self-seeking in place of neighborly good will; we send men to prison to get them out of our way, and that is criminal self seeking and ill will to the neighbor — delegating to hirelings our own proper business.

In attempting thus selfishly to extirpate crime, we commit the crime least of all forgivable — the denial of human brotherhood and responsibility. For that crime, no law sends us to prison; yet it is no sentimental notion, but the truth, that it is a crime worse than those for which we imprison men. Prisons are brimful of men less guilty before God than is the society that condemned them. You and I are not excused because we are not society — we are society. Society is not numbers but an idea — a mutual relation; we cannot shift our blame to people in the next street. "Am I my brother's keeper?" was an argument used long ago, and its reception was not encouraging.

Thoughts like these pass through a convict's mind when he discovers that he is on the last leg of his disastrous voyage. He then begins to see the whole matter in its general relations; what use was served? who is the better for it? "Prisons make a good man bad and a bad man worse," is the way I often heard the men at Atlanta put it. The situation, entire and in detail, is preposterous and futile. Grown men, from all ranks of life, or all degrees of intelligence and education, are herded promiscuously, and treated now like wild beasts, now like children. Discipline, in any condition of life, is a good thing, and no people need discipline more than we do; but in prison, discipline means punishment, and there is no discipline in the right sense of the word. A man is "disciplined" when he is starved, or clubbed, or put in the hole, or deprived of his good time.

Military discipline might be beneficial; it implies respect for rightful authority, and orderly conduct of one's own life. Officials in a penitentiary wear uniforms; prisoners wear prison clothes; but, in warm weather, officials go about, indoors and out, in their shirts and with the bearing of loafers; they have no official salutes, and the men are not allowed to salute them — to do so would expose them to "discipline." There is no drill in the prison, no soldierly bearing, no physical control of movement. The men are "lined up" to go to work, but it is a line of slouchers and derelicts; no spirit in it, no respect for themselves or one another, no decent example set by the guards. And yet armies in all ages and in all parts of the world have proved the value of discipline — its necessity, indeed — in all proper and intelligent handling and control of bodies of men; and it is as important for convicts as for soldiers. It would promote cheerfulness, smartness, efficiency; half an hour's lively drill of all the men in prison every morning and evening would do them good, improve relations between guards and prisoners, and lessen the danger of revolts. Why refuse it then? Is it because it would imply something human still lingering in convicts? or because it is feared that convicts taught to act in unison by military drill would combine more readily for mutiny? But order does not naturally lead to disorder but away from it, and mutinies are mostly impromptu affairs, contemplating revenge rather than escape. As for the other argument, a lie is not a sound basis to build on, and it is a lie that convicts are not human. To admit this would facilitate their management.

Physical exercise twice a day in the open air would diminish the sick line, produce better work, and help to put a soul in any prison. Desultory exercise — say two or three hours of baseball on Saturdays — does not meet the need — it emphasizes it rather. But at present the well-nigh universal aim seems to be to render the grey monotony of prison slavery as monotonous and as grey as possible. Any relief from it is opposed or made difficult. It is true that at Atlanta and elsewhere we have music (that is what it is called, and I have no wish to criticize the hardworking and zealous young fellows who produce it in and out of season; and some of the men may like it for aught I know); and that a vaudeville company performs for us occasionally. But I must look these gift horses in the mouth, and say that often we have them less for our own advantage than as an advertisement to the public of the liberality of prison authorities. And there to be sure at my prison, is Uncle Billy, who makes fiddles out of shingles, with nails, and plays on them, all with one hand. But he is — I hope I may now say, he was; for he was to have been paroled the other day; he was a lifer, and a picturesque and wholly innocuous figure — he was, then, permitted to pursue this industry, and visitors used to come and watch him do it; but he, too, was most useful to the prison press agent, and owed the indulgence to that functionary. On the other hand, there is a convict, also a lifer, who cultivated a most remarkable skill in inlaid woodwork, producing really beautiful and artistic boxes and other articles, and found some consolation for his awful fate in making them. But one day while I was there his cell was entered by the guard, his boxes and plant taken away and broken, and he was forbidden to do that work anymore. Visitors did not know about him.

This was malicious. But some of the things done by prison authorities are apparently due to sheer stupidity and ignorance. For example, there were some cows belonging to Atlanta prison, and some of them calved. So there were half a dozen calves more or less, with prospects of more to come. The authorities decided that the expense of rearing these innocents was not justifiable; there was nothing in the rule book about it; besides, the jail was not designed to harbor innocent creatures. The minutes of the conference were not given out, and we can judge of what passed only by the results. The order went forth that the calves be killed; and the killing was actually perpetrated, and the bodies were buried somewhere in the prison grounds. The story seems incredible, but it was corroborated by several men cognizant of the facts. Why not, at least, have turned them into veal?

I was speaking just now of the promiscuous herding together of prisoners in prisons generally. No effort is made to separate the old from the young, the educated from the ignorant; the hardened sinners from the impressionable youths or newcomers; or (at Atlanta, except in the cells), the Negroes from the whites. Association of Negroes with whites, on a footing of enforced outward equality, is bad for both; not because a bad white man is worse than a bad Negro, but because the physical, mental and moral qualities of either react unfavorably upon the other. The Negro, being the more ignorant as a rule, falls more readily into degraded vices; the white man, being as a rule the dominant element in the situation, masters the will of the Negro, but cannot or at least does not erect barriers against the latter's subtle corruption.

We must always bear in mind the abnormal conditions in a prison — the misery of it, the dearth of variety and relaxation, the terrible yearning for some form, any form, of distraction and amusement. The male is parted from the female, and from the resource of children; his nerves are on edge, his natural propensities starved, his thoughts wandering and embittered; he finds no good anywhere, nor any hope of it. He will seize upon any means of abating or dulling his cravings. The

Negro is pliant, unmoral, free from the restraints of white civilization. In the South especially, his subordination to the white is almost a second nature; but he involuntarily avenges himself (as all lower races do upon the stronger) by that readiness to comply which flatters the sense of power and superiority in the other, and leads to evil.

I wish to say, in passing, that my allusion to Negroes in this connection is by no means to be taken as reflecting upon them all; some of the men in Atlanta for whom I had the highest respect were Negroes; and I am inclined to think that the Negro in his right place and function is a desirable element in civilization, and, if we would treat him aright, would do us as much good as we can do him. But the Negro in jail is at his worst, just as white men are, and he is made worse by white companionship. There are more than two hundred of them in Atlanta jail, and some of them are the worst of their kind.

What is true of the association of Negroes with whites is not less true of the association of what are called professional criminals with the young and unhardened. Various prison authorities claim that they have made some effort to prevent this contamination; but the only sign of it that I could ever discover at Atlanta was that the old and the young are not commonly assigned to the same cells. Obviously, however, a man young in years may be old in crime; there can be no security in the age test taken by itself; and no pretense of adopting any other test in a jail is made.

A young fellow, without inherited or acquired criminal tendencies, is sent to jail for some inadvertent and insignificant infraction of law. He had always meant to live straight; he had no enmity against society; he had always thought of himself as well intentioned and law abiding. But here he is; and he is shocked, shamed and appalled at the sudden grip and horror of the jail. Upon a mind thus astounded and distraught the professional criminal seizes and works.

The man of the world — of the criminal world — befriends him, chats with him, heartens him, and soon begins to fascinate him with ideas which had never till now occurred to him. He preaches the injustice and hostility of all mankind, and the hopelessness of the convict once in jail ever again reestablishing himself in the world. He tells his pupil that he is damned forever by his fellow men outside, and that unless he be prepared to lie down and starve, he must fight for life in the only way open to him — the way of crime. Then he proceeds to show him, progressively, the profits and advantages of criminal practices. It is only too easy for the trained crook to overcome the resistance of the unhardened youth; his arguments seem unanswerable; and the wholly justifiable feeling that prison is wrong and an outrage aids the corruptor at every turn. A few months is often enough to turn an innocent boy into a malefactor; a year or more of such instruction leaves him no chance of escape; and many an innocent boy finds himself in a cell for what seems to him a lifetime.

Last July, a justice of a State Supreme Court sentenced Thomas Baker, little more than a child, to fifteen years in jail for — what? If your mother was blind and helpless, and your stepfather came in and abused her and beat her, in your presence, — a big brute with whom you could not hope to contend physically, — what would be your feelings, and what would you be prompted to do? Thomas Baker, trembling and sobbing with rage and anguish, ran out of the house to a neighbor's, borrowed a shotgun, and ran back and emptied it into the brute's body, killing him on the spot. Fifteen years in prison for that! Shall we rejoice and say that justice, at last, is satisfied? — But that is a digression.

No doubt, meanwhile, Thomas Baker's one consolation in life is the reflection that he did succeed in killing his stepfather; and he will be very ready to give ear to an older and more experienced man who tells him that the only difference between good and bad in the world is that those are called good who have power over those who are called bad; and that the only way for him to get even for his wrongs is to become a crook — and not be a fool!

The wardens and guards do not prevent these companionships; whether or not they try to prevent them cannot be affirmed; but to my mind it is plain that they could not prevent it, try as they might. It is an evil inherent in prisons and ineradicable. As long as we have prisons, we shall see judges like Thomas Baker's sending boys to jail for such "crimes" as his, there to stay for fifteen years, more or less, and there to be changed from innocence into diabolism. But Thomas was not innocent, you say, but guilty. What is guilt? I find him innocent of the guilt of standing inactive by and seeing that cruel fist strike his blind mother's beloved face.

Anything unnatural seems unreal. I remarked some time ago that when I was sitting in the court room being tried on charges sworn to by certain post office officials, the dull and sordid scenes would sometimes vanish before me, and I would say to myself, "It is an illusion — what is really taking place is very different from this appearance."

This thought often recurred while I was in prison.

At meal times, the men would file in and take their places at the tables; anon, the meal over, they would rise and file out — men whom I knew, creatures like myself, slaves of an arbitrary power acting in accordance with principles long since known to be false and mischievous. And I would see men whom I knew, men like myself, jeered, insulted, clubbed, dragged to the hole. I would see the dead bodies of men whom I knew, men like myself, rattled out of the gate to the dumping ground and dropped there and forgotten — men with wives and children still living or dead in poverty and shame, their pleas unheard and their wrongs unrighted. I would contemplate the long rows of steel cells, cages for me and men like myself, locking us in for months and years and lifetimes, for an example to others and for the protection of society against our menace. I would glance, as I passed, at the aimless toilers in the workshops, standing or squatting in the foul atmosphere under the eye and rifle of the guard.

I would consider that this dismal and inhuman pageant was going on age after age as a cure for crime — while crime, all the while, was increasing by percentages so astounding that we seek through immigration statistics and records of increase of population to account for it — and in vain. And I would tell myself, once more, that the thing must be an illusion; it was inconceivable that an intelligent nation should tolerate it.

If you found that you were taking bichlorid of mercury by mistake for a sleeping draft, would you go on taking it? or would you clamor for an antidote, waylay doctors for help, and disturb the discreet serenity of hospitals for succor? But the nation, made up of such as you, continues its prison nostrum, which slays a million for bichlorid of mercury's one.

A tragic farce — that is what prisons are. Enclosures of stone and steel are built, and a handful of armed men are given absolute control over several hundred beings like themselves. We, as a community, have erected a system of laws which places us, as a community, in the attitude of penalizing practices which we, as individuals, do not severely condemn. Our morality, as publicly professed, is in advance of our morals as privately exercised. When our neighbor steals or murders, we give him the jail or the chair; but when you and I are charged with such deeds and see the prison or the chair in our near foreground, we discover ourselves to be less convinced than we had imagined of the rectitude of our penal system. Of course, then, the faster we make laws to punish crime, and the more we punish criminals, the more criminals are there to punish. Our hypocrisy gradually is revenged upon us, one after another; one by one we fall into the pit so virtuously digged for others.

And criminal law, meanwhile, becomes constantly more searching and severe in its provisions, seeking to prevent crime by the singular device of employing the best methods for multiplying it. The victims of its activities are miserable enough in jail, and languish and die there, and, if they were not very wicked before, are furnished with every facility to become so; but they have not the consolation of feeling that their being thus immolated on the altar of an outraged but non-existent morality is doing them or anybody else any good. A prominent business man was put in a cell yesterday; a political boss arrives today; a college graduate, a judge, and a religious fanatic are expected next week. But business, politics, the Four Hundred, the Law and religion are no better than they were before.

The procession becomes ever more crowded; when is it to stop? Shall we build more prisons, enact more laws? A leading counsel said the other day, "Commercial crime is an effect and not a cause. The existing system is responsible. We should prevent conditions that lead to crime and resort to criminal courts as little as possible." And an ex-Attorney-General observed, about the same time, "I sometimes think that if we could repeal all the laws on our statute books and then write two laws – 'Fear God' and 'Love your neighbor' – we would get along better" – but he added, "If we could get the people to live up to them!" Yes, that is a prudent stipulation; and it applies just as well to the myriad "laws on our statute books" as to these two.

I call prisons a tragic farce, and am sensible of an unreality in them; but they are fortunately unreal only in the sense that they stand for nothing rational or in line with the proper and natural processes of human life. They are false, and the mind spontaneously reacts against falsity and denies it. But here are half a million (or some say, a million) men every year who suffer actual and real misery from this falsity, and many of whom die of it; that is the tragedy of the farce. And the fact that this falsity, prison, exists among us and has legal standing and warrant, tends to demoralize everyone connected with it, and, more or less, the entire community. If its misery and evil were confined within the circuit of its walls we might endure it; but it spreads outward like a pestilence. It creates little jails in our minds and hearts, though we never beheld the substantial walls nor heard the steel gates clang together. We become jailers to one another, and to ourselves.

There was a woman, the wife of a jailer, with a son four years old. At first, her husband had lived in a house outside the jail, but latterly he had been obliged to dwell within the jail walls.

His wife had seen and known too much of jails to be happy in such a residence. She thought of her son, growing up inside prison walls, and seeing the squalor and daily misery of convicts, and witnessing the cruelties of the guards – mere matters of routine, but horrible nevertheless. Her husband had come up from the ranks in prison life, and was an efficient officer. He had no thought of ever changing his occupation.

One day he left the jail on business, and did not return till one o'clock the next morning. Two keepers who had been left in charge heard four sounds like pistol shots about ten o'clock that night, but supposed them to be torpedoes exploding on the railroad that passed the rear of the jail. There was an interval of an hour or so, and then came two more shots. This time they made a search of the jail, but it did not occur to them to examine the quarters of the warden, where his wife and his little son were.

When the husband and father reached home, he went to his rooms; and there he learned the extent of the misery and loathing which his profession and his dwelling had created in the heart of the woman who had loved him. She lay dead, with a bullet hole in her temple. The little boy was also dead, shot through the heart by his mother's hand. On the floor was the pistol, and four empty shells were scattered about. Those first bullets she must have aimed at her son, but the horror of the situation had shaken her hand, and she had missed him. Then had come that interval, which the two keepers had noticed. What had been in her mind and heart during those endless, brief minutes — her terrors, her memories, her desperate resolve, now failing, now again renewed? If you who read this are a mother, you may perhaps imagine the unspeakable drama of that hour. At last, murder and suicide were better than the jail, and she fired twice again, and this time did not miss.

"Insane" was the verdict. But it is perhaps reasonable to ascribe the insanity to the conditions which found their black fruition in the woman's act, rather than to the despairing creature herself. She had all that most women would ask for happiness — a good husband, a darling little son, an assured support. But there was ever before her eyes the ghastly, inhuman spectacle and burden of the jail; she knew it through and through, and she could endure it no longer. She pictured her innocent boy growing up and following his father's trade. The idea tortured her beyond the limits of her strength, and she accepted the only alternative — death. She was not a prisoner — she was only a looker on; but that is what prison did for her. And our press, echoing our own will, and our courts, voicing our own laws, keeps on shouting, "Put the crooks in stripes; show them no mercy!"

Shall we not pause a moment over the bodies of this mother and her son, over this frenzied murder and suicide? They constitute an arraignment of the prison principle not to be lightly passed over, or commented on with rasping irony by witty editorial writers. That tragedy means something. We cannot lease the community's real estate to hell, for building hell houses and carrying on hell business, supported by our taxes and advocated by our courts and praised (or "reformed") by our penologists — we cannot do that without meeting the consequences. We see how the consequences affected Mrs. Schleth in the Queens County, New York, jail, last summer. It will affect other persons in other ways. But it will affect us all before we are done with it. Hell on earth is a tenant which no community can suffer with impunity.

If prisons are a good thing, it is full time they made good. If they are a bad thing, it is full time they were abolished. The middle courses now being tried in some places cannot succeed; no compromise with hell ever succeeds, however kindly intentioned. But the devil rejoices in them, recognizing his subtlest work done to his hand.

What shall happen if prisons are done away with? That question will doubtless puzzle us for a long time to come. I have no infallible remedy; but I shall touch upon the subject in my next and last chapter.

XVI

IF NOT PRISONS — WHAT?

*W*hat would you advise to check law breaking? A good practical answer to that question would save civilized humanity a great many millions of dollars every year.

The old answer was "jail" for minor cases and death for the others. There was much to be urged in favor of the latter. Dead men not only tell no tales, but they commit no crimes. Kill all criminals and crime would cease. The device has been tried — it was tried in England for a while — but the result was disappointing. It threatened to decimate the population; and in spite of logic, it failed to discourage law breakers. Criminals seemed to get used to being hanged, and drawn and quartered — they no longer minded it. There is a psychological reason for that, no doubt; though it is not so sure that psychology as understood and practiced today can find out what it is.

Moreover, the spy system, which always accompanies and thrives upon severe legislation, became so productive of informations that it was soon clear that the end would be the indictment not so much of a tenth part of the population as of all but a tenth — or even more. So a compromise was made; only murderers should be killed. That did not lessen the number of murders, and seems rather to have increased them; for the impulse to murder is commonly a very strong impulse, producing a brain condition in which consequences are not weighed. Also, when the community takes life for life, it appears to weaken the general respect for life, and men can be hired to do a killing job for small sums. Sentimental persons, too, insist on making heroes of convicted murderers, which in a degree, perhaps, counteracts the depressing conditions surrounding them. So we made another compromise.

This is not on the statute books, but it operates actively, nevertheless. It is the development of the appeal industry among lawyers for the defense.

"I will teach you to respect human life," says the judge, "by depriving you of your own."

"Don't worry, my boy," says the culprit's counsel, patting him on the back; "you'll die sometime, I suppose; but nothing is more certain than that it won't be on the day set for your execution by his honor. And I'll risk my reputation on your death being no less in the ordinary course of nature than his honor's, and very likely — for he looks like a diabetes patient — not so soon."

These anticipations often prove well grounded.

No one in the court room, therefore, is often more cheerful and confident than is the prisoner doomed to the noose or the chair. Besides, if all else fails, he may petition for pardon or for life imprisonment.

In short, the death penalty stays on the statute books, but the community does not want it, though it has not the courage to demand its abolition outright. It forfeits its self-respect, and the murderer draws the inference that it is safer to murder than to steal. A thoroughbred man does not compromise; he does one thing or he does the other, retains his self-respect, and commands that of his fellows, whether or not he be "successful." This nation is not thoroughbred as regards its laws, and is neither self-respecting nor respected.

However, there is agitation for the abolition of the death penalty; and possibly the futility and absurdity of such a punishment may finally strike the persons whom we have picked out as the wisest and ablest among us, and have put in our legislatures to tell us what to do and not to do. Absurd though legal killings may be, they are not so absurd as the persuasion that death is the worst thing that can happen to a man. It involves little or no suffering, and is over in a moment. Imprisonment involves much suffering, and lasts long, not to speak of the disgrace of it, to those who can feel disgrace. The serious feature about killing is, that it is final for this state of being, and when we do it we do we know not what. But that is for the community to consider, not the victim.

We cannot know what death means, but we can and do know what imprisonment means, and so far as our mortal senses can tell us, it is worse than death. But while we may abolish the death penalty easily, the suggestion to abolish imprisonment staggers us like an earthquake. Every moral instinct in our little souls leaps up and shrieks in protest; and if that be not enough, we fall back with full conviction upon the consideration of security of property. It is impossible to consider a measure which would leave crimes against property unpunished. And what other punishment for them than imprisonment is there or can there be?

Argument upon this matter evidently bids fair to drag in pretty nearly everything else — sociology, political economy, religion, politics, law, medicine, psychology, — the whole conduct of our life and history of our opinions. But I must content myself here with a few words, and leave volumes to others. That personal property has value is undeniable; whether it be worth what it costs us, in the long run, and from all points of view, may be left to the judgment of generations to come. Law in its origins is Divine; whether our human derivations from it partake of its high nature is debatable. Medicine and psychology, professing much, have not explained to us what or why we are, or what is our degree of responsibility for what we are and do. Politics sits on the bench and argues through the mouth of the public prosecutor; is justice safe in their keeping?

This age did not invent prisons, but inherited them from an unmeasured past. It is a primitive device. The mother locks up her naughty child in the closet or ties its leg to the bed-post. Society does the same with its naughty children, though with one difference — the mother still loves her child. She, following the example of God, chastens in love; but what do we chasten in? If not in love, then in hate or indifference, or to get troublesome persons out of our way without regard to harm or benefit to them. And that is not Godlike but diabolical, being based upon selfishness. The community being stronger than the individual, its selfishness is tyranny or despotism. Many of us indeed may be willing to admit that prisons are perhaps objectionable or altogether wrong in theory; but surely something must be done with malefactors, and if not prison, what?

The only answer hitherto is compromise — the old answer, fresh once more from the devil's inexhaustible repertoire. We are willing to abolish the death penalty, which is more merciful than imprisonment; but we are unwilling to abolish the latter, because in spite of its inhumanity, it seems to protect our property. In other words, we consider our own interests exclusively, and the culprit's not at all — though we still protest that our object in imprisoning is as much the individual's reformation, as our own security. The fact, however, that imprisonment brutifies and destroys instead of reforming is beginning to glare at us in a manner so disconcerting and undeniable, that we feel something has to be done; and in accordance with our ancient habit and constitutional predisposition, that something turns out to be compromise. We sentenced for murder, but put obstacles in the way of carrying the sentence out. On the same principle, we will now retain prisons, but make them so agreeable that convicts will not mind being committed to them.

That is the compromise; and it is already in operation here and there. In the first place, numbers of good men and women, with motives either religious or humanitarian or both, obtained leave to visit prisons, talk with the inmates, give them religious exhortations, supply them with some forms of entertainment, and in other ways try to lighten the burden of their penal slavery. These persons deserve great credit. It was not so much the exhortations or entertainments that did good, as the idea thereby aroused in convicts that somebody cared for them. Between, them and the community there was still war to the knife; but certain individuals, separate from the community, were not hostile but well disposed toward them.

A man fallen into evil may sometimes be redeemed by coming to feel this; he will try to be good for the sake of the person who was kind to him in his misery. I once asked a comrade in Atlanta whether if the warden were to give him twenty dollars and tell him to go to the town, make a purchase for him, and return, he would do so? He said, "No," and when I asked him why, replied that he would know the warden had something up his sleeve, and was not on the square in his proposition. I then named a certain benefactor of the prisoners outside the prison, and asked if he would do it for that person? After some consideration, he said that he would, because he "would hate to disappoint" that person, and would believe in the bona fides of that person's request. This man was held to be rather a bad case; but he was still capable of acting honorably, if the right motives were supplied.

But this is not enough. The great mass of convicts could not be reformed by "hating to disappoint" any particular person who had been kind to them or trusted them. Their personal gratitude to the individual would not stem the tide of their well grounded conviction that people in general were neither trustful nor kind; and the numberless and constant temptations of their life after liberation would prove too strong for them. There have been instances to the contrary; touching and beautiful instances, some of them; but they are far from establishing the principle that Christian Endeavorers, or Salvation Armies, or prison angels, or angelic wardens can effect the reform of men in prison. Some stimulus much more powerful is required.

The next step in compromise was to improve the physical conditions in the prison; to give more light and air and exercise, better food; to mitigate or do away with dark holes, assaults and tortures. There were many zealous critics of these leniencies; they said we were making prisons so attractive that criminals, so far from being deterred from crime by fear of punishment, would commit crimes in order to be sent to prison. And they could quote in confirmation cases of men who had accepted liberation at the end of their terms reluctantly, or had actually refused it, or of men who had voluntarily returned to prison after having been discharged.

There have been such cases; but they prove, not the attractiveness of prisons, but their power to kill the manhood in a man. What does it not suggest of outrage and degradation perpetrated upon a human soul, that he should come to prefer a cell and a master to freedom! There may be slaveries so soft as to invite the base and pusillanimous, but they are more rather than less depraving than cruelties to all that makes honorable and useful manhood. The deepest and essential evil of prisons is not hardship and torture, but imprisonment. If choice could be made between the two, every manly man would choose the former. No disgrace is inherent in hardship and torture; but imprisonment brands a man as unfit to associate with his kind. No mortal creature has or can have the right to inflict it, nor any aggregation of mortals.

This is a hard saying, but I will stand by it. There were criminals of all kinds in Atlanta with whom I was brought into contact. One had grown rich by organizing a system of "white slavery" on a large scale. He dealt in woman's dishonor and turned it into cash, and he saw nothing wrong in it. This man was advanced in years, he was incapable of regarding women in any other light than as merchandise, he was insensible to their misery, and laughed at their degradation. He was physically repulsive; his face and swollen body suggested a huge toad. It would be foolish to associate the idea of reform with such a creature. I felt a nauseous disgust of him; he seemed on the lowest level of human nature.

But, contemplating him during some months, I saw little touches of kindliness and good humor in him; he did not hate his fellows, nor wish them to hate him. If the other prisoners ostracized him or cursed him, he was painfully sensible of it, and even perplexed, and would try to win their favor. I perceived that he had always lived in a world of filth and sin, and knew no other. In that world, he had doubtless not done the best he might, but which of us can say he himself has done that? Had I been born and bred as he was, what would I be? What right had I to call him unfit for my companionship? I had no right to do it, nor had any other man. At last I shook him by the hand and wished him well.

There were men there who had committed merciless robberies, cruel murders, heartless swindles, abominable depravities. I have felt greater temperamental aversion from many highly respectable persons than I did from them. Their crimes were one thing, they were another. Not that crime does not corrupt a man – stain him of its color. But there is always another side to him, a place in him which it has not dominated. Given his conditions, we cannot affirm that he is not as good as we are – that he is unfit to associate with us. And it behooves us always to bear it in mind that to affirm the contrary is an unpardonable sin against him of whom we affirm it; it works more evil in him than anything else we can do, and places us who repudiate him in a truly hideous posture. Shall we be more fastidious than God?

All crime is hateful; but I came to the conclusion that there is only one crime which prompts us to hate the criminal as well as his crime itself. For this crime is one which originates in our heart; it is not forced upon us by need or passion or heredity. Therefore, it permeates every fiber of our being, every thought of our mind, every impulse of our soul; and we cannot say of it, this is one thing and we are another. It is an unhuman crime; and yet there is no punishment for it among human laws; rather, it is regarded as a mark of superiority. The most respectable persons in the community are most apt to commit it. And it was upon the suggestion and initiative of this crime that penal imprisonment was invented, and is perpetrated to this day.

Christ condemned it; Christianity is based upon its repudiation; we call ourselves Christians; and yet it is the characteristic crime of our civilization. The Law and the Prophets are against it; it defies every injunction of the Decalogue, for it takes the name of God in vain, it steals, murders, commits adultery, covets and bears false witness; but we clasp it to our bosoms, and actually persuade ourselves that it is the master key to the gates of Heaven. What is it? It is the thought in a man's heart that he is better, more meritorious, than his fellow.

It is engendered, most often, by a successful outward morality – conformity to the letter of the Commandments – the whitening of the outside of the sepulcher. But the stench of the interior loathsomeness oozes through. The only person unaware of that stench is the man himself. There is but one cure for it — what we call Regeneration; which makes us sensible of that deadly odor, and drives us freely and sincerely to detest ourselves in dust and ashes and bitter humiliation, to pity, succor and love our brethren, and to wrestle with the angel of the Lord for mercy. But we prefer to seek salvation from evil in the building of prisons.

Now, this crime may survive even in prisons; but it is rarer there than in any other aggregation of human beings. Therefore, there is a wonderful sweetness in the prison atmosphere. It is a sweetness which is perceived amid all the dreariness, stagnation and outrage, and it rises above the vapors of physical crime, for it is a spiritual sweetness. There men are locked in their cells, but the whited sepulcher is shattered, and its sorry contents are purified by the pure light of humiliation, confession and helplessness; there are no hypocrites there, no masks, no holier-than-thou paraders. Their crimes have been proclaimed, and branded upon their backs; pretenses are at an end for them. It was wonderful to look into a man's face and see no disguise there. "I am guilty — here I am!" This experience took the savor out of ordinary worldly society for me. I go here and there, and everywhere there is masquerading — the weaving of a thin deception which does not deceive. We were sincere and humble in prison; but that is a result which the builders of prisons hardly foresaw.

There was one more step toward compromise — to take the prisoner out of his cell and send him outdoors without guards or precautions, nothing but his promise that he would return when the work to which he was assigned was done.

I read the other day an agreeable account of this "honor system." The men were employed on road making chiefly, enjoyed the benefit of free air and the outdoor scene, and kept order and faith among themselves. But the prison walls were still around them, though unseen. They were told that any attempt to escape would be punished by deprivation thenceforth of all liberties — any attempt! and if the escape were successful, the fugitive would know that the chances of recapture were a thousand against one. Moreover, it was laid down that the escape or attempt of any member of the gang would react upon the liberties of all.

This made the men guards over one another; it was not honor but self-preservation that was relied on. And in any event, there was the prison at last; the chain might be lengthened to hundreds of miles, but it held them still. They were convicts; when their terms were up, they would be jail birds. Society had set them apart from itself; they were a contamination. "You are not fit to mingle with us on an equal footing."

Society might condescend to them, be friendly and helpful to them, but — admit them of its own flesh and blood? — well, not quite that! "We forgive you, but on sufferance; it is really a great concession; you must show your gratitude by good works."

Oh, the Pharisees! the taint of it will not come out so easily; and until it does come out, to the last filthy trace of it, prisons will continue to be prisons, and compromises will be vain.

I repeat — the evil of prisons is the imprisonment. You must not deprive a man of his liberty. His liberty is his life. He may, and probably he will, use his liberty to the endangering of your property or comfort; but has your own career been wholly free from infringement upon the rights of your neighbor? If you send him to prison, you ought to link arms with him and go there, too. You have not been convicted by a court, but your own secret self-knowledge convicts you. When the prison doors close upon you, you will discover that you have suffered an injustice — that you are the victim of a blind stupidity. Not in this way can you be reformed. All genuine reformation must proceed from within you — it cannot be compelled by locks and bars; freedom is essential to it. Locks and bars arouse only the impulse to break through them, and this primal and righteous impulse leaves you no leisure to think of relieving your soul from stains of guilt.

The only imprisonment to which a man can properly be subjected is that imprisonment of good in him which evil-doing operates automatically and spontaneously; any outside meddling with that operation hinders, confuses, or defeats it. Crime weakens and shackles you; to put shackles on the body is no way to remove shackles from the spirit. It is the gross blunder of a brutal and immature era, but we have continued it down to the present day. Jail is still the remedy.

The newspapers the other day told of a man who had been sentenced to forty years in jail for an assault. A woman, hearing the verdict, said, "Well, that's better than nothing; but he ought to have got life!" We are told in the Bible that we must not let the sun go down upon our wrath. The wrath of this lady could not be appeased with forty years. Think of what that culprit will be after forty years in jail. Assuming for the sake of argument the extreme absurdity that he is alive by that time, picture to yourself a fellow creature of his — and a woman — saying, "I won't forgive you yet." I pity her more than I do him, whose troubles in this world will probably soon be over. But when her time comes, with what face, on what plea, shall she ask forgiveness?

But if there are to be no prisons, what shall we do to be saved from crime?

I cannot for my part imagine any hard and fast plan being laid down in advance. But it would seem reasonable, to begin with, to free ourselves from the social crime of claiming superiority to our brethren. Having removed that beam from our eyes, we may see more clearly how to abate the motes in the criminal's. If we can bring ourselves to regard prisoners and jail birds as inferior to ourselves only in good fortune, which has kept us out of jail and put them in, we may find ourselves on the road to remedying their lapses from moral virtues.

The majority of prison crimes are against property, and are motived by want and poverty. If the man had opportunity to work for his living, he would as a rule abstain from stealing. Other crimes are committed in passion; but such criminals need education and training in self-control, and (often) removal of the provocations which set their passions afire. Many other crimes, and almost all vices, are due to physical or mental disease, or to actual insanity. It is the doctor and not the jailer who should seek the cure of these.

But there are also some persons, chiefly brought up or brought down in our cities, who practice crimes, apparently, for sheer love of evil. These gunmen gangs are the most depraved and malignant members of the community; they will not work, and they rob and murder not from want or passion, but because the suffering of their victims gives them pleasure and ministers to their pride and self-esteem. Most of these gangs, as we have too much reason to believe, stand in with the police, giving them a percentage of their plunder, and getting protection from them for their misdeeds.

These creatures, as I have already suggested, are the distillation of the various evils in our cities which society has failed frankly to face, or genuinely to attempt to lessen. They are not responsible for their existence, and, as they indicate a general condition, it can do no good to kill them or otherwise put them out of the way; others would take their place. They are not insane in the common sense, but they are the product of insane social circumstances, responsibility for which rests on us. They must be taken in hand individually, by workers self-consecrated to that duty, and deterred from doing evil, and showed the value of doing good. One might work a lifetime with some of them, and have little to show for it in the end; but it took a long time to build the pyramids and the Panama Canal, and to advance from the dugout of the savage to the *Mauretania*. It is work better worth doing than any of these.

Taking the situation by long and large, society must cease to be a sham and become truly social. The thing seems inconceivable, and still less practicable; but it is not. Nor has history failed to admonish us that it has sometimes been the most difficult and improbable things which have been nevertheless accomplished; as if their very difficulty, and the labor and self-sacrifice involved in doing them, were themselves a stimulus.

Europe, a handful of centuries ago, at the behest of a fanatical priest or two, forsook all else and spent a generation in journeying to Palestine and trying to get a certain city from the Turks.

The city was worth nothing to Europe; it was an idea that set them crusading. Nothing else seemed so unpractical and feeble as the gospel of Christ; but it crumbled the Roman Empire into dust, and has kept the world guessing and maneuvering ever since — never more than today. On the other hand, if you propose an easy job, something that can be done with one hand tied behind you, and your attention is diverted, it is apt to remain undone. Nobody can get up an interest in it. But talk of an expedition to the South Pole, or a flight round the earth in a biplane, with certainty of appalling hardships and all the odds in favor of death, and you are mobbed with volunteers. Human nature likes to test its thews and sinews.

Perhaps, however, nothing else was ever so difficult as to turn from our flesh pots, our dinners and tangos, our summer resorts and winter resorts, our business and idleness, and undertake to substitute for prisons our personal care and help for criminals — to remove the causes which led them to crime, to convince them of our good faith and good will, and to disabuse them of their suspicion that we distrust them, condescend to them, and despise them. For this prodigal brother of ours has become a very unsightly and unattractive object during these thousands of years of his sojourn among the pigsties and corn husks. He does not speak in our language or observe our manners or contemplate our ideals, or care for our refinements. We shall have to read again the fairy stories where the prince has been changed by evil enchantment into some uncouth and repulsive monster, but was redeemed to human form by sympathy. The evil spell was of our working, and it behooves us to overcome it. No one else can.

We must abolish the title of criminal as applied to any class or individuals of our race in distinction from others, and use those of unfortunates or scapegoats instead. They are our victims, and our salvation depends upon our making good to them the evil we have done them. It will not suffice to delegate the job to money, or to persons chosen for that purpose; we must do it ourselves — make it one of the main occupations of our lives. Riches and culture are fine things, but making good out of evil is better. Its rewards may not be so immediate or so visible, but they are real and permanent.

But I do not think morality will be enough to energize the effort;

morality should always be the incident and consequence of religious feeling, not an aim in itself. As soon as it becomes an aim in itself, it leads to self-righteousness, and paralyzes human love in its marrow. And it is love, far more than wisdom, that is needed here. Love God and keep His commandments; unless you first love Him, His commandments will be left undone, or done only in the letter, which is the worst form of not doing. But the way to love God is to love the neighbor, and the neighbor is the criminal.

Who shall have the immortal credit of abolishing prisons — ourselves, or our posterity? It will surely be done by our posterity if not by ourselves.

Appendix

*B*ubonic plague cannot be reformed; it is bad intrinsically and must be extirpated. Born in Asiatic filth, ignorance and barbarism, it now menaces modern civilization. While it killed millions in India or China only, we endured it, but when we hear it at our own door we turn and listen. The instinct of self-preservation, older and often more urgent than Christianity, says, "Destroy it or it will destroy you!"

We send our scientific martyrs to the front, who perish in the effort to solve the deadly riddle. We would pour out billions of money in the fight if need come. Rich men will spend all they possess rather than die, and see those they love die of it. Nations will do the same. Compromises are not considered; no one talks of reforming the Black Death. Unless it be jettisoned from the Ship of Civilization, progress and enlightenment go by the board.

And yet the disease is but physical — attacks the body only. It does not touch the immortal spirit. It has not rooted itself in the entrails of our social economy and order. It does not undermine our common humanity, or bankrupt human charity and infect it with indifference, suspicion or mutual hostility. It does not prompt law and justice to play the roles of persecution and oppression. It does not arrogate to itself the right to judge between man and his brother man, protecting the one and damning the other. It does not authorize us to say of the victim of sickness or circumstance, "Throw him to the lions!" and to affirm of his torture and death, "Serves him right!" Compared with such a plague as that, the Black Death would appear benign.

Penal imprisonment is an institution of old date, born of barbarism and ignorance, nurtured in filth and darkness, and cruelly administered. It began with the dominion of the strong over the weak, and when the former was recognized as the community, it was called the authority of good over evil. Man took the reins of government from the hands of the Almighty, and amended the Ten Commandments with statute law.

Evil is — to prefer the good of self before good of the neighbor; crime is to act in accordance with that preference. Every son of Adam is born to evil, and society is but his multiplication; but society could exist only by the compromise that the hostility of man against neighbor should mask itself as mutual forbearance. Impossible that everyone should possess everything; therefore dissimulate your greed and divide. But certain persons, missing their share either through non-conformity with the doctrine, or by force of circumstances, stuck to the old principle of each man for himself, and became "criminals." Their hand was against society, and society's against them.

In eras before society became integrated, some of these non-conformists prevailed over such strength as could be mustered against them, and by hearty and forthright robberies and murders came to be leaders and rulers of men — earls, barons, kings. The aristocracy of modern Europe is descended from such stout rebels. They became reconciled with, and organized, society, and aided it in war against the weaker of their own sort; and it was they who devised prisons for such captives as it might be inexpedient to kill outright.

All this did not alter the truth that all men are alike evil, and that such as are not also criminals, forbear — at the outset at least — from motives of enlightened selfishness. But in course of time, even enforced good behavior breeds good intent, and "good" people. For God rules us through our very sins, and will lead us, (with our passive cooperation) to religion and regeneration in the end.

But the segregation of a criminal class is manifestly human, not Divine; economic, not moral; illusory, not real. Consequently, pains and penalties inflicted by men upon other men, by society upon individuals, by the community upon "criminals," have no warrant of Divine authority, but only of superior numbers or physical strength. The only proper punishment for crime is the criminal's conscience, and if he have none available, he is liable to the natural contingency that violence breeds violence, and may get him in the long run — though it often happens that, measured by mortal standards, the run is not long enough for us to see the finish. We may console ourselves with the reflection that a finish, somewhere, there will be.

Meanwhile, it is for persons of intelligence and good will to consider whether, aside from physical penalties or jailing, we possess means for inducing criminals to abstain from crime. Let us leave abstract arguments and come to facts.

My license to speak in the premises is due to my being an ex-convict, sentenced to Atlanta Penitentiary for a year and a day, but recently released on "good time." I shall first give you a notion of what jail is, and of what is done and suffered there; then consider what has hitherto been done to alleviate prison conditions and abuses; and end with inquiring whether these measures, actively prosecuted, will prove adequate to the need, or whether something else and more is demanded. If so — *what?*

Purgatory is usually understood to be — as its etymology indicates — a place where persons encumbered with evil accretions may have them purged out of them, or stripped off from them, and so be fitted for the purity and innocence of Heaven. It is therefore a beneficent institution. Hell, on the other hand, was the inheritance of those whose evil is ingrowing and cannot be removed — a place where they may live out their diabolical or satanic natures and be punished and tortured by those of like nature with themselves.

Our prisons were, in the beginning, frankly hellish in their object; men who had incurred personal or society hostility were put in them to be tormented from motives of hate and revenge. But during the last few generations the humanitarian idea has come into being and has not only ameliorated prison conditions in some prisons and to some extent, but has caused prisons in general to cease being frank and to become hypocritical — to pretend that they are purgatories, aiming not at revenge but at reform. This pretense has been so industriously and sagaciously put forward that ninety-nine outsiders out of a hundred are misled by it, and believe that prisons are not, still, administered for the destruction of their inmates, physical, mental and moral, with such circumstances of cruelty and brutality as happen to suit the humor of the arbitrary and irresponsible guards and wardens; but that they are uniformly conducted with an eye to wooing away prisoners from sin and crime, and persuading them of the beauty and policy of honesty, gentleness and goodness. In fact it is probable that almost everybody believes this, except the wardens and guards, and the prisoners themselves — and a few Thomas Mott Osbornes and other prison workers who have had an amateur peep inside the walls and caught a fleeting glimpse of a horror or two before the discreet managers could get the door shut.

Not only so, but we read indignant articles in our morning paper about the coddling of criminals; and witty writers will have it that prisons are gentlemen's clubs where all the comforts of refined life are combined with a voluptuous idleness, or with only work enough to avert ennui. Criminals are depicted as waiting in cues at the gates of prisons for admission, like the public at the doors of a popular theater; though at the same time in another column, you may find the statement that, in view of modern legal technicalities, it has become almost impossible to get a man into jail. According to the logic of the witty writers, this near-impossibility should be more deplored by the technicality-inhibited criminals than by anybody else.

Prisons are not purgatories, nor gentlemen's clubs; they are just as much hell as they ever were, and as their managers can make them. Apart from any special leniency of local conditions, prisons are hell because they are prisons — because you are confined there and cannot get out; because you are a slave and have no redress; because your manhood is degraded; because despotic power is entrusted to the men who handle you, though they are never any better than you are, and are usually much worse, and regard you as an asset to make profit from, a thing to be driven and insulted to the last extremity and beyond it, and not as a human being. Prisons are hell because convicts are punished for trivial and whimsical reasons as much as for serious ones; and whether or not the punishment involve actual physical torture, the insolence, disgrace and injustice of it remain. Prisons are hell intrinsically, and always will be; and whoever doubts it has only to commit a crime and be sent to prison; that is the end of doubts.

Let every judge, attorney general, district attorney, and juryman at a trial spend a bona fide term in jail, and there would be no more convictions — prisons would end. Every convict and ex-convict knows that, and eternity will be too short to obliterate the knowledge in him.

The unctuous plausibility of the pretense that prisons are beneficent purgatories and not hells renders it the more sickening. Life is a God-given discipline for men, and at best a severe one; but if we believe in God, we know it is given in love, for loving ends. All mortal life is an imprisonment; the laws of it are essential and natural, and breaking them involves essential and natural penalties. God deputed this régimen of love to parents, and to those who deal with their fellow creatures from impulses of parental or brotherly love; but He never licensed any man to punish another from revenge or hate, or in mere indifference. He licensed no man to do it, nor any community or nation. And whoever does it, serves not God but the devil; and if any crime be unpardonable, it is that, because it is not essential or natural, but an usurpation against nature, and breeds not reform but more evil.

Prison officials, in their treatment of prisoners, are not actuated by love, but by indifference to suffering, or by animosity and brutality, or by desire of profit, and therefore their work is impious and wicked. And the longer they hold their office, the more hardened do they become to the spectacle of suffering and outrage; the more heedless of justice and mercy do they grow. They grow to disbelieve in any human truth and goodness; all men are to them criminals actual or potential; breathing and dwelling amidst crime, it enters into their own blood and temper. They will have their debt to pay; but neither may those escape who ignorantly or carelessly appointed them to office and hold them there — the Government, and the nation which creates Government as its representative. Ignorance does not excuse; knowledge on these subjects is a sacred duty. Man cannot break the bonds of his brotherhood with man; the blood shed will be required of him, and the usury of misery and tears.

"Throw him to the lions! — serve him right!" Most of us have joined in that barbarous cry upon occasion. But some of us have sickened at the slaughter, and are for paring the lions' claws, or at least exhorting them to roar less savagely, and to devour their prey in secret. But the lions, with their attendant hyenas and jackals, have so long been accepted as indispensable to the order and majesty of the State, that no one likes to stand up to his God-given intuitions, and demand the abolition of the whole prison circus. We hardly realize that the harm criminals do society cannot equal the harm that society does to itself by its handling of them and attitude toward them. The circus must go on, of course; but — let us ameliorate its coarser features!

Let us make our prisons hygienic — larger cells, drainage, air, exercise; let us select nice, kindly persons for guards and wardens; let us give the convicts useful industrial occupation, which will not only keep them happy and sane, but pay the cost of their keep to a tender-hearted but economic state; let us even be very venturesome, and — with reasonable precautions — put the men on their honor, suffer them to run out a little way and labor in the free sunshine, upon their promising to remember that they are not really free, and to return at night to their cages. And after they have served their terms, and the souls within them are moribund or dead, let us get or solicit jobs for them, and at all events keep a sentimental eye on them for a while. All this — only let us keep our prisons! For think what would happen if those terrible creatures were let loose upon us, to keep on murdering and robbing us with impunity! Remember that they are a class apart, unlike ourselves, whose perverted nature, though it may be lulled by gentleness and tact, can never become truly human.

No: the Laodicean spirit will not serve! I do not ridicule or belittle the efforts of generous and genial men and women who give their spare time, or their whole time, to bettering the plight of convicts. But the diabolical spirit of the prisons sneers at them, and sits undisturbed. Let air and sunshine come to outer courts and clean-swept cells; the star-chambers and the secret dungeons remain. Let the outraged creatures out, to stray to the extent of their honor-tether; they are slaves and prisoners still. There were compassionate reformers in Ancient Egypt, who tried to make the lot of the captive Israelites easier; but the heart of Pharaoh was hardened, and God Himself must intervene before he would let the people go. Nor does it help that the slaves themselves are grateful for hard-won privileges, and that we read urbane descriptions of smiling and rosy felons working on state roads in "Don't Worry" camps. Is it ground for congratulation that the very victims of the specious pretense of the eternal right and necessity of prisons should have succumbed to that delusion? Does it not prove a need yet more urgent to be up and at them? Is it not humiliating to know that men, our brothers, partakers of our common nature, can be so abased as to kiss the rod, and joke about their fetters, and accept as favor what none is entitled to deny them?

Prisons are hell — we come back to that; and they are not and cannot be made purgatories. Men competent to make them purgatories are not to be had at Government prices; no duties more onerous than those of a fit conscientious warden exist under the state; and how can we look for such a man at a four or five thousand dollar salary? Twenty-five or even fifty thousand would be moderate, and the men who are worth that are in some other business. The foremost citizens of the nation would not be too good for the job, and we content ourselves with ward heelers and rough-necks, who undertake it not for the salary, but for the graft that goes with it and exceeds it. Politics and graft sit in the warden's office, and walk the ranges in guards' uniform, and crush the manhood out of our brothers for money, and out of sheer wanton inhumanity. Of all the inmates of the jail, these men are the veritable and incorrigible and unpardonable criminals; for they were not driven to crime by passion, hunger, drink or ignorance, they have not been reduced to the state of desperate pariahs, outcasts and scapegoats of the race, but they willingly embrace the function entrusted to them — the Government license to steal, bully, torture and murder — with a grotesque sanctimonious leer for the public, and for the convicts — what! The régimen of hell!

This writer's statements seem a trifle emphatic, do they not? May we not surmise that they are motived by some personal grudge? have we not heard an old adage — "No thief e'er felt the halter draw with good opinion of the law?" Would it not be prudent to take all this with a grain of salt? Shall we be driven to rash measures by the objurgations of an ex-convict?

Of the right or wrong of my conviction and sentence I am not to speak here, nor do they specially interest me now, except as illustrations of the working of the machine. But personal grudge against officials of my prison I have none. I was treated with consideration and lenity. I came out in better condition upon the whole than I went in, both of body and spirit, though nothing would have been easier than to murder me under the forms of routine prison discipline. What was the reason of this? I was never informed; I might guess at it, but I don't know. Nevertheless, the sweetness and light of the prison dispensation as regarded myself did not blind my eyes or stop my ears to what was being done to others, not elected to dreams thus beautiful. I saw men beside whom I sat at meat or labored in the vineyard, fading and failing day by day; I saw some of them die of broken hearts or broken bodies; I heard their stories and was certified of their truth; I saw the cart rattle out of the gate with the pine box containing the body of the man who could only thus find freedom; I visited the graves of those who had been needlessly and sometimes wantonly slain. I could not ignore these things because I myself escaped them. After a few months of durance, I went forth free, leaving behind me men as good as I or better, sentenced to serve years, lifetimes, under treatment which I cannot imagine myself as surviving at all. My grudge is deep, but no personal one.

I shall not at present discuss Government measures of so-called mitigation — suspended sentence, parole, indeterminate sentence. In the intention of their originators they may have appeared beneficent; in practice, they proved sinister and abominable means to cruelty and despotism. There can be no compromises with hell.

But can I pretend to solve the age-long problem of the right handling of crime in the community? I am not wiser than my fellows, but I have felt and known at first hand more of certain grievous wrongs than most of them have, and even those who have known and felt may not possess the opportunity or facility to speak that I have. I must say what is in me, and leave to the collective judgment of the nation, and to the further teaching of time, what shall be changed, abolished, and done.

One thing seems plain — there must be an act of faith. Worldly wisdom and enlightened selfishness have been tried out thoroughly and are thoroughly discredited. Their proposal was first to cure crime, and only after that was done, to abolish prisons. But it turns out that prisons generate, teach, perpetuate and inflame crime; never extirpate it, though they often deter specific persons from continuing a criminal career by either killing them outright, or destroying in them their effective spiritual manhood. Therefore the selfishly enlightened and worldly-wise shake their heads and declare that crime in criminals is ineradicable. If medicine for crime be futile, save as a temporary physical preventive, all that is left to us is to continue it as a preventive, while admitting its impotence as a cure. Protection of society is the paramount consideration.

Yes: but is society protected by prisons? John Jones has been jailed for burglary, it is true; but straightway Tom Brown, Jem Smith and Reginald Montmorency start in as train-robber, murderer and confidence man. We have sown the dragon's tooth, and reap three for one. Lynch your Negro, and before the smell of roast flesh is out of the air, several fresh cases of rape are reported. — But there is no visible connection between alleged cause and effect — it just happens so. — Yes, but if it does happen almost invariably, we cannot avoid the suspicion that a connection, even though invisible to the outward eye, there must be.

Moreover, on what grounds does society claim protection against evils for which its own constitution and administration are responsible? The greatest happiness of the greatest number? — Are we so happy, then? The happy man has been sought for long, but the seekers still delay to return. To what end shall we cut the cancer out of the body politic, if it sprout again in a more vital spot? If we could only reach the cancer germ! — But the germ is not found by the knife. There are more criminals than there ever have been heretofore. The jails are overcrowded; we must either build new ones, or transform those we have into castles of refuge to which good people may fly to escape the criminal nations outside; there will be no overcrowding then!

Let worldly wisdom and enlightened selfishness retire, and listen for a while to believers — fanatics even. An act of faith: that is to say, first abolish jails, and then see what can be done with criminals! It is vain to beat about the bush; we must face the alternative. The syllogism runs thus: criminality is incompatible with true civilization — with a normal and secure society. Jails are a crime; society makes and warrants jails; therefore society is criminal. And the abolition of jails — repudiation both of the principle and of the concrete fact — is the only way to social redemption.

The one escape from this conclusion is, of course, denial that jails are a crime. I will not further contest that point, but only repeat: Let the deniers and doubters try a year behind the bars, themselves, and then register their revised opinion.

But, obviously, though jails are a crime, they are not the only crime; there are also the specific crimes of individual malefactors; and it seems inevitable that by relieving these of prison restraints, we must increase the prevalence of crime in the community, however much we might be absolving the community itself from its characteristic crime of jails. Is there any answer to that?

I am not logically constrained to make any, because if jails are a crime they should be abolished, let the consequences be what they may. But I will suggest two considerations. Individual crimes are the outcome either of a pathological condition in the agent, or of conditions in his nurture and environment which are due to social negligence or hardness of heart. These conditions tempted him beyond his power of resistance, or reduced him to desperation; in other words, no sane and normal man commits crimes for the fun of it, and as not he but society created the conditions, the latter must shoulder its part, at least, of the blame. And this implies that it should devote itself to so improving these evil conditions as to give the criminal a fair chance.

That is easily written, but it involves nothing less than a radical readjustment of our whole attitude toward life. It also brings me to my second suggestion — that this should be accomplished. We must embark upon a great adventure — the greatest, so far as I know, ever undertaken in this world. We must overcome the anti-human prejudice that there is a distinct criminal class; we must recognize the latent criminality in us all, and regard those in whom from latent it has become active as such men as we, but for fortunate circumstances, would have been. There is no other distinction between them and us.

Can brotherly companionship and trust reform them? If all of us sincerely and practically united in trusting and companioning them, — so sincerely as to convince them of the fact — I would have small misgivings. But we can expect no universal revolution to kindness. Many of us, probably the vast majority, would fail to rise to the height of the occasion. Yet I can believe that many would achieve that faith and stanchness; enough to make a beginning of success. And I have no doubt whatever that, so far as the kindness was credited by its objects, they would do their part. Few men that I or anyone have known in jail have been incorrigibly wicked at heart. There are indeed incorrigibly wicked men, but they are at least as frequent outside as inside jails, because the crime of wanton hatred and cruelty to others which is theirs, comes only accidentally if at all under the cognizance of our law.

When jails are razed and their inmates let forth, they are not to be left to shift for themselves. They are to be taken heartily and unreservedly into the community, made a part of us, protected against want and against their sinister propensities, given work to do, taught how to work, compensated for it, and shown by constant example the wholesomeness and beauty of good and decent living. Will they rob and murder their hosts? Such calamities will no doubt occur here and there; there have been martyrs in all great causes, and will be in this. But blood so shed will not be wasted. And if the nation, or a considerable part of it, turns resolutely and persistently to its mighty task, it will not fail in the end.

There is nothing original or startling about the Golden Rule as a proposition; but it will seem to tear us to pieces when it is put in practice. But that will do us no harm; we have been long enough compacted together in error and selfishness. The revolution will come; it is still for us to say whether it shall be outward and terrible, or spiritual and benign. Penal imprisonment and all that it implies is not sane nor safe; and the cry, To the lions — serves him right! — belongs to the dark ages, and not to the future. — *Reprinted by kind permission from Hearst's Magazine for February, 1914*

The Wall

The long, high wall that shuts out life —
That death-in-life holds in its coil —
Its height and reach cannot prevent
The sky, nor check the immortal strife
We wage with hungry Fate, nor spoil
Our desperate hope, nor circumvent
Dreams, that redeem our aimless toil!

What Fear and Ignorance have built
Shall pass, with Ignorance and Fear,
Before the breath of Love; and men,
Casting aside the mask of guilt
That baffled, mocked and cursed them here,
Shall know each other once again!
— And must we die, release so near!

Written in Atlanta Penitentiary,
October, 1913

www.ingramcontent.com/pod-product-compliance
Lightning Source LLC
Chambersburg PA
CBHW030505260626
47157CB00005B/1657